N

NEAREST *and* DEAREST

CAROLINE JOLLY

authorHOUSE®

36 / 5491

AuthorHouse™ UK
1663 Liberty Drive
Bloomington, IN 47403 USA
www.authorhouse.co.uk
Phone: 0800.197.4150

Published by AuthorHouse 04/07/2016

ISBN: 978-1-5246-3091-1 (sc)
ISBN: 978-1-5246-3092-8 (hc)
ISBN: 978-1-5246-3093-5 (e)

Print information available on the last page.

Any people depicted in stock imagery provided by Thinkstock are models, and such images are being used for illustrative purposes only. Certain stock imagery © Thinkstock.

This book is printed on acid-free paper.

Ch. 1

'Ethel McIver?'

Effie sighed, gathered up her belongings and pushed ruminations about her daughter aside. She held her stomach muscles taut as she walked into the consulting room. At least she could make an appearance of being fit.

Dr Gordon greeted her with his usual rather tired smile.

'So how are we today?'

'I am fine' she replied cheerfully, placing her ample backside on the faded leather chair.

'Let's see' he muttered as he produced the blood pressure machine, peering at the dial as the apparatus tightened.

'Sleeping OK?'

'Not particularly.'

'Bowels OK?'

'That bit of me's fine.' Which was true and something Effie prided herself on since it accorded with her view of herself as a well-organised person. It had become something of a running joke in the family that she would disappear into the bathroom exactly twenty minutes after her first cup of coffee in the morning. Even Jack had been known to boast that he could set his watch by his wife's bowel movements. Typical of his crude sense of humour.

The band round her arm was slackening and Dr Gordon caught her eye for the first time. 'Blood pressure is still a bit higher than it should be. Nothing to worry about but keep taking your pills and perhaps think about your lifestyle. Watch the diet, gentle exercise, you know. Keep an eye on the alcohol. Maybe get out a bit more?'

Effie felt her face going red under the scrutiny and cursed to herself. So did he see her as a pathetic old lady who stayed home watching the box and hitting the bottle? And what was wrong with that anyway? She knew her life was a bit dull but the discovery that blood pressure mattered and could not be so easily controlled had come as a bit of a shock a few months ago. She certainly didn't feel old, just a bit tired some of the time. Not particularly young either. Get out more?

Dr Gordon was still fiddling with the Velcro armband as Effie juggled her view of herself in her head. He finally extracted the strap with a tug and as he did so his hand brushed against her breast. He hardly appeared to notice as he wound up the machine, but Effie registered a sudden skip of her heartbeat. Actually, he wasn't so bad looking... a definite flicker of excitement which was quickly followed by a flop into self-deprecation. Perhaps she <u>was</u> pathetic, if this was the nearest thing to a man touching her in a remotely arousing way that she'd experienced in several years. How galling to admit that she was going downhill? Yet while she had been sitting in the waiting room it had been she who had been looking at the other patients, at their drooping blank-looks, depressed submissiveness, convinced that she was the perky one.

Time to go. She rolled down her sleeve and made a cheerful 'bye' as she exited the consulting room, glimpsing at her watch. Exactly 9 ½ minutes. That's half a minute less than last time and... she made a mental note to stop herself from automatically calculating the number of minutes the doctor would save if all his patients were seen for a half minute less. Numbers were so fascinating, steadying.

She needed her wits about her for the coming evening when she was going to baby-sit for daughter Cathy, picking the two girls up from a neighbour and putting them to bed. She enjoyed her role as regular baby-sitter even if it could be exhausting. Her grandchildren, or grandchild, as it was then, were the one thing that had kept her going after the bastard Jack had walked out on her some six or seven years ago. She considered this and the doctor's comments as she drove herself over to fetch the girls. It was all very well for him, the doctor, to suggest she needed to watch her lifestyle, but life was tough for a single, not so young woman. She needed her indulgences. My god, life without the occasional glass of sauvignon blanc would be quite unbearable. Not to mention the not so occasional indulgence in large chocolate-covered cappuccinos with the odd almond croissant, just to bring out the flavour. No, she needed her breaks, and particularly tonight when she anticipated that by the time the girls were washed, brushed and had been read to, she would be gasping for a glass of wine.

As expected, bath time turned out to be a hugely energetic and wet affair. Daisy would insist on demonstrating what she called the 'arky meenies principle' which had been mentioned in her school science lesson, by jumping in and out of the bath, cheered on by an excited younger sister and a partially enthusiastic grandmother who was pleased to encourage the child's scientific interest. A marathon story-telling followed, Effie knowing perfectly well that she was being exploited shamelessly by her grand -daughters. The soft touch in contrast to their mother who stuck firmly to bedtime rules.

By 8.07 she was breathing a sigh of relief as she sat herself down at the granite breakfast bar in Cathy's kitchen and poured herself a large glass of Chilean Chardonnay. Well-earned she thought, stretching her aching back and enjoying the sensation as she swallowed the cool liquid, feeling her body relax. She had half an hour or so before the parents returned. They had separate engagements this Tuesday and Effie was not sure who would return first. If it was Cathy, she hoped she'd be in a good mood. She had been quite touchy recently, and if it was Jim, well, he was always considerate and kind to her. She rather prided herself on having a good relationship to her son-in-law, not too close, not too distant.

Either way, she was looking forward to having some time to herself before their return. She settled herself down on what Cathy called 'the bum stools' which had tractor seats moulded into the shape of a bottom which were surprisingly comfy, turned the dimmer switch to a pleasant glow and sipped her wine. She had brought a book to read which was billed as a story of modern-day life amongst a group of young hopefuls living in London, which turned out to contain passages of erotic explicitness. An office romance was developing between Bradley, the boss, and Paula, his PA. Not really her normal cup of tea, but she plunged in now as she drank the wine and felt warm in the kitchen glow, the children asleep, safe and sound upstairs, no-one about.

'Bradley was working late and Paula was helping him with the last details of a project. Her pen slipped from her slim hand and as she bent down to retrieve it Bradley's arm was already there, reaching not the pen which lay by her red high heel, but the delicate ankle which he touched lightly. Her foot did not move. The hand moved slowly up from the ankle, up the shapely calf, stroking it, hesitating as it reached the hem of her skirt. Still she did not move and her own hand reached down to touch his dark hair as his head came closer. The silence and tension were broken only by the sound of beating hearts as his hand continued on its journey up into the hidden crevices, and she let out a whispered 'yes - yes' as he caressed her secret part.....'

The steamy detail gripped Effie and the pace quickened as Bradley's hand wrestled with the zip of his trousers, his mouth seeking Paula's, covering her face with kisses, her neck, her throat and gasping with desire as he nuzzled her delicious bosom. 'yes – yes' she was pleading now' and on Effie read with the couple finally falling back on the floor behind the office sofa, exhausted but laughing furtively.

Pretty crude stuff, thought Effie, but she was aware of an excited flickering in her lower regions, and found herself reading the passage again. The wine was having an effect. She shifted on the bar stool, eyes closed for a moment, opening them and reading the steamiest passage again.

'Yes – yes, cried Paula as his hands struggled with the buttons on her shirt and his eager mouth sought her full lips...'

Eyes closed once more and imagining the scene, she let her hand slide between her thighs, moving rhythmically, tightening, releasing, enjoying the sensation. Yes, still there. It could be Jack's hand. In the subdued light she sat perched on the stool clenching her thighs and her eyes at the same time, willing something to happen: 'yes – yes - let it happen'.

'Hi, Effie.'

She sat bolt upright. Jim! Oh God! She touched her cheek. Thank god for low lights.

'Hi there, Effie. All quiet?'

'Yes, fine, fine. Not a squeak. We had a lovely time. Lots of swimming at bath time with plenty of splashing and only half of it went on the floor.' Effie laughed as she brushed her hair back from her face, hugely self-conscious, praying Jim would not notice her heightened colour. She eased herself off the stool turning to take a glass out of the cupboard, glad to have a reason to move away from the light.

'I was sampling the Chardonnay. Not bad. Want to try some?'

'Yes, sure', and it was only now that Effie noticed he was rubbing his shin. 'Something the matter?'

'That damn garage door. Just too narrow. I always bash something when I get out. This time my shin hit the fender. It's got a bloody sharp edge.' He winced as he rubbed the offending area again. 'Anyway, never mind that. So how've you been. Cathy tells me you're going to the doctor tomorrow.' He sipped his wine and smiled, attentive to Effie.

'Well, yes, today actually. Just my usual check up, checking the blood pressure, you know. So difficult. I mean you know me and food, not to mention drink. Actually, I think I've lost a few pounds' she said optimistically as she poured herself another glass, ` and I've no idea why unless it's the running around with the children every week. I guess they do keep me on my toes. Bless them.'

'You can have them any day as far as I'm concerned. Little beggars are still waking about six. Just never get a really good night's sleep, and Rosie's been up a few times in the night with bad dreams, monsters and things.'

'Goodness, poor darling. Wonder what that's about? What does Cathy think?'

'Oh she just thinks it's a phase... she'll grow out of it. I mean don't all children have bad dreams from time to time? I certainly did, and still do.'

Effie looked at Jim. The idea of him having bad dreams was a new one to her. She supposed she didn't often think of him as a child. He just seemed to be someone who sailed through life without too many difficulties. She'd always thought that it was her children who had the problems. Yes, Cathy had been quite difficult when small, argumentative and unbiddable. Jim by contrast seemed to be a shining example of calm self-assurance, a peaceful man, and a kind man, thank goodness, who had the added attraction of loving her daughter and his children. She felt safe in the warm glow of this thought, raising her glass. 'Cheers. And listen, I'm sure the dreams are nothing to be concerned about.'

Jim laughed. ` God, I'm not concerned so much as flipping fed up with them! They're basically fine, but we've been woken up three nights in a row. - - and... damn...' he reached down to rub his leg again.

'Jim, let me have a look at that. It really hurts doesn't it? Here sit down and roll up your trouser leg.'

Jim protested it was nothing, but sat himself down as directed and pulled up his trouser leg for Effie to inspect. He revealed a livid looking gash on his shin. 'Nasty!' she exclaimed and proceeded to busy herself searching for disinfectant and plasters. She ran some warm water into a bowl, poured in the disinfectant and dipped the cotton wool, squeezing it out before applying it to the raw wound. She gently wiped away congealed blood, dabbing and squeezing till the cut was clean. Jim was silent, watching her movements, the firm but gentle pressure, her concentration. Once clean she inspected the wound, holding his leg in her hands, a strong muscular leg. 'I don't think you need stitches, it's not so deep, a nasty one but it should heal on its own.'

'Well, I didn't know you were a nurse. Great stuff', he started to get up.

'Hold on, I'm not finished. You need a plaster to keep it clean and protected.' 'Yes, matron,' he smiled, and Effie returned the smile glimpsing up now at her son-in-law, catching his eye, rather lovely eyes, blue eyes, and a nice mouth too. A very attractive man.

She focussed back on his leg, the rolled up trousers, a glimpse between his legs and found herself clenching her thighs. That feeling stirred. Her eyes closed. That down there stirring. Oh god!

'Effie?'

'What? Sorry, just making sure it's OK' and she hurriedly stuck the plaster in place and got up clumsily to take the bowl to the sink. She turned the cold tap on forcefully, hardly aware that Jim was speaking, expressing his thanks. And then another sound, heard vaguely. Another key in the door. Cathy was back.

'Hi mum. Hi there. How's things?' Cathy bustled in dumping her stuff on the way. 'Wow, what a day,' she exclaimed, not giving them a chance to speak. `You two boozing I see? Well, come on then. Can't I join in?'

Ch. 2

It was a decision she came to lying in the bath. Relaxing in the warm water in the privacy of her own bathroom she could think. Two forbidden men stirring her up in one day must mean something. And after months – years - of having felt nothing but browned off about the opposite sex. All Jack's fault she muttered to herself as she wrung out her flannel, mentally throttling him with her bare hands.

'He's a bastard, he's a bastard,' she fumed, twisting and squeezing a last drop. One final 'he's a bastard' and she hauled herself out of the water. Time to take stock. She stood naked in front of the mirror, narrowing her eyes to scrutinise the image facing her, casting her eyes down from her breasts, definitely droopy, to be expected after three babies, to what the children called 'the muffin top' underneath, a soft roll of flesh, to her waist which was barely visible, to her thighs which she liked to call 'Rubenesque' and her legs which were in good shape so long as she didn't turn round to reveal protruding varicose veins behind the left knee. The vision was topped by a face with fine features, age lines softened by a slight plumpness, grey eyes and a head of thick grey hair which framed her face. Not bad for a woman about to enter another decade?

There were in fact two decisions made that evening: one was to join a gym and the other was to venture into the world of dating. If her sexuality had been merely in hibernation for the last few years rather than totally extinct she could see her moment of weakness with Jim not so much as sinful as a wake-up call. She had a vision of a squirrel exiting its burrow after the freeze of winter, nibbling a nut and fluffing its tail in the warm spring sunshine. But such feelings needed directing. She would have to think carefully. What to do?

The first answer she gave herself was – ring Susie, who, on her third marriage, she considered a fount of knowledge about life. The second answer, instinctively, was to tell herself to be careful what she said to the children even though, or perhaps because, they were all grown up. Should she tell them? With these thoughts and having arranged to meet Susie the next day she took herself to bed to sleep fitfully and to dream of a grey squirrel busy burying a huge pile of nuts that kept popping up out of the ground as fast as it dug a hole.

The following day was Saturday and the sun was shining. Effie had arranged to meet Susie at their favourite haunt, Cafe Contini. They ordered skinny lattes from the Italian-looking waiter, Marco, who was actually from Bulgaria, and settled themselves at one end of the long wooden communal table where from behind an array of pots of jam and honey they had a vantage-point view of the establishment.

'Nothing to eat for the madams today?' queried Marco.

'No grazie, Marco, not today.' Effie patted her stomach, and turned to her friend 'I hope you're impressed by the fact that I have not ordered an almond croissant.'

'Bowled over. So? You're either not feeling well or Dr Gordon has finally made an impact?'

'Neither, but... well, maybe it is partly because of him. He did tell me to get out more. So I've been thinking' and Effie leant across the table, lowering her voice. 'Do come closer, Susie, I don't want the whole cafe to hear. So what do you think about me trying to find someone. I mean a new man in my life?'

'Why darling, of course you must have a man in your life' exclaimed Susie loudly. 'What a marvellous idea. I've been wondering what you've been waiting for?'

'I didn't know I <u>had</u> been waiting' said Effie, 'just felt like it all went dead when Jack left, and there were the children, and Daisy's arrival, you know...'

Susie 's heavily made-up eyes opened wide. 'But having children in your life isn't a reason not to have a man in your life.' She stirred her latte vigorously. 'I mean, look at me. I've never found it difficult to find a man even though I do have two hulking great grown up children. There are lots of men out there over 50 still looking for a gorgeous mature lady.'

'Susie, you know perfectly well I'm about to turn 60.'

'So? Give or take a few years. You look great for your age. A bit too fat but you can't have it all.'

'Thanks. Anyway, the other thing is, you'll be pleased to hear, I've joined a gym...' Susie's eyes widened again 'and to prove my good intentions, I'm cutting down on unnecessary sugar, least...' she paused to hail Marco 'the trouble is, going to the gym makes me feel hungrier than ever. Shall we at least share a croissant?'

'Effie, you've got to take this business seriously, you know.'

'I have?' Effie sighed and ordered the one croissant. 'Did I ever tell you about the woman at work who wanted to lose weight? She thought she could get skinnier by drinking umpteen skinny lattes.'

They laughed, and with the arrival of the pastry began to plot a campaign of action so that by the time Effie reached home that evening she had rekindled some enthusiasm which she knew was necessary if she was to brave the reality of on-line dating. Somewhere in her mind was a dormouse scurrying back into its hole. She sat at her computer staring at a blank screen. Susie had regaled her with the names of dating sites, newspaper dating pages and agencies and told her to get on with it. 'Not so easy' complained Effie. 'I don't know where to begin. All very well for you with a steady devoted husband behind you.'

'They weren't all devoted! Third time lucky for me. And maybe for you it'll be better second time round.'

And so Sunday found Effie ensconced with her computer, her phone and a pile of papers, names and numbers, trying to sort out some sort of search strategy, only to find after one hour and ten minutes that her computer was playing up, refusing to follow instructions despite every effort to click, re-boot or shift material. In utter frustration Effie did the thing she had told herself she would not do, that is, ring one of her children. Leo was the obvious person to consult as the IT man of the family and she felt she simply couldn't wait. Enthusiasm could be fickle.

Leo responded with alacrity to his mother's call for help.

'Leo, darling, sorry to bother you on a Sunday but I've got this awful virus..'

'Oh, Mum, poor you. You should have told me you weren't well '.

'No, no, <u>I'm </u>fine, but the computer isn't. You couldn't give me a hand could you?'

True to form, Leo soon had the technical problem sorted out. 'Is this what you wanted, Mum?' he asked as the words 'Dream Dating' flashed up at the top of the screen.

'I 'm afraid so' Effie grimaced, apologetic. 'I'm just sort of trying to brush up my social life. I mean, you don't mind, or think it unsuitable, do you?'

'Mum, not at all, but I think I'll leave you to it.' And with this stamp of approval, he rose to go, giving Effie a fatherly pat on the shoulder as he left.

'You will be discrete, Leo, won't you' she called after him 'I mean, you know...'

'My lips are sealed, Mum.'

Half an hour later, however, there was a call first from Cathy and then from Jane. 'So what's this I hear? Dating?' exclaimed Cathy. 'I hope you know what you're doing.' A more encouraging 'fine, so long as you promise never to talk about sex' from the latter. So the next Saturday afternoon, with Susie's help, Effie got down to the task of finding herself a mate. She sat at her computer at the living room table which was strewn with papers, files, mugs, a teapot, a plate of biscuits. This was serious business. They started by reading the weekend newspaper dating columns before moving on to a dating agency called 'Arcadia' that had sent Effie a bundle of profiles of prospective partners and they were sifting through them, placing them into three piles: 'no-hopers', 'possible but unlikely', and 'give it a go'. The pile of 'no-hopers' was growing with alarming speed. 'How can there be so many duds?' complained Effie. 'I mean I may be a bit fussy, but even so... This Felix sounds Ok but just look at his photo. That great bristly beard and funny shaped head. It'd be like going out with a toilet brush.'

'Well, try the papers. There's not so much to read there, and the photos come later.'

'OK then, how about this' and she read... 'John is a sensitive man who is looking for an equally sensitive lady to share his aesthetic appreciation of the exquisiteness of nature and the finer qualities of life...' I'd be scared of putting a not so delicate foot in it.'

Susie raised an eyebrow behind her tortoiseshell glasses, 'But listen to this one: 'Romeo of mature years eager to meet an equally mature Juliet, hoping to change Shakespeare's tragic ending into a happy ever after story.' well he's hopeful' she chortled as she put him in the 'unlikely' pile and Effie screeched with laughter. 'God, I just want somebody ordinary.'

'We carry on' commanded Susie ` there must be somebody here who grabs your interest.'

Effie sighed but continued her task. The result of it all was a large pile of 'no hopers', a smaller pile of ` possible but unlikely', and a mere two in the 'give it a go'. Effie sank back exhausted, glimpsing at her watch: five to six. 'I think we can open the bar five minutes early tonight. We deserve it' she said as she opened a bottle of Chardonnay, 'even if it's not much of an outcome. I mean, Susie, do you realise that between us we've looked at thirty to forty profiles, read fifty to sixty ads and flicked through six sites and about a hundred entries. Out of all that we've settled on two which is something like a one percent success rate and I haven't even met anyone yet which suggests that... 'Effie was warming to her task as she poured out two large glasses...' assuming there is a considerable drop out rate amongst the people I actually meet, I'm going to need to cast my eyes over the details of maybe a couple of thousand men. Cause to celebrate?'

Susie, not to be deflected, replied with some irritation that everyone knew statistics always got something wrong and Effie should control her calculating urges. 'A hundred years ago a woman of your age couldn't possibly have done this sort of thing'. Which was quite unnecessary for her to point out, but if Susie thought Effie ungrateful she needed to smooth things over and she gave her friend a comforting pat on the arm. 'I do appreciate all your help, Susie, couldn't do this without you. Here, have another glass.'

So the evening finished amicably with agreement that first place would go to a man called Simon whose picture they both liked, clean – shaven, relaxed expression, regular features, who described his interests as classic cars (always useful), classical music (cultured), climbing (adventurous) and caring for a collie dog (good to be caring). All 'Cs', too, which appealed to Effie's sense of order. He was in his early 60s, five foot ten and worked in the area of the media (films, television?)

Simon had been extracted from one of the Arcadia profiles and Susie was explaining the procedure. The next step was for Effie to send back her choices and if all went well and there was a match the agency would set up a rendezvous for the two at a particular restaurant.

'You mean, I take myself to this unknown restaurant to meet an unknown man?'

'Exactly, but he sounds OK. He's not too anything. You said you wanted ordinary. Come on, let's send them off.'

Effie slept surprisingly well that night. No dreams. She considered this on her way to work the next day. There was definitely some sense of relief to have done something. She was looking forward to meeting some new people, and hoped she would get to meet this Simon even if he wasn't likely to be the love of her life. She was wary of letting herself get too excited anyway after Jack. His departure had been such a crushing blow to her ego, her confidence, her sexuality. She rose to get off at her stop as the branch of a cherry tree heavy with blossom brushed the bus window and for a moment she felt touched, delighted by its blousy beauty. Life had its beautiful side and she felt better today than she had in a while as she set off on the familiar route to her office. A small flame of excitement about life opening up was flickering. And if she kept her focus firmly on Simon, she could anticipate some relief from that uncomfortable niggle she had experienced on visiting Cathy since those wayward feelings of the other week. She hated the word 'guilt', but that's probably what it was, that hard little peanut.

Ch. 3

A small, not-so-smart restaurant confronted Effie: her first rendezvous. It was the result of an arduous journey by bus, tube and a nine minute walk to a suburb on the other side of town. Her mind was whirring with calculations of how much time she would be spending on the extra travel involved in dating over the next few months, assuming she stuck at it. The resulting total was not reassuring, and to waste any time at this stage of life was a sin. On the other hand the process of calculating had a calming effect despite the speed at which her brain was working. She like the control and certainty of it faced with the uncertainty ahead.

Feeling chilled by a cold March wind that had buffeted her during the course of her nine-minute walk from the tube she greeted the Bistro d'Oro with a sigh of relief although she couldn't see much about it's dull brown quasi -tyrollean facade that looked the least bit 'd'oro'. She had allowed masses of time to reach the place. She dreaded being second to arrive and not having time to go immediately to the ladies room to put herself straight before being seen. After all that wind she was sure her face was red and her hair wild. The first embarrassing thing had been to say she was from Arcadia, the euphemistically named introduction agency. Did the waiter express a barely suppressed smirk as he ushered her over to a table? 'Here we are. This is the Arcadian table.'

Resisting the temptation to tread on his foot, she sat down and attempted to take stock. The other diners were solidly in couples, not even foursomes, and she felt she stood out like a sore thumb as a single woman. Or could they all be happily joined up protégés of Arcadia? A middle-aged couple next to her were laughing together, sharing a joke. Her own mood was something between adolescent excitement and old age cynicism: 'now's your chance' or 'don't kid yourself – I mean just look at you!' She was clearly nervous and needed to seek refuge in the ladies room, check her face and hair, re-do her lippy. There was still plenty of time, fifteen minutes to go. Her bladder was taking the strain of her nerves. She had already been three times at home in the course of getting herself ready, a process which had taken several hours of indecision, of changing four or five outfits, settling on a sixth and then taking everything off again because she had a suddenly panicked that her underwear ought to be clean, just in case her bra straps showed from underneath the black top she had chosen. It only struck her now as she stared in the mirror in the ladies room that a black bra was hardly likely to show the dirt. In fact even the black top which was decently high necked was covered by a grey fitted jacket. Simple but smart and definitely not too sexy had been the mantra agreed on after discussion with Susie who turned out to have strong views on such matters. The outfit was completed with a pair of slim line matching trousers, black patent leather shoes with not too high a heel - don't want to look small but not too tall either - and some silver jewellery that jangled to complete the ensemble.

Looking at herself in the mirror, she thought the image was OK if a little sombre, all that grey and black, even silvery hair, but nothing for it now. She needed to get back to the table so that she would be able to view Simon as he came in. Much better to be the one already there, sitting down, though she hoped he wouldn't be late. She was dying for a drink to calm her nerves but thought she had better wait, not wanting to look too keen about the joys of alcohol. What if he was TT? That was quite a sobering thought, and something that had not been mentioned in his profile. She could at least order a bottle of fizzy water.

The waiter, however, was studiously ignoring her despite Effie's best efforts to catch his eye. She became convinced that he was deliberately taking no notice with the result that she was both frowning and waving her arms wildly to attract attention when a man suddenly appeared at her side.

'Effie?'

'Goodness, you must be Simon'

'That's me.'

'Great... sorry about that. I was just trying to get myself a waiter, I mean some water.'

Simon smiled, sat down opposite Effie and hailed the waiter who responded immediately. 'Some water for the lady please and shall we have a look at the wine list?'

This was music to Effie's ears and she immediately felt more relaxed and able to take in her companion. He was neither tall nor short, neither handsome nor ugly, fat nor thin and in possession of a moderate amount of greying hair. An ordinary man she thought, at least to look at, but he had a nice smile and she had liked the way he had handled the introduction. She just prayed he didn't feel as awkward as she did and wished the waiter would buck up with the wine list.

They exchanged a few pleasantries about the journey and the difficulties of finding the restaurant until the waiter finally returned with the wine list which he handed to Simon. 'Right, let's see' he muttered as he put on a pair of horn-rimmed spectacles. 'You will join me, won't you?'

'Oh please.' Effie tried not to sound too eager.

Simon was scanning the list as though he knew what he was looking at which appealed to Effie. 'I think the Sicilian ones are good and this is basically an Italian restaurant, isn't it?'

'Fine by me'.

'So shall we have a glass each? Or could we manage a bottle? We're neither of us driving are we?'

'I'm easy' she lied.

'Let's go for a bottle then.'

Effie perked up, gratefully swallowing a large mouthful as soon as the wine arrived, grateful, too, that he suggested they have a look at the menu although that too had its difficulties. It had been made clear by the agency that on first dates clients would pay for themselves. That made sense to Effie but it still left her with the issue of what to choose wanting neither to appear too affluent – the grilled lobster – or on a diet – a salad - or too greedy - the lasagne. So she hesitated, hoping to get a cue from Simon who was studying the menu with the same seriousness he had adopted with the wine list.

'So, the ravioli sounds good' he finally pronounced 'I'll go for the one with the meat filling.'

'Good idea. I'll have the same, or, perhaps the one with ricotta and spinach. That's an old favourite of mine.' Which was true. At least she'd not have to eat her way through something she didn't like. The wine, too, helped her to control the occasional strong desire just to be back in her own home watching the television.

'Cheers, Effie'. The order had been given and Simon was at last looking at her. There was a sense of getting down to business. 'So tell me about you, Effie?'

'Me? Well, not much to tell. At least, I think I mentioned in my - in my profile -' she had almost said 'CV' - 'I got divorced some years ago, three children and...' did the mention of grandchildren make her sound too old? She gulped down a large mouthful of Chardonnay and pushed on, leaving her last sentence hanging having decided that grandchildren were not for the first meeting. 'Job-wise, I'm sort of an accountant, work for Ledgers, have done for years. I look after a group of hotels. Lots of adding and subtracting I suppose' she laughed. Simon did not, but raised his rather bushy eyebrows 'that sounds impressive. I like a lady who can do her sums. Never my forte, I'm afraid. Not that I didn't want to make money when I left school. That's why I went into property.'

'Property?' I thought you indicated you had something to do with the media?'

'Ah yes. That was a few years ago. No, I'm now attempting to make my fortune in the rather cut throat world of property development. Worked for the Beeb for a while but it was too political, too back-stabbing and I certainly didn't make much money.'

'I see' said Effie as she pronging a piece of the ravioli that had just arrived and looked good. Her appetite had suddenly returned and she was anxious now not to drip sauce onto her front. 'So how about the cars you said you enjoy? Is it vintage stuff? Racing cars?'

'Sadly, not even a Polo. That too is something that has had to pass into my personal history books. You see, I did have a couple of beautiful classic cars, an old MGB and a Ford, but when I moved out of the media I needed some capital to invest in a development. Had to sell pretty well everything and the fact is I'm still waiting for a return. I found I didn't really need a car anyway. Hence the trek here' he laughed.

This seemed to be the cue for both of them to pause and for Simon to refill their glasses. Effie rested her fork on the side of her plate and addressed him. 'So what about the classical music?'

'Ah, yes, I once joined a choir, but had to give that up I'm afraid. Just haven't had time recently.'

'So do you still climb? That sounded exciting.'

'Sadly no. I fell and broke my leg. Years ago actually. No a brisk walk to the river and back is about as much exercise as I allow myself these days.'

'And the collie?'

'Poor chap died last year. Got a bit carried away when we were out in the country. Some sort of throw back to his sheepdog mother, except he wasn't, a proper sheep dog, I mean. He went charging off that afternoon rushing after a flock of pregnant ewes, went absolutely mad, yapping and all hyper. Nothing I could do, and the irate farmer shot him. Understandable but sad, damn sad.' He took a large mouthful of ravioli and chewed it pensively. 'Lovely dog.'

Effie spoke with caution: 'so, basically, Simon, all the things you mention on your profile aren't relevant any more?'

'I suppose not. No, you're right. It's all just a bit out of date. The fact is, I wrote it a while back when things were different. I first went to Arcadia some years ago. Met some lovely people, and they've just sort of kept me on their books.'

'I see.'

So what did she see? It was difficult to tell since the man sitting in front of her was not the man she had been led to believe he was. There was a whiff of stale goods, of someone second hand and much used. The food suddenly did not taste as good and Effie lowered her laden fork.

'Well, perhaps you'd better tell me a bit about your up-to-date version'. But she knew her interest level had plummeted and she more than ever wanted to be home and not have to go through another course and possibly coffee – did they serve chocolates with it? - just to be polite. The whole situation was so untried and new, however, that Effie felt quite paralysed about doing anything other than what she usually did, which was to be polite, and the food was quite palatable she decided as she picked up her fork again. So she sat it out for another forty five minutes, ordered a tiramisu, which she knew she shouldn't, followed by a double espresso, which she knew would keep her awake all night, and accepted Simon's suggestion that they finish off with a limoncello which he assured her would make her sleep like a baby.

There was nothing acutely wrong with Simon. His story wasn't even entirely ordinary but Effie found his apparent lack of concern about having given her the wrong impression hard to digest. Or was it strangely compelling? What a way to get through life, simply not letting things bother you. The fact was that it did bother her, that instead of being an adventurous, dog-owning media man he turned out to be a property developer with a highly uncertain future and no dog at all.

The rich mix of chocolate, cream and alcohol on top of a hefty pasta was also taking its toll on Effie. Time to go. Her feet were aching and she longed to be soaking herself in a warm bath. Simon made no protest when she took the initiative and asked for the bill which they shared as instructed, agreeing on a suitable tip. Their coats were retrieved by the smirking waiter who insisted on helping Effie get hers on. 'I hope madam enjoyed her evening'. To which she struggled to think of a suitably crushing response, only able to come up with a feeble 'yes she did thank you'. 'So...?' Simon was hovering at the door 'Well, I enjoyed the evening Effie.'

'You did?'

'Oh yes, one of my best to date.'

'Right...'

'I'd really like to get to know you better. Such an interesting life you have. I mean, I'd love to meet up again if you would?'

'Well, yes, that'd be nice' she lied for the second time that evening.

'I've got your number. I'll give you a call some time?... Maybe we could do a film or something?'

'Yes, sure. A film would be good.'

And so the evening ended with a degree of bathos for Effie whose gut feeling told her he would not ring and she didn't want him to anyway. Not a complete disaster of an evening but she seriously wanted to get home now to nurse her aching legs and buffeted psyche.

All was not finished, however, at the door of the restaurant. Having made their farewells, with a cheerful smile and a peck on the cheek from Simon and a nod from Effie, they turned to start the journey home, only to find that they were heading in the same direction. 'So where do you actually live?' he enquired, one question that neither of them had asked so far. 'Oh, I live in Earl's Park. A small house off the High Street.'

'Goodness! So do I. I mean, I live in Earl's Park too. A flat in the block overlooking the park. What a coincidence. So I guess we're going the same way. And we could have met much nearer to home for both of us.' Effie laughed, finally able to see something funny in the evening, that huge long trek through the wind and the rain when they could have met round the corner in the local Indian. And now she had to reckon on a further three quarters of an hour of small talk with her companion on the journey back. It was in fact forty seven minutes until Effie could put her key in the door and a further twenty one until she was lying back in the steamy warmth of a bath with a cup of peppermint tea balanced on the edge. Not a total washout for a first meeting, but tiring, exhausting. Perhaps she was too old for this sort of thing after all. She certainly must not wear those shoes again, even if they weren't too high they had proved miserably uncomfortable. Death to her varicose veins.

Her phone buzzed. It was half past eleven. Only Susie would ring this late, but she did not answer. She would have to wait until tomorrow. She was far too tired and too sober to engage in a de-briefing with her friend. Or would it be a post-mortem?

Ch. 4

Date number 2 was the second post-mortem. 'Retired antiquarian' Henry Braithwaite was relegated to the 'duds' box with little hesitation. Effie quickly realised as they consumed a full-scale English tea in a small cafe – his choice – that her interpretation of his profile, which included a variety of acronyms, had been fatally flawed. 'SOH' did not stand for ` Sense of humour', of which she thought she had plenty, but for `Student of Horticulture', which was not her strong point, and 'view to LTR' did not mean he was aiming for a `Long-term relationship' but 'learning to rumba', which was definitely not one of her talents. 'Looking for TLC' referred not to tenderness but to his search for a `Tall lady companion', which Effie could not really claim to be at five foot five. But the main reason for his fall into the flop box was the look of him. He turned out to be carrying a sizable paunch with a completely bald head and a huge bushy grey beard which, by the time he had munched his way through a plate of toasted tea-cakes, was strewn with crumbs and other debris, which deeply offended Effie's sense of hygiene and order, although he seemed to be finding the whole encounter highly amusing, laughing heartily occasionally for no obvious reason that Effie could discern. No, this Falstaffian character would not do.

And so to date number 3. This was Oliver who according to the profile was in his early 60s, a widower, tall and slim with a full head of hair, ran his own business, though was in the process of handing over to younger colleagues, was interested in historic buildings and antiques, theatre and films. He claimed to be looking for someone with similar interests and a good sense of humour. Oliver's provenance was another site called 'College Comrades' and was meant to sift off a more intellectual group of people. 'You might as well go for someone with a bit of a brain' had been Susie's recommendation. 'I mean it's so easy to get bored when the sex stuff has run its course.'

'Must you!' Effie straightened her posture. But 'Oliver, interested in history and antiques', sounded all right and they had exchanged a few emails so that she knew, this time, where he lived – not so far away – and she had agreed to meet him at a pub near his house. 'I'll be wearing a tweed jacket and I have glasses' had been his aid to recognition. There was no photo.

'He's telling you he's an intellectual' said Susie excitedly. 'Sounds like a good one.'

Effie was not so sure but prepared herself, nevertheless, taking care to wear what she thought was appropriate attire for an intelligent working woman of mature years, a skirt and top, shoes with a moderate heel, not her red jacket. Quietly attractive, was the idea. This time she drove, on the theory that it gave her a greater degree of control and there was no risk of an awkward trek home with a strange man. It was Friday night and the pub was full of noisy people celebrating the end of the week. How on earth was she going to recognise him? She pushed her way forward through the throng attempting to scan the horizon for a man with hair, glasses and a tweed jacket. She managed to reach the bar which she decided was a central spot, grabbing a stool as a definitely gorgeous young girl lifted her elegant bottom from it, and flicked her hair in Effie's face as she ran her hand through long blond tresses. 'Bitch' muttered Effie making no attempt to disguise her comment amidst the din. The girl glared at her briefly and disappeared into the melee on the arm of an adoring young man. Effie hoped she had heard. Not a great start she thought as she placed her own ample bottom firmly on the bar stool. Daft place to meet.

She continued to scan the heads she could see but nothing matched her image. There was something to be said for Arcadia where at least she was surer of the meeting place. I'm too old for this, was her thought yet again and she was just about to cut her losses and order herself a drink when the man who was leaning on the bar beside her, who seemed to be well away, turned to her and laid his hand proprietarily on her arm. 'Can I get you something, m'darlin'' he enquired in an Irish accent. 'Well,' replied Effie who had a soft spot for the Irish, ` that's very kind of you. Perhaps I will.' And within a few minutes, perched there with a glass of Sauvignon Blanc in her hand and a gently drunken Irishman on her left who was soon making her laugh with his stories of life in rural Ireland, she could kid herself that she was one of the young city crowd milling around her.

Some twenty minutes passed in this fashion and Effie really was enjoying her Irishman whose name was Brendan when someone tapped her on the shoulder. 'You're not Effie are you? I'm Oliver.'

She turned and faced Oliver. A man more than middle aged, half bald with wisps of pale orange hair plastered down on his pate, tortoiseshell glasses perched on a long nose over light gray eyes, cheeks with high colour and, indeed, wearing a well-worn tweed jacket. Effie absorbed the impact in a flash causing her to mentally put a large negative slash across her fantasy man. Another dud. She glared at the 'full head of hair'. Maybe twenty years ago. These men and their vanity. But the glass of wine and Brendan's company had put her into a basically good mood so that she could respond graciously. 'Hello there. Yes, I'm Effie. And this is Brendan. I'm afraid I rather gave up on finding you in this throng. Friday I guess.'

Oliver smiled amiably and nodded at Brendan. 'Yes, I'd forgotten how crowded it can get. Sorry about that. Took me a while to find you. I see you've had a drink already.' He eyed the empty glass on the counter. 'Look why don't we go back to my place where it's quieter and we can talk.'

'Good idea' said Effie, throwing caution to the wind, easing herself off the bar stool. Her instant gut feeling was that this man was completely safe. 'Nice to meet you Brendan and thanks for the drink.'

'Pleasure, m'darlin.' He emptied the remains of his beer in one gulp. 'so, Oliver, you've got yourself a lovely lassie here... another pint, John, please, another pint.. '. and he turned away to the pleasures of his beer.

It had been a long time since Effie had spent any time in a pub, let alone perched on a bar stool chatting to a strange man at the same time as she was introduced to another that she barely knew. This was a half formed thought in her mind as they negotiated a path through the noisy throng, Oliver ushering her along protectively, a gesture which softened her initial dismissive response. It had been so long since a man had offered her this kind of attention, and it felt good. She knew where he lived, a quiet street of semi-detached houses with small front and rear gardens frequented mainly by young families and the odd retired couple. It was a street which had a well-worn feel about it as though, once there, people stayed. Oliver had revealed in his emails that he had lived there for twenty six years with his wife and three children who had all now left home. A daughter lived just round the corner and popped in from time to time. His wife had died some four years ago after a long illness so that it was eventually something of a relief when she died. He sounded matter-of-fact about it for which Effie was grateful.

Number 37 was not one of the smartest houses in the street but looked homely enough as Oliver opened the front door revealing a hallway which was cluttered with coats and a pile of shoes and wellington boots. He ushered her into the living room which had a similar rather cluttered appearance. There were shelves covered in nick knacks, books, CDs, papers in no particular order. The sofa, where Effie perched herself, looked as though it had seen better days. She disliked the candelabra wall lights and the chairs covered with a pink chintzy material - old fashioned - but her scan of the room hovered briefly on a handsome cut-glass decanter and a cabinet housing some elegant champagne flutes. She had to admit that she did need the reassurance of a drink to help settle remaining nerves. The decor was far from her own taste which was for cheap and cheerful contemporary design, a preference which she dated back to her parents' house in the north of England which had been furnished with heavy dark furniture and dull wallpaper that had only added to the rather oppressive family atmosphere. This brief moment of reverie and then she was back with Oliver who, thank god, was offering her a drink.

'So, what can I get you, Effie? I've a not half decent scotch – my preference – or a sherry – medium I think?'

Sherry! Effie had no idea it still existed.

But Oliver was peering at a green bottle which looked as though it had been dug out from the back of a cupboard. 'Yes, medium... or perhaps there's some gin here somewhere. Alice always liked her gin.'

From which Effie gathered 'Alice' was the dead wife. And here she was again, faced with having to make a decision in tricky circumstances because what she really wanted was a glass of wine. Her tactic, was to wait for a cue.

'Might be something else back here,' from Oliver who was still rummaging in the cupboard.

So am I the first date he's had since his wife died? she wondered.

'Ah', exclaimed Oliver, extracting his head from the cupboard and in the process scraping the top of his head on the shelf above and dislodging the orange wisps of hair so that they hung like damp string at one side of his face, a sight which was both pathetic and comic and which precipitated Effie into an explosive guffaw. Oliver stared at her in surprise but did not seem to take offense. He flicked the offending hair back into place and suddenly grinned.

Effie, however, felt the need to apologise. 'So sorry. I guess I am a touch nervous.' She grimaced as though to prove the point.

"Oh quite all right. Here, you do need a drink and so do I. Would the gin do?'

'I don't suppose you've got any wine?' Somehow the guffawing had made it easier to ask.

'Oh, wine! Why didn't you say! Hang on, I think there's a spot in the fridge.' Upon which he disappeared into what Effie presumed was the kitchen, returning a few minutes later with a green bottle in hand. He held it up to the light. 'Yes, there's a bit in there.' How long's it been there, she wondered, but had already decided that she would drink it whatever it tasted like. She had never yet suffered from drinking elderly wine. Oliver was waving the bottle around as though he was searching for something. A glass?

'Can I help?' offered Effie, eager to speed up the process.

'yes, yes – in the kitchen. Glasses in the cupboard by the stove.'

So Effie entered the totally strange kitchen which had an even more cluttered appearance than the hall, and having negotiated a dog bowl placed strategically right in front of the cooker, she opened the cupboard to reveal a selection of glassware, mainly tumblers or beer mugs plus a couple of chipped wine glasses, one of which she grabbed. With a satisfied 'aha...' she turned on her heel only to send the dog bowl skimming across the kitchen floor scattering debris as it sped. 'Damn!' She crashed the glass down on the table shattering it. More mess! She bent down to pick up the broken pieces, but where to put them? There must be a dustpan and brush somewhere to sweep up the remaining shards of glass. A panicky feeling impelled her to brave a rummage in the dark depths under the kitchen sink, with no success. Nor could she see a broom and in desperation she opened the nearest door. Surely it was a broom cupboard? It housed an old boiler but no broom. She was shutting it as quietly as she could when Oliver made her jump. 'What <u>are</u> you doing, Effie?'

Fifteen minutes later the floor was back the way it had been, Oliver having finally produced a rather tatty old broom at Effie's insistence and they had between them swept up and disposed of the offending dog food. Effie had still not had anything to drink since Brendan and breathed an audible sigh of relief as she sat down again on the chintz sofa sinking back this time into its soft cushions finally able to swallow a deep gulp of Chilean Chardonnay. She felt as though she had been with Oliver for hours and had hardly spoken to him. She also suddenly realised she was hungry and it was not at all clear whether a meal was on the cards. She foolishly had only snacked at lunch time and the wine was rapidly going to her head. But Oliver seemed in no hurry to suggest eating. He wanted to talk about Alice telling Effie much more detail than she wished to hear about her illness describing a nice comfortable sounding lady, an amateur artist – Effie had to admire paintings on the wall – a dog lover - so where was the dog? - and an excellent mother. Effie made appropriate noises about the photos of happy smiling children scattered around the room.

'But no point getting too down about it' he asserted once the tale was told. 'so tell me a bit more about you, Effie'. So she in turn tried to tell a bit of a story about herself, her work doing accounts for the hotel group, her children, a quick skate round her marriage and, in an attempt to steer the conversation round to food, describing her interests as 'cooking' and 'going to restaurants'

'I maybe didn't tell you that bit in my emails.'

At last Oliver picked up the cue. 'Restaurants? Well, you must be hungry. But I thought we'd just stay here now. I've got some stuff in the fridge. Let's see.'

What Effie soon saw as Oliver busied himself digging around in the fridge – was this man obsessed with having his head inside small spaces? – was the remains of a shop shepherd's pie which he pulled out triumphantly. Effie stared at the foil container inside of which clung bits of half-burnt potato and scraps of brown matter.

'Just bring down a couple of plates, would you?' Oliver's mood was cheery and he dived again into the recesses of the fridge producing this time some wilting leaves and a couple of drooping carrots. 'Can we have these raw?'

No we certainly can't, was her thought, but she gamely took her cue and fished around in a grimy pot by the sink till she found a vegetable peeler and sharp knife, prepared the offending items and stuck them in a pot of water which Oliver pushed in her direction.

'It's so nice to have someone who knows about these things' he breathed excitedly. Effie inwardly shrugged and set about making the place fit for a meal which was obviously what was wanted. She found out how to work the stove, transferred the remaining pie into a smaller cleaner dish and stuck it in the oven for twenty minutes which she assessed would be long enough to kill off germs without burning it completely. Oliver meanwhile pottered around pushing the objects on the table to one side in order to make a clearing in which he placed a couple of old knives and forks together with a much-dripped candle. The talk became more relaxed as Effie got into her stride and they even shared a few jokes so that when they finally sat down together to sample the shepherds' pie and two veg the scene could have been mistaken for an old married couple dining in their own homely kitchen.

Oliver was putting on the kettle in order to make coffee when there was the sound of a key in the door and a loud panting noise followed by a burst of barking. Here then was the missing dog. A black Labrador bounded into the kitchen and went straight for Effie, tail wagging as though she was his long lost friend. The poor creature is missing Alice, she thought, letting it jump up on her excitedly. She was so busy with the dog that she only gradually took in the person who had brought him in, a young woman with short brown hair and a fresh face, Oliver's 'round the corner' daughter, June.

'Hi there, Dad. Hello Effie,' she said, quite at ease, as though she'd known Effie all her life. 'So how was the pub?'

'Marvellous' came the enthusiastic response from Oliver. 'Effie and I have had a great time. So nice to have someone around again.' He beamed at Effie who responded with a gentle smile but said nothing. What she wanted to say was that she wasn't Alice, she wasn't the least bit like Alice. She couldn't be the same as this woman who liked chintz covers and had a messy kitchen. She wasn't going to be sucked in to being a replacement Alice, even if the last part of the evening had been pleasant enough. Pity, since the daughter was friendly and she liked the dog.

Ch. 5

Daisy pirouetted around the hall. It was Saturday and she was going to dancing. A new venture in her young life and one which she had grasped with a powerful enthusiasm. 'See what I can do, gran'ma. Look. Look.' She spun round, her golden hair in a tight bun high on her head so that she looked like a spinning top, Effie said. Cathy was bustling around gathering up shoes and jackets. 'I don't need a jacket, Mum. It's hot.' and she ducked to avoid the proffered garment. Cathy shrugged and shoved the offending item in her large flowery bag. 'Now come on, Daisy. You can't go out in those ballet shoes. You put them on when we get there, you know very well.' Daisy reluctantly took them off complaining to no one in particular. She was keen to get going and for once did not argue.

Effie was taking the younger Rosie to the park while Mum accompanied Daisy, and Jim had promised to come and pick Rosie up from the park later. The May sun was out and the lilac was flowering in the garden, beautiful blousy purple blooms exuding a heavenly scent. Effie breathed it in as she ushered the excited Rosie along the path. It was good to be outside and she was looking forward to having some time on her own with Rosie. She had decided to give dating a break this weekend and had arranged instead an outing with her old friend Agnes, a single lady like herself. The idea of spending an evening with someone she knew well and did not have to fuss about was an entirely pleasurable thought.

But first there was Rosie and the park which the child loved. She raced ahead on her scooter which she had insisted on bringing despite Cathy's discouragement. Sensitive to the implied criticism that she, grandma, wouldn't cope with a scooter, Effie made conscious efforts to encourage the child to use it though as Rosie flew off into the distance she momentarily regretted her decision: the perils of pride.

When pushed, however, Effie could set up a fair old pace and she was soon catching up with her young granddaughter who was happy and laughing. 'I beat you! I beat you,' she trilled. 'Oh no you didn't. We're not there yet' said Effie as she shot past Rosie aiming for the playground at the far side of the park. Rosie grabbed her scooter handles and right leg flying raced the machine after her grandmother, half laughing and half crying. 'Wait for me - wait for me!' Effie gradually slackened her pace, grateful to let Rosie win. 'Wow, you're a star, you're a shooting star, poppet. I think you deserve an ice cream.' 'Ooh yes!'

Rosie couldn't believe her good luck to be allowed an ice cream before anything else. 'Mummy always says I've got to do something before I get sweety things.' 'Well,' said Effie conspiratorially 'you're out with me today and we do things grandma's way, so you can certainly have an ice cream right now if you want.' Rosie jumped excitedly and sped off towards the cafe. She chose a triple-decker cone with boules of chocolate chip, green pistachio and red berry symphony: Effie chose a double-decker - a concession to her waistline - of pecan nut crunch and mango madness. The two of them sat on a bench, silently licking. 'It's 'licious' pronounced Rosie as she grasped the heavy cone in her small hand, her little pink tongue busy. 'Now no need to eat it all if it's too much.' Effie was beginning to wonder if she had been a bit foolish to give the child carte blanche. But Rosie showed no sign of giving up, licking round the colourful dome of the ice cream with care and skilfully catching the drips as they melted and slid down.

Ten minutes later she was down to the last piece of cone, now not so crunchy, but she was clearly not going to leave a single bit and gobbled up the last soggy morsel with a sigh of satisfaction. The older woman and the little girl sat there for a few minutes not speaking but utterly content. Effie closed her eyes briefly and absorbed the heat of the sun on her face, the lingering sweet flavours in her mouth and best of all, the warm wonderful sense of being close to her granddaughter. Give me this kind of love any day, she thought. So much simpler than sex.

Her reverie did not last long. Rosie had recovered from the mountain of ice cream and was now on something of a sugar high, tugging at

Effie's sleeve to get her to go on to the playground which was brimming with happily screaming children. They started at the swings, moved to the big slide and a variety of climbing frames. Rosie was fearless, refusing to be put off by her small size. Effie helped her where she could, giving her a hoist here and a push there. She was amazed at the child's agility and lack of fear. So unlike me at that age she thought. There was a large sandpit at one end of the play space and abandoning the climbing apparatus Rosie soon settled down in the sand where she was quickly chatting to another little girl and finding tools, a spare spade and a bucket. They busied themselves digging and patting what shortly Rosie informed Effie was a sand house. 'You can come in when we're finished,'

'OK darling. I'll sit here and watch.' She seated herself on a bench at the edge of the sandpit with the other lazily watching guardians.

The afternoon moved on and the sun was going down so that shadows lengthened in the sand as Effie watched, closing her eyes occasionally, but careful not to drift off. It was peaceful, despite the noise of the children. She noticed Rosie looking up every now and again in her direction. Just checking I'm here, she thought and pondered a while on her younger grandchild. A feisty little girl who was jostling for position with a dominating older sister. Not as self-confident as Daisy nor as vain, though coming a close second. She couldn't really blame them. The shops were stuffed full of fashion items for children and she knew she herself could succumb to purchasing items which were unnecessarily adult and too sexy. But the children always leapt on such purchases with enthusiasm. Strange really because Cathy had never bothered about that sort of thing. Even as a teenager she had steadfastly taken a defiant stance against the prevailing fashion. And now, venturing into the world of dating had forced Effie to take her own appearance more seriously. With Susie's expert advice and blunt criticism she had added a few items to her wardrobe, was wearing skirts one size smaller and spending longer on her makeup than she ever remembered from her adolescence. She was all too aware that the three dates so far had all looked her over quite carefully, and she dreaded looking silly. Mutton dressed as lamb came to mind.

Her rumination was interrupted by a tap on the shoulder and a cheerful 'Hi Effie'. It was Jim. He looked relaxed in casual clothes. He had already picked up a touch of tan on his face and gave her a smile revealing strong white teeth. He stood for a moment looking for his daughter. 'So how's things? She looks as though she's enjoying herself. Who's the friend?'

'Oh I think it's Charlotte, her new friend. They've been busy together for an hour. It's been lovely.'

'Let's see what they've made' said Jim as he moved across. Effie followed. The girls had constructed a dug out of a house with four 'rooms' with sand beds and sand chairs. They had a kitchen with a bucket for a sink and leaves and twigs were arranged on the sand table. A deeper hole led off one of the rooms which Rosie claimed was 'the loo'. There were lumps of wet sand and bits of bark in the loo. 'We don't know how to flush it away' explained Rosie's friend and they giggled together. 'And that's where the daddy sleeps when they have a row'. Rosie pointed to a small dug-out area.

'Oh, do they row?' queried Effie, but at that moment a young woman appeared who turned out to be Charlotte's mother. Neither child wanted to go and some ten minutes passed in negotiating an extraction. The friend cried and wheedled and so did Rosie till finally, Jim's patience wearing thin, he promised her a quick visit to the adventure playground. 'For big kids like me' pronounced Rosie. 'Yeh, well, if you go there you've got to behave like a big kid and not cry like a baby,' said Jim, taking Rosie firmly by the hand.

'Well, I think that's my cue to get going, Jim. I'll just walk over with you and then make tracks.' Rosie, happy again in her minor victory, was chatting away to her father as she scooted along. Effie listened, impressed by the speed with which the child's mood could change from apparent catastrophe to a kind of happy insouciance. Oh to be a child and recover so fast.

Jim stopped at the entrance to the adventure playground. They made their farewells, he gave her a friendly peck on the cheek and Effie headed off for home feeling good about her afternoon. So good to have Rosie on her own for once. She put her hand up to the cheek where Jim had deposited the kiss and strolled along the path admiring the flower beds, the profusion of colours, fresh smells. She bent down occasionally to inspect a bloom and smell it. The sun was still warm on her back and she felt life really wasn't too bad. She carried these pleasing feelings with her as she exited the park and made her way to the bus stop to wait for her bus home. A young girl was already in the shelter and gave her a smile. Nothing like a fine day to make people friendly she thought. She noticed the girl's earrings, pretty gold rings with a purple stone, probably amethysts, a stone she liked. The sun, now low in the sky, caught the gold and glistened brightly. Effie's mobile rang. She tutted as she pulled it out of her bag to answer, the peaceful spell broken. It was Jim and there was panic in his voice. 'Rosie's fallen off – cut her head – can you come, please.'

Ch. 6

Effie reached the adventure playground sweating and panting. She quickly found them. A small group of people were huddled round the pair and Rosie was crying with a high pitched frightened sound. Effie threw herself into the crowd calling out: 'Rosie, gran'ma's here.'

The little girl was sitting on the ground cradled by her father who was holding a bloody handkerchief to her forehead and trying to sooth the distraught child. Her dark wavy hair was soaked in blood on one side sticking to the child's white distorted face, her eyes scrunched shut. Bright scarlet stains covered the front of her pale pink t-shirt. Jim was ashen: 'thank god. I think it's all right but I can't tell. It's all right, darling, it's all right.'

The small crowd moved aside to let Effie take her place next to the injured child. 'It's going to be all right, it'll be all right.' Effie took in the situation quickly. The child did not seem to have any broken bones or other injuries apart from the head, and heads, she knew, bled a lot. Jim was explaining.

'She just tumbled down off the top, hit the side of her head on the metal, a great whack.'

'It went bang like a drum' said a solemn-looking little boy standing close to Jim.

A lady tugged at the boy's arm. 'Come away now, George' she said pulling him out from the gawping crowd.

Effie ignored everything but Rosie and slid an arm now round the little girl's waist, easing the sobbing child on to her lap. 'Now I need to take a look, Rosie, just a little look so we can make it better.' She spoke softly but firmly rocking the child now and resting her cheek gently on the side of her head that was not bleeding. Jim held the handkerchief

33

in place and Effie made no attempt to move it until Rosie gradually calmed and the terror left her sobs. She stayed like this for several minutes continuing to rock Rosie as she spoke soothingly. The crowd began to drift off sensing that things were settling and there was no tragedy to stare at.

'There we go, darling, now I'm just going have a peep and make sure we don't need to let the doctor have a look. See what you get up to when gran'ma's not looking.'

'She just fell. My back was turned for one minute. I don't think I could have caught her anyway.'

'No, no, Jim. No one's fault. Now let's see, poppet.' She took the bloody handkerchief from Jim and examined the damage: a nasty gash which was still bleeding. The head bleeds such a lot, she told herself again. 'I think this one does need a bit more attention, Jim, just to be on the safe side. Now Rosie,' she addressed her grandchild quietly but seriously. 'Rosie, we're going to take you to a special place where a doctor can have a quick look and make you better very quickly.' Rosie whimpered. 'It's nothing to worry about. I promise it won't hurt and we'll stay with you. Promise.'

Now that Rosie had calmed down Jim was on the phone trying to get through to Cathy. 'Damn it. She's not answering. Where is she?'

'Never mind, Jim, come on. We've got to get this one to the clinic as soon as possible,' said Effie taking charge, easing Rosie onto her feet. 'Let's see if that bleeding stopping.' She tutted as a sliver of bright red new blood trickled down her cheek. 'Here, I know what we can do.' She pulled a flowery silk scarf from her handbag and wound it twice round Rosie's head covering one eye so that she looked 'like a pirate' Effie joked hoping to lighten the child's mood.

'And I'll be your pirate ship' said Jim as he gathered up his daughter in his arms and strode off towards the car park. By the time they reached it Rosie had stopped crying although she looked pale and shocked so that Effie sat with her on the back seat keeping her arm round her and talking quietly. She fished out a story book from the children's debris scattered around in the back of the car and started to read as Jim sped off, his phone clamped to one ear as he tried again to contact Cathy. 'Why the hell doesn't she answer?'

The experience at the clinic was straightforward enough; a late afternoon lull before incidents involving young people out on the town on a Saturday night kicked in. Jim was tense when they arrived, raising his voice when he heard they would have to wait half an hour or so. 'Wait!, but she's only four years old. I think someone should look at her immediately.'

'But we have, sir. I've taken a look and my assessment is that she will be fine until the doctor is free to come and do the sutures.' The nurse's voice was patient but firm. No special treatment here, thought Effie. No, you wait your turn. Her role clearly was to keep Jim calm as much as Rosie. She suggested he went and bought them a cup of tea and a juice for Rosie who was sitting quietly and unusually still, her little face white except for smears of now drying blood which Effie thought it was best to leave for fear of upsetting her further. Cleaning up would come later.

Jim returned, his neck crooked to accommodate his phone while he balanced two steaming paper cups and a packet of juice. He was explaining to Cathy. 'Look, I think it's OK now, your Mum's here and they apparently don't think anything too serious. What?... No, no, she didn't fall right on her head... she knocked it on the metal side of the slide when she fell.... No, they don't think she needs an x-ray, at least, that's what the nurse said.... No, better you stay there with Daisy. I'll call if any news... yes, I'll hand it over. She might like to hear your voice.'

Jim held the phone to Rosie's ear, but the moment she heard her mother's voice she burst into tearful sobs. 'Oh don't cry, darling'. Effie could hear her daughter's tense voice. 'Poor darling, it'll be all right.' More sobs from Rosie. 'It'll be all right, darling...' Jim took the phone away leaving Effie to comfort the little girl again while he paced up and down continuing his conversation with Cathy, arm and voice raised now. '... she just fell, I couldn't reach her... Yes, Cathy, I did.' Jim was frowning when he came back to where Effie and Rosie were sitting. His colour was high showing through the tan. Effie tactfully concentrated on trying to soothe Rosie.

'There, there, my pet,' she crooned as she rocked Rosie gently. The little rigid body softened and gradually allowed herself to sink into Effie's chest. 'We'll see Mummy very soon. We'll be home as soon as the doctor's made it better. Look, daddy brought you some juice. Shall I help you put the straw in? No?'

Effie started humming in rhythm with her rocking motion. Rosie quietened and put her thumb in her mouth. Effie continued to sing softly watching as Rosie's eyes flickered and then closed. Jim was sitting opposite, bending forward, brow furrowed as her stared at his daughter. 'She'll be all right,' Effie reassured him. 'Believe me, she'll be all right. It's not as bad as it looks.' And she flashed him a smile which she knew he registered, his blue eyes lifting briefly from his daughter to meet hers.

'So stupid, Effie. We only went to the damn place because she was making a fuss. So stupid...'

Rosie Cunningham. A voice echoed Rosie's name round the waiting room. There was a slight stirring and heads looked up briefly. 'Cubicle three, please' the voice called. 'Thank goodness,' said Jim as he reached down to carry Rosie into the allotted cubicle. Rosie opened her eyes but did not start crying again and the three of them were ushered into the small space by a large smiling nurse. 'So what have you been up to?' she beamed at Rosie.

'Now let's have a proper look. It won't hurt but I just need to make sure it's all clean,' she intoned as she pulled on a pair of surgical gloves. 'The doctor wants to have a look and he'll be here in a minute. Just finishing stitching someone up next door. That one fell off a ladder trying to reach his cat stuck in a tree. Nearly killed himself' she cackled. 'Twenty one stitches.' She cackled again while Rosie stared wide-eyed. The nurse pulled off the temporary dressing and, still chortling, peered at the gash which had at last stopped bleeding. She dabbed around the wound with cotton wool and a strong smelling liquid. Effie could see Rosie's lip wobble.

But at that moment diversion arrived in the form of the doctor, a young man with dark hair cut short and glasses who looked as though he was only recently out of medical school but who seemed to know what he was doing and managed to put Rosie at ease by letting her play with his stethoscope. He seemed in no hurry, allowing her to put the earpiece in her ears and hold it against his own chest. 'See that's my heart. It's noisy isn't it?' Rosie smiled for the first time since the accident. 'OK, then, Rosie. Now I want you to be very grown- up and lie still while I fix that nasty cut you've got. I'm going to give you something so it doesn't hurt.' He turned to Jim. 'Do you want to stay?

'Yes of course. I'll hold her hand.'

'Fine. Let's get on with it then.'

So Jim sat at the head of the bed holding Rosie's hand while the doctor and nurse busied themselves with the medical paraphernalia. Effie sat at the bottom of the bed, wishing it was over and they could go home. She hated seeing the little girl in such pain and distress. Yes, hard to think about, and as a diversion she let herself calculate how many stitches the doctor would stitch in a lifetime assuming he did twenty to thirty stitches every hour for maybe twelve hours a week for x number of years. She briefly drifted off into four figures when she was aroused from her ruminations by Jim who staggered past her looking white.

'Sorry, Effie. Need some air. Can you take over?'

Effie edged round to take his place at Rosie's head. 'So what happened?'

'Oh, I think he felt a bit faint,' said the doctor not raising his head, intent on his work. ` Not easy for parents to see their nearest and dearest stitched up. Fainting at the sight of blood's quite common.' He laughed and gave Effie a quick glimpse. `I don't imagine it's the first time you'll have seen someone's sutures?'

In other words, I'd better not faint too, thought Effie. ` No I'll be fine,' she said squeezing Rosie's hand. Rosie responded by gripping hers firmly. But she stayed still and quiet and did not seem to be in obvious pain. Good girl, thought Effie. She knows when to co-operate. So keep talking, keep her distracted. And so Effie talked about the earlier afternoon and the big ice-creams they had devoured and her new friend and the house they had made together and the fact that the sun was shining (even though it had gone now) and how bulbs she had planted with her grandmother were now flowering, yellow tulips, Rosie's favourite colour because it made her think of sunshine and the lovely golden sand they had seen last summer when they went on holiday down to Cornwall, and so on until the doctor snipped his last piece of thread and raise his head with a satisfied 'there we are, Rosie. All done. Five lovely stitches. I've made them as small as possible,' he said addressing Effie. 'you'll need to come back next week and have the nurse take them out but after that there should be very little scarring. Children's skin is very good at recovering. And you, young lady, are my star patient today.' Rosie, now sitting up, grimaced but Effie knew she was pleased and the colour was coming back into her cheeks.

'Yes, an absolute star. I wish some of my grown up patients were as good as you. Here...' he swivelled round in his chair to fish around in a drawer from which he produced a jar of brightly wrapped sweeties. 'You deserve one of these.'

After a moment of hesitation Rosie reached out her hand and rummaged around until she found one in a shiny golden wrapper.

'I'm sure she's allowed' said the doctor, looking at Effie again. 'A bit of sugar'll do her good after all she's been through. But you be careful now, Rosie. No more falling off slides. Off you go.'

And that was that. What had briefly seemed like a tragedy had shrunk to more of a minor incident in Rosie's short life. The doctor did not think a scan was necessary nor that there would be any further problems. He advised Effie to keep her quiet for a couple of days and just to be vigilant lest there were any sudden or persistent headaches. He's speaking to me as though I'm her mother, she thought as they exited the cubicle. She had almost forgotten about Jim and was surprised to see him sitting outside slumped in a chair. He still looked pale and quite shattered in contrast to Rosie who was beginning to recover her spirits and was happily chewing her sweetie.

'thank god she's all right! Come here, darling. Let me give you a hug' and he reached out to pull her towards him. 'I'm so sorry,Effie. I just couldn't stand the sight of him sticking that needle thing into Rosie. So sorry.' He hugged her even more tightly until she protested. 'Daddy. y. y... wan'a go home now. I wan'a see Mummy.'

'Sure, let's go' and off they set, Jim holding one of Rosie's hands and Effie the other. Now that all was well Effie could let herself enjoy the nice feeling of being with two people she loved and with a good sense that she had been helpful, secretly grateful – awful thought – that nothing terrible had happened while she had been in charge.

She did not stay long once they got back to the house. Cathy was waiting anxiously and quickly enveloped Rosie in her arms, while even Daisy seemed pleased to see her sister in one piece and readily admired the stitches that Rosie showed off. Jim's colour had returned and he recounted the story while Cathy tutted occasionally as she rocked Rosie on her lap.

'Your mother was great' came a full compliment from Jim as he rounded off the story 'I don't know what I'd've done without her.' He spoke quietly but as though he really meant it, looking straight at Effie with those lovely kind blue eyes of his. Grateful eyes, thought Effie, nodding in response. It was good to be appreciated by her family. She had noticed that Jim had not mentioned fainting in the clinic. It had not been a good afternoon for him and the episode was between her and him, unless Rosie said something which she didn't think she would.

Time to go home, to her own home. She turned down the offer of a lift from Jim. No, she'd rather get some fresh air on a fine evening. She also experienced a definite feeling that it would be unwise to accept such an offer. So she made her farewells and walked herself down to the bus stop, picking a daisy as she went so that she could pluck off the petals, counting them to see if she could guess the number.

Ch. 7

Date number 4 was a friend of a friend. After her three not so successful experiences with the dating agency and websites, not to mention the emotional ups and downs with the family, the idea of this 'friend' really appealed. Susie, as ever eager to express an opinion, was reassuringly positive about it. 'A friend is bound to be better. I mean you feel you already know something about them. They're sort of vetted.'

'They're not sick animals, Susie' replied Effie as she stirred the chocolate into her cappuccino. 'Anyway, I don't know him. He's someone Vanessa knows. Or even someone Vanessa knows knows. I'm not raising my hopes.'

'Oh go on, Effie. Relax.' said Susie sprinkling sweetener over her latte with gay abandon. 'He just might be your dream man, so you'd better be ready.'

'Dream man! I don't have dreams like that any more. That's something Jack stole from me when he decided that my best friend was his dream girl... that skinny bitch Helen !' Her spoon stabbed through the frothy top of her cappuccino, furious at Jack, annoyed at herself that he could still upset her. 'OK, Susie. I'll go. But it's suddenly striking me that in a way this is a more awkward one, I mean, the fact that Vanessa knows him makes it all seem much more public.'

'So? It's a natural human urge to want to be with someone. And I'm sure it doesn't occur to Vanessa to think it is anything but totally normal.'

'Well, I wasn't suggesting it was <u>abnormal,</u> just a bit exposing. Anyway, I said I'd go. I've told him I'll come. And I'll tell you one thing about this guy - he's called Quentin, by the way - he's rich.'

Susie put her cup down and gave Effie her full attention.

'Yes, Vanessa tells me his family are pretty loaded, very successful family business which he inherited. But he's no shirker. He sold off the family business after a while at some huge profit and then started up another one which is also doing well. Quite talented at making things work and gathering in quite a fortune in the process, or so Vanessa told me over the phone. She was surprisingly frank for someone I hardly know myself. Anyway, perhaps at least this time I'll get taken out to dinner.' The two women laughed and sipped their coffee thoughtfully.

Prospects looked good. Quentin had called her and she liked the sound of his voice, deep, warm and very polite. He got 7 out of 10 for initial presentation. Effie was a hard marker. He suggested they went to 'Le coq rouge' for dinner and his score soared. 'Le coq rouge' was a first rate restaurant with an excellent reputation and Effie felt hungry just thinking about it. After putting the phone down she couldn't resist immediately phoning her friend to tell her the news. 'My god, Susie. So far he's done everything right.'

This time it was Susie who voiced a note of caution. 'Great, darling, but hold your horses till you actually meet him. He might turn out to be fat and sweaty with bad breath.'

'I don't think so.'

The rendezvous was to be the following Friday and Quentin would pick her up in his car. As the day in question approached there was no doubt that Effie was experiencing an unaccustomed excitement – or was it nerves? She found herself drifting off at work imagining likely scenarios. What to wear also became a preoccupation. She scanned her wardrobe for the umpteenth time and on this occasion Susie was no help. Her suggestions were always for short skirts and bright tops which Effie felt ignored the all too evident fact that her legs were definitely on the plump side, if shapely, and too short a skirt risked revealing the varicose vein on her right leg, apart from looking silly. In desperation she consulted her two daughters.

The ever romantic Jane suggested her mother wear a dress – 'something filmy, better at disguising excess flesh', while practical Cathy went for trouser suit and boots – 'Best to cover your legs. More comfortable anyway.' After these encouraging comments - how could she expect the girls to take her dating seriously? - Effie decided to take the matter into her own hands, and paid a visit to Halter & Gusset where she tried on fifteen bras before exiting with a lacy black affair and a pair of 'tummy tightening tights'. Her wardrobe was subject to one final scan at 6.35 on Friday night leaving her precisely 55 minutes to get ready, which should be ample time, she told herself, although she had not calculated with a lengthy struggle to get in to the extremely tight tights. Once in place she was pleased with the result even if she could hardly breath and by 7.30 she was able to stand in front of the mirror and look with a degree of satisfaction at her reflected image: a fitted black skirt down to the knee, a red silk polo neck top, black tights and her highest pair of heels. Her hair gray but shiny and sleek, enough eye-makeup to bring out her grey eyes and a touch of light apricot lipstick. Not bad. She slipped on her black fitted jacket as she heard a car draw up and the doorbell ring.

The first thing she noticed was the car. She didn't know what it was but what she did know was that it was something special. For one thing it was incredibly low and she had to bend right down to get in. Once she had undertaken this manoeuvre with as much grace as she could muster she was able to give her attention to Quentin. He looked nice. In fact he looked very nice. He smiled revealing a set of perfect white teeth. He put his hand through thick gray hair. Not a sign of balding. He beamed kindly, two brown eyes looking at her. And then there was the voice which in reality sounded even more attractive than on the phone. It was a deep, quiet yet penetrating voice which had no trace of hesitation. She summed him up as a man at ease with himself. She, on the other hand, felt a disturbing thrill of excitement which was far from easy to handle. Why did some men get to look more attractive as they got older?

She had only a vague memory of how they got to the restaurant or what they talked about, she felt simply overwhelmed by her senses. This attractive looking man, the plush car seats, the purring engine, and then the assiduous attention of the maitre domo at Le coq rouge who welcomed Quentin as a familiar client and smiled politely at her. None of the ill-concealed sneering of the waiter on her date with Simon. They were seated at an excellent table and in a quietly authoritative voice Quentin suggested they start by looking at the menu. 'Let's get that dealt with shall we?'

And what a menu it was. 'Have whatever you like' he reassured her in a way that left Effie feeling he really meant it so that her eye automatically shifted to the more expensive items on the list. She rapidly calculated the likely cost of the meal, the digits in her head moving rapidly to three figures as a glass of champagne was placed temptingly by her right hand. She chose a starter of smoked salmon mousse served on a bed of courgette flowers, followed by lamb noisettes en croute with a mint and basil coulis. 'Excellent choice'. Quentin nodded approvingly. He chose a lobster bisque to start followed by fillet steak au poivre. 'Not as adventurous as you' he smiled, to Effie's delight. He raised his glass and Effie realised that she had been so absorbed in what was going on that she hadn't even thought about her normal need to drink in order to put herself at ease. 'Cheers' she said with a clink of cut glass. Quentin sat back.

'So, Effie, I understand you're a friend of Ursula.'

'Ursula?'

'Yes, Ursula Hammond.'

'Well, no. I'm a friend of Vanessa.'

'Vanessa?'

'Yes, Vanessa Campbell'.

'Ah. So you don't know Ursula?'

'No – no, I don't know her... but I do know Vanessa and I think she knows Ursula.'

'Ah. So you haven't spoken to Ursula?' He sipped his drink thoughtfully leaving Effie feeling awkward and mildly guilty for not knowing the right person. She gulped her champagne which went straight to her head.

'So, to the missing link' she joked as she raised her glass, hoping Quentin would smile again, which after a second or two he did, raising his eyes from their apparent preoccupation with a loose thread on the table cloth. 'Well, you'd better tell me a bit about yourself I think.'

So Effie recounted something of the basic facts of her story, her family, her divorce and was moving on to say a bit about her job when the first course arrived looking absolutely delicious. Her spirits perked up considerably. The food was indeed quite splendid and Quentin quickly finished his plate of soup. 'So how about you?' queried Effie, 'I don't know a great deal about you.'

Quentin laughed and sat back in his chair. 'What to tell...? At that moment his phone rang. 'Ah, sorry, I'd better take this. Excuse me.' With which he got up and disappeared towards the men's room. Effie finished off her mousse and was quite happy to savour the delicious flavours once finished. A waiter hovered and refilled her glass as it emptied. About five minutes passed and Effie checked her watch. Yes, more than five minutes. She wished he'd come back. Another ten minutes went by before he returned, profusely apologising.

'Sorry. There's a business deal I'm nurturing. It's American time - six hours behind us. It always happens just when I'm starting something. Bad timing I'm afraid. Anyway, enough of that. Where were we?' he asked, placing the phone on the table beside him.

'You were just about to tell me about you.'

'Me? Well, where should I start? I guess I'd hoped Ursula might have filled you in a bit. I'm not the greatest at talking about myself.'

There was a pause. Effie hesitated. This reticence was unexpected from a man who seemed so self-assured and obviously successful. Was she expected to step in and say something? She wished he'd put that phone away. It was periodically winking. In her experience, most people liked talking about themselves if given half a chance. Should she give him a few cues: I'd love to hear about your work, or even, do tell me what your interests are? These flash thoughts were rescued from the need to make a decision by the arrival of the main course which Quentin greeted with a hearty 'ah ha'.

The conversation turned to food which was a topic dear to Effie's heart, while Quentin was clearly equally at ease. He became quite voluble, expanded at length on his considerable experience of restaurants and his 'dabbling' in cookery. Effie could not compete on the restaurant front. Even during her married life they had rarely ventured out to eat, Jack preferring to eat at home, but as a result, Effie had developed into an extremely good cook and she could talk about food with enthusiasm. Quentin seemed to be genuinely interested in her culinary skills and was soon asking her about recipes as he sliced his way through his succulent steak.

'I always use a bit of good old-fashioned lard when I do savoury pastry. It actually makes it lighter I find',

'Really? But isn't it the flour you use that makes the difference?'

'Well, that's hugely important, of course, but...' The phone rang and Effie stopped in mid-sentence. A name flashed up on the screen and she had just time, reading it upside down, to make out 'Gloria..'

'Ach. Sorry, Effie. Have to take that. Just when it was getting interesting. This'll be a quickie. Don't want to mess up the deal.'

I'll bet you don't, was the angry thought that gathered in Effie's head as she watched him talking in the lobby, phone to his ear and arms gesticulating. If Gloria was merely a friend why not say so? Was this another man out to deceive her? By the time Quentin returned four and a half minutes later, profusely apologising again, Effie had worked herself up into quite a lather inside about his Macavity-like performance, the ready 'alibi', the unreliability of men in general and, of course, the principle culprit, her husband with the feet of clay. She had not experienced quite such a rage since the bad days after Jack had left on the arm her best friend. She glowered at the waiter who was brandishing a menu. 'Dessert, madam?'

'Oh yes, Effie, we must have dessert. I can see you need something sweet after my unforgivable rudeness.' He flashed her a smile. 'And what I recommend is the hot raspberry soufflé. They do it to a tee.'

'They do?'

The idea of a hot raspberry soufflés was definitely tempting and Effie's angry ruminations subsided. He really was most charming, and perhaps Gloria really was just a friend. She had no claims on Quentin anyway, and wondered why she had felt so annoyed. Quentin was looking at the wine list again and was discussing a dessert wine with the waiter. 'We absolutely must have at least a small glass of Sauterne with this dessert. The two go together like, well...' he hesitated 'I was going to say like in the old song about love and marriage but perhaps not appropriate for either of us. I believe we're both divorced. Maybe it's more like good food and France.'

'But the French have rested on their reputation far too long and have got careless' Effie asserted with a degree of certainty that surprised her. 'I really think the Italians have got the edge with their marvellous pastas and simple roast meats not to mention the best hard cheeses in Europe.'

'Yes, but the basic attitude to food in France is different, it's serious and such an important part of daily life and, well, there are so many superb restaurants, like this one,' he smiled. 'And just wait till you try this divine soufflé' he added as the waiter emerged carrying a tray on which perched two little white dishes capped and overflowing with crispy mounds of pink froth tinged with golden-brown and smelling of heaven.

'Wow!' Effie could not help exclaiming.

'Voila' from Quentin 'you would't get anything like that in Italy.'

They raised their long silver spoons, and to Effie's surprise the phone did not ring. The soufflés were quite delicious but fleeting. Effie's was consumed in three minutes twenty two seconds, but was memorable. She sat back and sipped the equally delicious sauterne and felt much more benign towards her companion who had eaten his dessert even more quickly than she. He raised his glass to her. 'Here's to a great meal and to the best cuisine in the world, and I think I can also toast a small victory in my own life. That last call has just about clinched the deal. I don't think anything can go wrong now. Yes, here's to Glorianna.'

'Glorianna?'

'Yes, it's the name if the company. Pretty crumby name but not my choice.'

'I see.'

'Oh I'm sure you've never heard of it. We deal in some totally unnecessary products to do with airport hygiene. Nothing very exciting.'

Effie realised that this was the first piece of solid information she had received from Quentin apart from the brief reference to divorce and a quantity of insights into his gastronomic tastes which were clearly partisan. She rebuked herself for having got Gloria wrong and wasted emotional energy on unnecessary anger. She suddenly felt tired and a bit old, worn down by the strain of having to be sociable with someone she did not know. The initial thrill, like the soufflé, had subsided and she did not feel much the wiser about Quentin. Not an easy man to get to know and perhaps not that interesting underneath the trappings of success. More immediately, the mixture of excitement and tension, the rich food, not to mention the growing discomfort of her stomach increasingly complaining against the constriction of the tights, was beginning to play havoc with her digestive system and she longed to get home. Quentin, however, had summoned the chef into the dining room so that he could express his admiration and gratitude for the delicious meal and all things Gallic and carried on an enthusiastic conversation with 'Pierre' in appalling French that grated on Effie's churning stomach. The two men appeared to have forgotten all about her and the continued talk about rich food was beginning to make Effie feel heavy and a bit sick. Desperate measures were called for. It was only when she managed to make herself sneeze extremely loudly that the two men stopped their conversation and looked at her.

'I 'ope madame eez not catching the cold?' Pierre asked considerately as Effie dabbed her nose with a pink tissue.

'Oh non, ce n'est rien - un peu trop de bonnes chose ce soir - la cuisine etait vraiment superbe – l'agneau magnifique et le desert - je n'ai jamais goutte un desert comme ca – le soufflé aux framboises etait parfait - hors du monde - et merci.' She waved her arms as she spoke in true Gallic fashion.

By the time Effie finished this little piece of theatricality Pierre was grinning and Quentin was looking distinctly less pleased. 'Well, Effie, for someone who speaks such good French I'm surprised you aren't more in favour of French food.'

'Oh I never said I didn't like it. I really did enjoy the meal tonight, but I just think there are other kinds of cooking and I <u>am</u> quite keen on Italian It seems to suit my stomach better. Talking of which, I think I'd better get back if you don't mind.'

'Ah yes, of course'.

The journey home was quiet and Effie had the sense that she had definitely put a foot wrong somewhere, either by not being sufficiently Francophile or by demonstrating that she was better at the language than he was. Either way, she was not surprised that when he dropped her off there was only a vague reference to doing something again and a quite petulant parting shot: 'I'm sorry if it was too rich for you. It really is the best of its kind in this part of town'.

Half an hour later, her stomach at last released from the stranglehold grip of the terrible tights, she sighed with relief as she sipped a cup of Dr Davis's digestive detox tea in the vain hope that consuming it would guarantee her a decent night's sleep.

Ch. 8

Ever the optimist, Effie had decided to make the most of her experience with Quentin by trying to re-create the amazing raspberry soufflé or something equally impressive. It was Friday morning, her day off, and she had invited some of her female friends round for a light supper that evening. Dissatisfied with what she found in her own collection of recipe books she had gone on line only to find that her computer stubbornly refused to work and was stuck with a bug. Her usual rescuer for such a glitch, son Leo, was working and could not help. Her solution was to catch a bus and go to her local library.

The building had recently been refurbished and had the pleasant clean feel of fresh paint about it. One end of the large rectangular room was now set aside with twenty or so computers at long tables. There were also bays in which were wooden desks and work tables which on this particular day were half full with people either using the computers or reading. Effie liked the place which did not feel too much like a public building. Young people from the nearby comprehensive used it as well as a medley of locals. She found the atmosphere of quiet study stimulating, and it also satisfied a certain voyeuristic pleasure in being able to sit and watch the life that passed through the doors of the establishment. The chance to enjoy a private laugh at the goings on was rarely disappointed.

Today she felt purposeful and went straight to the shelves where she knew she would find recipe books. She carried three heavy tomes across to the free computer space she was allocated by the librarian, an amazingly young-looking girl with long slim legs poking out of a tiny stretchy skirt that clung to her buttocks like sellotape. Tiny pert breasts protruded from an equally clinging top. She peered at Effie through a pair of John Lennon glasses and two heavily made up eyes. Her voice, however, was perfectly grown up.

'You can have it for an hour.' She flashed a smile revealing pearly white teeth. Effie dutifully sat at the appointed desk conscious of easing herself as elegantly as possible onto the seat under the gaze of the nymphet. Goodness, I could get two of her into me, she thought as she watched the girl walk briskly away on a pair of equally insubstantial kitten heels. Well, if you insist on making rich desserts, was the annoying thought.

Effie sighed but opened a book and was soon absorbed in her search. She logged on to her computer and entertained herself with browsing through a series of photographs of tempting –looking dishes which made her mouth water. A dark chocolate cake caught her attention. It looked moist and inviting. Too rich. Stick to the idea of a fruit soufflé or definitely something fruity. She flicked on to the section on fruit tarts and flans but was distracted by the sight of a man who was trundling a laden supermarket trolley round the room muttering to himself from time to time. He had a straggly beard and wild gray hair while he sported a coat that looked as though it had once been smart which was now ragged and tied round the middle with a piece of string. The nymphet took no notice, continuing to tap away at her keyboard. In fact nobody took much notice and Effie guiltily cast her eyes back to her screen. The tramp proceeded to push his trolley slowly round the room, pausing occasionally to inspect a book on a shelf, still muttering as though engaging in a private commentary.

Effie turned her attention back to the computer and continued to flick through the recipes, stopping at a picture of a magnificent frothy edifice which appeared under the heading of 'pistachio and greengage soufflé '. A huge greeny- gold dome of froth rose like the Taj Mahal above a white porcelain dish.

'That's a beauty' drawled a loud well-educated voice beside her that shattered the discrete quietness of the library. Momentarily everybody looked up in Effie's direction. It was the tramp, who had decided to park his trolley next to Effie and was bending to inspect the picture on the screen.

'Yes, it is rather fine,' said Effie as quietly as she could. The tramp was silent, apart from breathing noisily. Effie was aware of a distinct odour coming from the tramp's proximity. Doing her best to ignore him, she flicked on to the next page praying that he would go away. He, however, was clearly interested in the images and had no intention of moving. He stood there, silently, as Effie flicked the controls at mounting speed, her eyes glued to the screen. Why did he have to pick on her? She was aware that the rest of the assembled company had all returned to their studies and were obviously going to leave her to deal with the situation. She tried glaring at the man sitting opposite, willing him to look up and come to her rescue. But his eyes stayed resolutely down. Bastard!

The tramp began to rustle paper in his trolley within inches of Effie. She did not dare look for fear of what she might see. She was beginning to break out in an uncomfortable sweat and feared that she too might be smelling. Concentration was impossible. Prayer seemed futile. Rational argument? It could be you, she told herself, reduced to tramping around with all your possessions piled up in a trolley. And with this attempt to take a more benign view of the situation Effie turned to him. 'So are you looking for something?' Her voice was calmer than she felt.

'Looking for something?' His voice boomed out, and he turned his head towards the window, staring for a while. 'Now that is one of the deep philosophical questions of the age' he intoned. 'We are, all of us, undoubtedly looking for something. We search. We ponder. We search again. And sometimes we find.' His gaze came back to Effie. 'And you, fair lady, no doubt are no exception. You have the air about you of someone who is searching, searching I think not just for the culinary delights of this world but also for its masculine pleasures. Yes, a fair lady in search of her gallant knight.' With this he took a deep sigh and stood quite motionless, eyes fixed on Effie.

She shrank inwardly and outwardly. The damp feeling under her armpits was now a trickling stream and she knew her face was scarlet. What to do? Get up and go? Engage him in conversation? She shot a furious glance over to the nymphet who was still doggedly ignoring the drama despite the penetrating voice. Eyes flicked down as Effie's glance roved angrily around the room. Was chivalry completely dead?

The tramp seemed to be transfixed to the floor as was his gaze fixed on her as he muttered to himself and occasionally laughed lightly. He raised his arm and for a terrifying moment Effie thought he was going to stroke her hair.

Her phone rang and at this sound the nymphet's head shot up. She stared accusingly. 'Please, no mobile phones'.

Effie grabbed the phone and marched herself out of the room into the corridor, glaring at the nymphet as she passed, but hugely grateful to see that it was daughter Jane who had come to her rescue. 'Thank god, darling, I'm being propositioned by a tramp and it's not my thing.'

Jane was suitably sympathetic and chatted with her mother for several minutes. 'But, Mum, don't turn him down on my account.' 'For god's sake, Jane, it's no laughing matter. I don't fancy him and he won't go away. Any suggestions? I can't go till I get my stuff.' Effie was peering through the glass door of the reading room. 'Hang on, I think he's moving. Damn. He's coming this way. Must go.'

She jammed the phone in her pocket and dived into the ladies room which luckily was close by. Surely he wouldn't follow her there? She hovered behind the door trying to hear if he was moving off. There was a shuffling noise outside precipitating a further retreat and flight into one of the cubicles locking the door firmly. What now? She felt angry, a bit frightened and utterly ridiculous, a prisoner in the cubicle, but she did not dare go out until she was quite sure he had gone. For the moment she could only hear her own breathing and heart thumping. Was that the door? Wasn't that a familiar bad smell? She had seen in the movies people caught in situations like this and knew that the tell-tale fact was that your feet could be seen under the door. She quietly put down the toilet lid and hoisted herself up keeping her head down for fear it would be visible over the top of the cubicle. Someone was running water and it sounded as though they were washing their hands. She stayed still, her thoughts racing. The water continued to run. She crouched precariously on the loo seat and tried to calm herself by calculating the amount of water that got flushed away if the loo was used every twenty minutes eight hours a day... and wasn't that a waste of public money... and wasn't it a waste of her time being stuck in a public lavatory, a conclusion which triggered a seriously angry thought about

Quentin. After all, it was because of him that she was trying to do the damn soufflé in the first place, and her fault for trying to impress the girls. Oh woe the sin of pride, or was it vanity, we are meant to avoid?

At that moment there was the sound of someone humming, and humming in a female voice. The water had stopped and there was the buzz of an electric hand dryer. Effie dared to peep over the top of the cubicle whereupon a pretty young red-head screamed: 'My god! You gave me a shock!'

Effie clambered down and opened the door, apologising as she did so and hastened to explain her behaviour as best she could. The girl shrugged. 'Well, there's no one out there now.' Which there wasn't, so that Effie was able to return to her desk with comparative dignity to gather up her things and flee the building leaving a trail of cookery books behind. There was no way she was going to attempt a soufflé tonight. No, it would be fruit salad and half-fat crème fraiche, a healthier option anyway. And no raspberries.

Her spirits were down, however, as she walked home from the supermarket, a shopping bag in each hand. It was hard not to feel discouraged by the events of the day, although she could imagine that recounting the story of the tramp would raise a few laughs from her friends that evening. But for Effie it only succeeded in adding to her feeling that the task of finding herself a suitable partner was becoming something of an emotional minefield.

She reflected on the cast of characters she had met so far – admittedly only 4 - 5 if she included the tramp - but it felt like a multitude. In her present mood she could only see them as oddballs, flawed or inadequate and she was not at all sure that her friends that evening could help her shift her view to see them less harshly: could they be intriguing, impressive, novel? The funny thing was that the most perceptive person she had met to date was the tramp.

Ch. 9

Effie decided to stop counting after Quentin and the tramp. This was partly superstition. Wasn't there something about the number 4 or was it 5? Also, she disliked the feeling of the shopping list applied to people. Her girlfriend's had advised her to keep going but to take a more relaxed approach and definitely not to count. Effie replied feebly that counting things just came rather easily to her. It had been a disappointing Saturday. As a treat for the largely recovered Rosie, she had taken the two girls to a pizza parlour for lunch and they had not behaved well, spilling their drinks and arguing, and when she dropped them off back home Cathy had looked grim-faced and barely thanked her mother. Jim was nowhere to be seen and she offered no explanation. An afternoon visit to the gym did nothing to improve Effie's mood. She came out feeling exhausted, hungry and depressed that her weight had not shifted and so it was with some gusto that on returning to the house the first thing she did was to chuck her pile of 'duds' into Monday's recycling bag. A light was flashing on her answer-phone. She eyed it warily. She had intended to have a girl's evening with her friend Bea but she wasn't at all sure if she could face going out again. Thoughts of a soak in the bath with a glass of wine and some tele were tempting. There was a good film on later. She wanted to ignore the winking light on her desk but curiosity got the better of her and she pressed the button.

It was Oliver. She had almost forgotten about him. It was a good two weeks since their encounter and Effie had not been encouraging about the possibility of meeting up again. She had, however, given him her phone number, grudgingly, because he had asked for it while his daughter was standing there and it seemed rude not to do so. Susie and she had relegated him to the 'duds' box. There was no way she was going to step into a dead woman's shoes and, besides, she had most definitely not forgotten the pathetic left-overs that had served as dinner.

So here was Oliver again, his voice quite chirpy and not unpleasant.

'Hello, Effie? This is Oliver speaking. I hope you don't mind me ringing on a Saturday but I thought I'd call. Short notice I know, but I wondered how you were fixed for tomorrow and whether you'd like to pop over for a spot of lunch. My brother and his wife are coming. She's a damn good cook and has offered to do the cooking... lovely if you could join us. I did enjoy our evening together. Anyway, you know my number. Give us a call, or I'll call again later. Hope all well.'

Effie glanced at her watch. Already after 7.00. Bar's open and the water's hot, was her immediate thought. No need to do anything about Oliver just yet. Ten minutes later she was lying in a fragrant froth of bubbles with a glass of red Shiraz perched on the side of the bath. She breathed a sigh of pleasure as she sank back feeling her body relax in the warm water. Her thoughts wandered back to the incident with Rosie who was clearly none the worse for wear after her fall. Such an adventurous child, which was admirable, but had its costs. She remembered her brother Victor who had been a daredevil if ever there was one, rarely without a cut or bruise and never cried. He used to call her a cry baby if she did. There'd been absolutely no concession to her being younger and a girl. Only once she remembered him shedding a few tears when he crashed his bike into a concrete wall and gashed his ankle almost through to the bone. There had been raw flesh and blood everywhere. It had been shocking and sick-making. Not just the ghastly sight of the damaged leg but to see her heroic brother with tears that he couldn't prevent from silently oozing from his eyes on his contorted face. She shuddered even now to think of it and felt a chill despite the hot water. She sipped the wine, and another wounded leg, Jim's leg, came to mind.

The phone was ringing, interrupting her ruminations. Knowing perfectly well she did not have to answer, Effie hauled herself out of the bubbles and wrapping a large towel around her shuffled through to the bedroom. You never know, it might be an emergency. Rosie? But of course it was Oliver. She gave him top marks for persistence.

'Effie? Ah, you're there.'

'Yes, yes. Hello Oliver. I just picked up your message. How are you?'

'Oh fine, quite fine, yes. So... shall I see you tomorrow? I'm sure you'd like my brother and my sister in law. She's a super cook, as I told you, and she's really looking forward to meeting you.'

'She is?'

'Yes, I've told them all about you.'

'You have?'

'Of course.'

'I see.'

'Can't wait to meet you.'

'Right. Well, I guess I'd better come then.'

You idiot! She told herself as she shuffled back to the now cold bath. The sensual pleasures of the evening were spoiled and all she could picture were the unappetising remains of the shepherds pie clinging to the sides of the dish. So why had she said yes? Because you are weak and can't say 'no'. All too complex, was her defence as she pulled the plug. I need to get out of here. So she called her friend Bea in the expectation that she would still be on for a drink, which it turned out she was so that Effie was able at least to off-load some of her thoughts about being pursued by someone she did not find attractive while avoiding going into the more confusing area of her deeper feelings.

Oliver had left a message instructing her to come for a late lunch at 2.00. The day was overcast but dry and Effie spent a lazy morning catching up with emails and tidying the house. She rang Cathy, half hoping for a reason not to go through with the planned lunch, but her daughter was brusque, making unveiled references to the girl's having behaved badly after yesterday's pizza outing. 'We've had enough excitement recently, Mum, what with broken heads and things. I think we'll have a quiet day tomorrow.' and then, as though relenting 'but have a word with Rosie. She's right here.' The receiver was passed over and Effie had a three minute chat with her grand-daughter which was long for Rosie. She sounded her usual chirpy self. Nothing wrong with her. Effie found herself wishing that her mother could be half as resilient as her daughter who frequently demonstrated her capacity to bounce back from adversity. Cathy, even as a little girl had tended to catastrophise when something went wrong. Still does, which was a sobering thought for Effie as she mounted the stairs to her bedroom in order to change for the lunch outing. She doesn't take kindly to things going wrong and definitely not if her mother's anything to do with it.

She switched on the radio in the bedroom to listen to the news as she changed into clothes suitable for a casual Sunday lunch. Fitted trousers – not too smart - and a dark sweater over a pink shirt. There were reports of heavy rain in the west country but the sun here was beginning to peak through lightening the clouds as she snapped herself into her seatbelt and headed for Oliver's house.

It had been dusk when she had paid the previous visit and the house had seemed gray and disorganised, but today with the sunshine it looked brighter and she was surprised to see how much of the clutter had disappeared from the hallway when she entered the house ushered in by Oliver who also looked rather more spruce, apart from the strand of hair which was still plastered across his dome-like head. He smiled, pleased to see Effie and conducted her through to the living room which today had a door open on to the garden. It too looked tidier. A middle-aged man and a woman were bending over a book, an album of photographs, and laughing. The man looked like the spitting image of his brother except that his hair, also gingery, was cropped close to his head making no attempt to disguise the baldness. The woman was slim and neat with not a hair out of place so that Effie involuntarily put her hand to her own hair to smooth it down.

'Effie, this is Frank, my brother, and Sally. So... now what would everyone like to drink?' Oliver reeled off a list of possibilities which surprised Effie considering that last time he had revealed a pretty bare drinks cupboard.

'I'll get them' said Sally raising herself from the sofa. 'I've got to see how things are going in the kitchen anyway. Perhaps you'd like to come and give a hand, Effie?'

Happy to avoid any possible awkwardness at finding herself in the middle of three unknown people, Effie followed Sally into the kitchen, only to be amazed yet again at the transformation. Firstly, there was a delicious smell coming from the oven and, secondly, the place was spotless and tidy. She couldn't stop herself from exclaiming, 'wow!'

Sally smiled. 'Yes, probably not what you found last time. Poor old Oliver. He simply hasn't coped since Alice's death. Not that she was particularly well-organisēd. But Olie has just let everything go. I don't think he particularly notices. He just seems to be quite helpless without her or someone to tell him what to do. Mind you, I think he was always a bit like that.... But Frank sort of keeps an eye on him and occasionally we come over and tidy up and give him a decent meal. Anyway, enough of that' she added brusquely. ` I'm sure you don't want to hear the whole sorry family saga. Now try this, Effie, it's a wine from the Loire region we think is rather good.'

Effie gratefully accepted the proffered glass and soon the two women had relaxed into an animated discussion of the lunch menu. Sally was clearly very knowledgeable about food and wines and Effie was sufficiently interested not to feel envious. She noticed how Sally had everything neatly laid out on the kitchen table which looked as though it had been recently scrubbed. An ordered row of equipment and ingredients was laid out in a line: a tin of flour, a rolling pin, a pat of butter, sharp knives and a spatula. There was a row of herb pots: marjoram, thyme, chervil, black pepper and sea salt. On the draining board lay a pair of yellow Marigolds beside the now shiny sink. This woman was clearly a perfectionist, thought Effie, but she could not help admiring her and the smell coming from the oven was delicious.

'We're having a bit of beef fillet in a lined pastry crust, or beef en croute I think they call it. One of Oliver's favourites. I think he only eats meat these days when we come over. God knows what he does the rest of the time, and the state of the place! Takes me a couple of hours to get it half way clean enough to cook in' she laughed. 'Personally' she added as she sipped the wine, 'I don't know how he can stand to live in the place the way he does. But there we are.' She looked at Effie suddenly serious. 'I hope I'm not putting you off.'

No chance of that, was Effie's thought, because I'm not 'on' anything I could be put 'off' from. The brother seems OK. Pity he's not more like him.

As though he had heard her thought, Frank entered the kitchen at that moment, a mug of beer in hand. 'Come on, ladies, now what are you up to in here? Smells good, Sal. When do we eat?'

'Twenty minutes exactly. Make sure you and Oliver are sitting down with the knife good and sharp. Now don't get under my feet, Frank. Why don't you show Effie the garden and you could top up her glass I'm sure.'

So Effie allowed herself to be topped up and ushered out of the kitchen to enter the garden from the open French window in the living room. The sun was still shining and as the sensual pleasures of the day began to work their effect Effie could view the unkempt greenery as a romantic wild place. The bright white petals of a late magnolia caught her attention, then a flash of red in the undergrowth, a rose, quite perfect. She breathed in its heady scent closing her eyes and letting herself dream a little until she realised that Oliver was speaking to her, directing her away from the dreamy stuff towards a pile of rocks almost hidden behind long straggly grass.

'Come and look at the pond, at least I think there's still a pond. Haven't actually been down this end of the garden in a while.'

The three of them negotiated a path through the long brown grass and various sticks and stones, Effie treading gingerly in her high heels. Oliver, it seemed, was enjoying his role as gallant pioneer, helping Effie with the scrambling and cutting a swathe through the undergrowth. When on earth did he last come down here, indeed! Effie could not restrain a quiet oath under her breath as her heel caught in a crack between stones. It was Frank who instantly grabbed her arm to prevent her from falling; Oliver just stopped and stared. 'Goodness, are you all right?'

Effie extracted her shoe and dusted herself down. 'No harm done. I'd have worn my walking boots if I'd known.'

Frank laughed while Oliver just looked crestfallen so that Effie guiltily felt she had to rescue him by being cheerful. 'Come on then,' she took the lead. 'If we're going to see the pond let's go.'

So the party continued on its way with Effie now in front followed by Frank with Oliver bringing up the rear, which somehow seemed to be the natural order of things. But it's not what you want, was the niggling thought in her head. What you want is a man to sweep you up, take charge and carry you off. The tramp was right. And what have you got here? Even his sister-in-law did not paint a glowing picture. Are you mad to be here?

Oliver piped up from behind her. 'Careful, Effie. I think it's just here. Ah, yes' he said pointing at a clearing in the grass. A patch of bright green was visible under the arch of brown vegetable matter which surrounded the pond. A few patches of dark water were visible openings in the green stuff which on closer inspection turned out to be a slimy-looking substance which covered most of the pond. Like so many things to do with Oliver, was Effie's unkind thought. What she said was `I can see it must have been rather nice once.'

'Yes, it was, it was.' He spoke slowly. 'Alice used to like it' and he sighed.

The ever practical Frank had picked up a stick and was bending to catch up some of the offending green matter to clear a larger water area. 'Hey, look!' he exclaimed. 'Tadpoles.'

They all bent down and there, indeed, were lots of little black tadpoles swimming about in the murky water, some of them with legs already appearing, some still attached to a lump of jelly which Frank explained was the spawn they had come from and which kept them alive till they turned into frogs. Effie was fascinated and delighted when she spotted a tiny frog hopping along a blade of grass at the pool's edge.

Oliver was grimacing as though he did not like what he saw. 'My god, frogs.' He stepped back while Effie moved closer, peering into the depths and remembering how as a child she had kept tadpoles in a jam jar and had cried when they died. For some reason she felt hugely moved to see these little creatures, the ones that had actually sustained the transformation from little black blob to a delicate green and yellow frog which was not much bigger than the end of her finger.

Her ruminations were interrupted by the sound of Sally calling from the house. 'Lunch is rea..a...a....dy.' Frank immediately laid down his stick.

'Come on, folks, better not keep Sal waiting.'

Effie edged back from the poolside, careful not to tread on any of the tiny creatures which were so difficult to see against the undergrowth. 'So don't you like frogs?' she asked Oliver.

'Well, I don't really think about them much.' He grinned but Effie was pleased to note that he did seem to be taking care not to step on them. 'I think more about dogs' he said.

'Well, of course you can't take a frog for a walk, but really...'

Frank was laughing. At least he's got a sense of humour, thought Effie, whereas Oliver... He is a bit of a pain. I mean how can you not like frogs! She continued an internal argument with Oliver as they retraced their steps towards the house so that by the time they reached it she was definitely irritated by Oliver which she knew was not very fair because he had actually said nothing particularly hostile about frogs and in fact was quiet as they negotiated the route.

Sally was waiting impatiently in the kitchen, brandishing a lethal-looking carving knife which she aimed at Frank. 'So where have you all been? Come on then, Frank, let's see what you can do with this. It needs to be really sharp to cut the pastry without spoiling it. And here' – she handed a bottle of wine to Oliver – 'how about keeping an eye on our glasses.'

'Yes, of course. That is if you're ready for some more, Effie?'

'Of course she is' said Sally before Effie could say anything ' and me too. I've been slaving over this damn meal for hours and I need some refreshment.'

Effie was impressed with the way Sally handled her brother-in-law and felt more cheerful. The lunch smelled delicious and she anticipated a good meal. She did not mind Sally organising them all like children and obediently sat down where she was told next to Oliver. Frank was making a drama about the carving knife, honing it to perfection on an old carborundum that Sal had produced from the depths of a kitchen drawer. He tested it with his finger and was finally happy. 'Could cut the hairs off an elephant's arse with that.'

Oliver glimpsed at Effie. Goodness, was he prudish? But everything else was soon forgotten as they tucked in to Sally's marvellous meal. The boeuf en croute cut like a dream and was accompanied by tiny new minted potatoes and strips of glazed carrots. The meat was cooked to perfection: a darker ring shading to pink in the centre, surrounded by a creamy mushroom stuffing while the pastry itself was light and crispy. Frank had opened a bottle of Burgundy which sported an impressively old date which did not disappoint. In fact, Effie felt she had never tasted such delicious wine and what with that and the gastronomic delights of Sally's cooking she was soon feeling quite euphoric and forgave Oliver for she wasn't quite sure what.

The whole party warmed up and even Oliver mellowed to the point of daring to tell a vaguely dirty joke which everyone laughed at. Frank was obviously enjoying himself and, Effie thought, much in love and possibly in awe of his talented wife. There did not seem to be anything that Sally could not do, and what she did she obviously did extremely well, not just cooking. She looked good too, somehow managing to stay incredibly slim despite tucking in like the rest of them. Effie's hand involuntarily went to her stomach as she sat back allowing the pleasant sensations of good food and drink to permeate her body, listening to the conversation and thinking about the company: Oliver, not so far impressing her, too needy and even a bit mean? Frank, the livelier brother, better looking too. He got the long straw, or had Oliver just not developed his talents? And why was she being so critical anyway when she felt so good? And then there was Sally. Such a confident person. She patted the roll of flesh around her midriff as she contemplated Sally. How on earth did she escape being lumbered with this deposit of unwelcome fat? What's more, her conversation was witty, she was obviously cultured, looked good and had talent. To cap it all she was so damn nice. Effie could not fault her. Except that mischievous imp envy was hovering somewhere not completely out of sight, poking its sharp nose into some vulnerable hole. Her ankles are too fat. No they aren't !

Effie's attention was pulled back from this fruitless argument by the arrival of the dessert which caused Oliver to exclaim. 'Wow, Sal, that's magnificent.'

Which indeed it was: a pyramid of chocolate covered profiteroles standing high in perfect formation on a silver platter. Beside it Sally placed a dish of fresh raspberries and a bowl filled with the flesh of passion fruits. The profiteroles, of course, were home-made.

'Oh it's easy to make them' insisted Sally,' you just mix up a bit of choux pastry, bung some cream in and pour some dark chocolate over it all. Must use good quality chocolate though.' She smiled.

Much as Effie wanted to hate her for this brazen show of confidence the moment her mouth was full with the sweet pastry her resistance sank. It was no good. She could not hate a woman who could make such marvellous creations. So Effie allowed herself to savour the delicious dessert and join in the conversation, and found herself recounting some stories about her own life and opinions. She skimmed over her divorce, praised highly an exhibition of abstract art showing at the neighbourhood gallery and allowed herself a brief rant about the local council's planning committee. Oliver was critical of the exhibition and defended the council but the mood was one of cheerful debate and Effie found she was beginning to enjoy the engagement with him when Sally rose from the table and suggested they continued next door. 'Who's for coffee?'

'Can I help?' offered Effie who surmised that coffee making was a comparatively disaster-proof task.

'No, honestly. You three go and sit in the living room. I really do prefer to do these things myself' she said, disappearing into the kitchen. Effie dutifully followed Oliver who began muttering to himself and was soon bending down, burrowing in the now familiar drinks cupboard. Effie wondered what he was going to produce this time. To her surprise after a few minutes of rummaging he straightened up with a triumphant 'Aha!' brandishing a large bottle of Cognac. 'Just the job. Effie, will you try some? It's been in there a while but I suspect all the better for it.'

On this occasion Effie thought he was probably right and although she knew she shouldn't she accepted his offering held out in a cut glass whisky tumbler. 'Sorry I haven't got any of the proper ones left. Tastes all the same though.'

And has the same effect, thought Effie, lying back in the comfy old armchair, absorbing the warm feeling spreading down her throat. She observed Oliver through half-closed eyes: could the warmth extend as far as him? He was somehow improved by the presence of his brother and sister-in-law. And what a sister-in-law. Impressive. Quite something to live up to. She watched as Sally placed the coffee tray on the table and accepted a glass from Oliver, tutting at the glasses.

'Honestly, Oliver, we must get you organised. You can't go on putting 12-year old brandy into Woolworth glasses."

'They're cut glass, my dear Sal. Alice's favourites.'

'Yes, well, I only meant they aren't brandy glasses.'

'Tastes just as good' said Effie, unexpectedly coming to Oliver's defence. Sally's attention to detail could become tiresome.

'Alice and I bought those glasses when we got married. We got them in a sale half price I seem to remember.'

Sally crashed the coffee cups down on the table and noisily sorted out a medley of assorted cups, saucers and spoons.

'Coffee, Effie?'

At this point Effie had the distinct impression that Sally was discouraging Oliver from reminiscing. Would she mind a man who was still so wrapped up in a dead wife? Who wasn't wrapped up in something? She was quite wrapped up in her job and her children, not something Oliver had said much about. So in her warmly well-fed state, sipping her brandy, she ventured to ask him:

'So, Oliver, tell me about your children. I met one of your daughters, didn't I?'

'Oh yes, so you did. That was June, the one who lives round the corner. Married with a dog.'

'A dog?'

'Yes, a golden Labrador, lovely animals. Gentle you know, wouldn't hurt a fly. Yes, Alice and I used to have a golden before we got a black one...'

Whether or not it was the obvious evidence that Oliver's fallback position was, indeed, his lost wife, or the effects of the extremely good meal, but as Oliver droned on about his wife and the lovely Labrador Effie began to feel a distinct movement in her stomach which rumbled around for a while, settled, and then started churning again, until there was no doubt that something would have to be done about it. She inwardly cursed, the euphoric feeling dissipating into irritation and a degree of embarrassment. She told herself there was nothing embarrassing about it but the fact was it did feel awkward to have to undertake a major call of nature in this strange rather odd house.

'Sorry, Oliver. Sally, can you show me the loo?'

The loo turned out to be in the hall right behind the living room door which had been left open during the lunch which meant Effie did not feel she could push it shut. Sally wafted her in with the comment 'can't answer for the state of it. I did my best.'

God, she's even cleaned the loo for Oliver was Effie's thought as she gingerly closed the lavatory door. The small room bore the evidence of her cleaning efforts, a sparkling white toilet bowl and wash basin, folded towel and a couple of neatly hung jackets on hooks behind the door. Thank god, there was a full roll of loo paper on the dispenser. Effie hovered a moment, listening to see if she could hear the conversation outside. How thick were the walls? She could pick up a murmuring. But the pressure to go was powerful and she had to get on with it. She lowered herself gingerly onto the wooden toilet seat, praying she would be able to control the evacuation and not, dread of dreads, make a farting noise. She clenched her sphincter muscles as tightly as she could but inevitably had to let the thing go which it did with a deafening 'plop!' She held her breath as though this would soften the impact of the sound. Oh god. She reached out to unwind a long stretch of loo paper from the holder which squeaked as she pulled. She hardly dared wipe herself. The flush was a handle on the side of the cistern and even this rattled as she pressed it down.

A gush of water swirled around in the bowl before settling only to reveal that the offending object was still there bobbing around in the water. Aghast, Effie waited for what seemed an hour for the cistern to re-fill noisily like an old steam engine. She turned on the basin tap hoping to merge the sounds of running water and flushing. At last it seemed to be full and Effie pushed the handle again firmly. The fact was that the cistern did not hold much water and Effie's turd simply refused to be flushed away. As the waters calmed again there it still was floating around merrily in the pan. When a third and even a fourth effort produced the same result Effie was visibly sweating and panicking at the thought that she would be stuck there forever or, worse still, have to go and get the perfect Sally to help her. It was just too humiliating. She was aware that all this waiting for the cistern to fill up each time meant she had been ensconced in the lavatory for quite a life time and her absence was no doubt noticed. All she wanted right now was to be back in her own home. What a fool she'd been to come. She felt like weeping.

Pull yourself together, girl, she commanded herself. Now, think. There's a physics principle here. Her mind flashed back to school days in the science lab. Something about density and water displacement? If only she'd paid more attention. Or was it surface area? Perhaps the damn thing just wasn't heavy enough, with which thought she pulled off a reel of loo roll paper, folded it into a sort of wad and placed it on top of the devilish object. The idea was that the wad would absorb water, becoming sufficiently heavy to weigh down the object so that it didn't stand a chance when she next flushed.

She was suddenly calm and resolved: one more try. I'll get you this time. She pressed down on the now slippery handle. A familiar gushing noise heralded the cascade of water. Effie held her breath as the flow lessened and became still. The water was clear at last.

'I say, are you all right?'

It was Sally.

'Yes, fine, absolutely fine' she called through the door as she hurried to put her face straight, touching up her lipstick, powdering her cheeks to cover their flushed appearance. Flushed indeed! She laughed to herself before opening the door to find Sally hovering with a concerned expression. 'We were beginning to wonder what had happened to you. You're not unwell are you?'

'No, no. Just got into a bit of a tussle with the flush, you know.'

'Ah, so it doesn't work then?' She advanced into the small space and dropped a piece of rolled up paper into the pan before pressing the handle down. 'Let's see.' The cistern obediently cascaded a large gush of water and neatly disposed of the paper roll. 'Seems to be OK; you just have to know the knack. But come on, we thought we might take the dog for a walk. He's back.'

But the thought of a walk with an excited dog did not appeal to Effie. This was not her afternoon and she reckoned an eight to one risk of saying the wrong thing, and a six to one risk of treading on dog poo. No, the most sensible thing was for her to go home, lick her wounds, recover her composure and start again. She made her farewells to a clearly disappointed Oliver: 'oh Effie, Milton (the dog?) was so looking forward to you coming with us.'

She had made up her mind, however, and her head was throbbing with disturbing images of full lavatories, so much so that she was convinced she must have a stain on her pale trousers or be smelling. No, the only way of ridding herself of these troubling thoughts was to have a long deep bath at her own home. Did Sally have her nose in the air when she said goodbye? And did Oliver give her a pathetic pat as though she was the damn dog? She did her best to give them all a cheery goodbye, waving as she sped off in her powder blue Golf. Her route took her past the pub where she had met Oliver a couple of weeks before, coincidently named The Oliver Cromwell. Being a warm day people were sitting outside on wooden benches and she noticed a familiar face: it was Brendan sitting there with his pint of bitter looking the picture of contentment.

If she had not been so eager to get home she would have stopped and said hello. He was quite fun, was her passing thought. Another time perhaps. Meanwhile she had the task of restoring sanity and sanitation to her mind.

Ch. 10

'My god, Effie. How ghastly!'

'Awful, shaming beyond belief.'

It was Monday lunch time and Effie was regaling Susie with the experiences of the weekend and the whole sorry saga of her battle with the cistern. The two women were seated in a corner of their favourite cafe, sipping lattes. Effie was also indulging in an almond croissant since, as she explained, she needed the sugar after all the excitement of the past few days.

'I used to think I led a rather ordinary boring existence, and, now this! First a tramp takes a fancy to me, then my granddaughter nearly kills herself falling off a slide, and then I get stuck in a strange loo where I have to do combat with a piece of shit. I swear I have never been so embarrassed in my whole life. God! You should have seen Sally's face when I came out.'

Effie bit into her croissant causing the almond paste to squirt out over the table.

'Now come on, darling, no need to repeat the situation. So what about Oliver? Have you heard from him since?'

'Oliver?' An image of his hangdog expression came to mind. 'No. No phone call and I haven't dared check my emails since. I know I should say a thank you, or do I need to apologise? Or maybe he should apologise to me for having such an ancient old clapped out loo. Allowing me to use it was like inviting me into Guantanamo Bay. I really thought I'd never get out, like that old lady who was stuck in the lavatory from Monday to Saturday.' The childhood rhyme played in her head.

'Now don't get too sorry for yourself' Susie laughed 'it was only a mechanical failure. Some of the day sounds OK. I mean, take Sally.

She sounds interesting even if she is too perfect for words?' Susie sipped her coffee ith furrowed brow. 'Let's think logically. A man who has a brother who's not half bad and a sister in law to die for can't be a total loser.'

'He can't?'

'I don't think you should score him off completely.'

'But you were the one who assigned him to the 'duds' box.'

'That was before the lunch. I just mean his family seem interesting and maybe he's still so sunk in poor Alice he comes across as worse than he really is.'

Effie was not convinced. She wasn't sure what she thought at all apart from wishing that life was simpler, that Jack hadn't left her, that she wasn't having to expose herself on a daily basis. Today she felt absolutely no desire to try anything new and just craved peace and quiet. She resolved to do some gardening when she got home from work. She also wanted to go round to Cathy's house to check on things there. She'd pay a quick visit before Jim got home. He often worked late.

Susie was talking, something about her work and someone she'd met. Susie had an elegantly un-stressful job running a small dress shop which gave her definite business skills immense satisfaction without the need to make a huge profit since her husband's ample salary removed that need. This knowledge occasionally niggled at Effie who was not immune from envying her friend both the financial security and the fact of having a man in her life, not to mention a twenty four inch waist. Yet, there were genuinely warm feelings between the two women and Effie knew she could rely on her absolutely when needed. It was Susie who, after Jack's departure, had helped her pick up the shattered pieces of her life. Her very lightness was a blessing. Right now she was peering quizzically at Effie.

'Sorry, Susie. I was just thinking about Rosie, I might pop in tonight on my way home, see how they all are.'

'Good idea, darling, but if I know Rosie she's absolutely fine and I want to get back to you. What are we going to do about you?'

'Do?'

'Yes, 'do'. You can't just leave things because it got a bit steamy yesterday. I think you need to contact Oliver to say your thanks and see where it goes from there. And in the meantime, you obviously didn't hear what I said about this man who came into the shop.'

'Buying a dress?'

'No, sweetie. He was with his daughter. She was looking for something for a wedding. Anyway, we got talking and he said that his wife had died a while ago and that he had to sometimes do things like go to shops with his daughters, both grown up I gathered. But he was nice, really nice.'

'Oh Susie, not another widower.'

'But he certainly didn't give the impression he was all wrapped up in a dead wife. Far from it: he sort of oozed confidence about life.'

'But do I want someone who is oozing?'

Susie put her cappuccino mug down firmly. 'Honestly Effie. If you're not prepared to try. I mean what have you got to lose?'

'My dignity, my self-esteem, my sense of self, to mention but a few... thank god, not my virginity,' she ended with a laugh. 'You realise, Susie, that all this activity could mean that I end up having a sex life again?'

'Yes, my dear' cackled Susie 'and much the better you'll be for it.'

'Yes?' Effie stood up scattering pastry crumbs on the floor. 'Anyway, must get back to work. I'll think about it.'

'You do that. He's coming back with the other daughter end of the week. You might like to pop in, anyway, to have a look at my new stuff? Some super dresses. Stunning materials.'

'Maybe.'

......

Effie was not accustomed to experiencing such uncertainty about so many different things and was not enjoying it. As she hurried back to her office she could imagine herself years to come looking back at this period in her life and laughing, but right now she had no such vantage point. She was drifting in choppy waters. There was that envy again of Susie and the settledness of her life. Not that it was necessarily more certain. She knew that very little was absolutely certain. She had thought she was certain that Jack loved her, that they'd grow old together. The fact was, she hadn't been doing too badly in her single life and she had really only herself to blame for where she found herself now. Didn't it all stem from that fatal moment when she had allowed herself to have an incestuous thought, which she couldn't now un-think? All she could do was not encourage it, to try and make it smaller. She remembered reading somewhere about how to mentalise a troublesome thought by imagining it as an object which could then be dealt with, such as a weed which could be pulled out of the ground. She recalled a friend who had found she had a massive fibroid growing inside her which had probably been there for years, unbeknownst to her until she had a bad period one month. The size of a grapefruit she'd been told. They'd cut it out and she was fine. Perhaps if she could think of her bad thought as a fibroid she could excise from her mind or at least reduce in size from a grapefruit to more of a hazelnut, or what about a peanut? She'd had those dreams about squirrels and nuts. Perhaps Susie was right. She shouldn't give up because she was pretty sure that if she did manage to find a new and interesting man in her life the problem of the grapefruit or the hazelnut would recede.

She sat down at her desk in a better frame of mind, pleased that her instinct to seek out her friend today had been correct. There were two things: she would try imagining her bad thought as a hazelnut and secondly she would take up Susie's suggestion of dropping in at the shop. Friday was her day off and she could easily hang around there with Susie over a cup of tea.

At half past five she closed down her computer and headed for Cathy's house. The girls would be back from swimming where they went after school on Mondays and she was looking forward to seeing them. It was Daisy opened the door.

'Hi, Grandma. I did back crawl.'

'Clever you!'

Effie was always sincerely impressed with her grandchildren's achievements on the physical front, Daisy's dancing, their swimming skills, Rosie's gymnastic agility. It delighted Effie to observe that her own somewhat slothful attitude to such activities did not appear to have been genetically passed on to her grandchildren. Daisy was pink-faced, damp hair clinging to her scalp as she danced around chewing a bit of toast. Rosie was sitting at the kitchen table, her hair quite dry.

'So didn't Rosie swim?' she asked Cathy.

'No, still being a bit careful after the fall. Whatever they say, I think it's best she keeps out of public swimming pools for a week or so. But she's fine, aren't you, poppet?'

Rosie grinned at her grandmother and did, indeed, look well despite the criss-cross marks at the side of her head. 'Hi, gran'ma.'

Cathy was ladling fish fingers and peas onto plates for the girls as she talked. 'Come and sit down, Mum. Here, some tea.' She topped up the mug with milk as Daisy came to join the party at the table and for several minutes the children were quiet as they ate, obviously hungry.

'You know, Jim was really upset by the business in the park, still feels guilty I think. Rosie is just a bit too confident sometimes, aren't you, darling?' she turned to her daughter. 'You know you've got to be more careful in future, don't you?'

'Well, I like the slide' replied Rosie with her mouth full 'an' Daddy didn't say I couldn't.'

'Well, he should have done' Cathy said firmly.

'Should not!'

'Young lady, he should.'

'Not!'

'Rosie, don't argue about it.'

'Oh, it really was just bad luck' Effie couldn't resist intervening.

'In my book, Mum, Rosie is still too young for that playground and I'd really rather you didn't take her there.' To which Effie was about to point out that it had not been <u>her</u> that had taken Rosie to the big playground but her father, but she stopped herself as she noticed that Rosie had put her fork down, and her lower lip was beginning to wobble. A tear rolled down her cheek. Effie waited to see what her daughter was going to do, resisting the instinct to scoop Rosie up in her arms and tell her everything was all right.

Cathy sighed, and for a few moments mother and daughter looked at each other across the table, Rosie silently tearful and Cathy silently serious. Daisy stared at the half-eaten fish finger on her plate. Effie held her peace.

The silence was broken by the sound of a key in the lock. It was Jim.

'Well, hi everyone. What's up?'

Cathy sounded impatient as she explained that she was trying to make Rosie understand that she had to be more careful about what she did, that she was not quite a big girl yet so that she had to accept there were some things she could not do, like going on dangerously high slides. There was the obvious unspoken criticism of Jim for having let her do it. Effie said nothing. Let Jim defend himself.

'I think Rosie knows that, Cathy. You don't need to rub it in. Come on darling, there's no need to cry now' he said sitting down beside his daughter and lifting her onto his lap for a hug. 'Now you are going to be careful, aren't you, and Daddy's going to be careful too. So no more tears. Come on, let's have a look at that head.' He dabbed her wet cheeks with a piece of kitchen roll as he inspected the wound. 'Looks fine to me, Rosie. I came home early 'specially to see how you were after swimming.'

'She didn't go swimming' said Cathy firmly. 'We agreed we'd wait.'

Rosie by now had stopped sniffing and was allowing herself to be rocked in her father's arms. Cathy had not yet smiled but she went over to the kettle to make another cup of tea which she placed in front of her husband.

'I know she's Ok but it's just a case of what might have happened... it could have been...'

'I think it's enough for Rosie this afternoon, Cathy. Let's leave it till later. Come on, girls. Hey, Daisy, eat up or you won't get any pudding.'

Effie stayed a further half hour but made to leave as Cathy was about to run their bath. Her daughter was still looking serious and was uncommunicative, giving Effie the definite sense that she, too, was somehow responsible for Rosie's accident. Whatever the truth, Effie knew she would have to wait till Cathy was in a better mood before it could be discussed. The tension between husband and wife was troubling too and a reminder for Effie that her daughter's skin was thin when it came to things going wrong, that she took things to heart and was slow to recover.

She gave the children a farewell hug, a particularly warm hug from Rosie, a more rigid one from Cathy, and was just leaving the house when Jim appeared.

'You off then, Effie? Have you got a minute?'

'Yes, sure.'

'I just wondered, I mean, about the business with Rosie. I don't know... Cathy's giving me a hard time about it and I just wondered what you thought?'

Her thought was, you poor man, you're feeling guilty about the fall, which wasn't your fault, and you feel bad about fainting which you haven't told Cathy about but wasn't really your fault either. You're just a human being, and a rather nice one too. She said something to this effect, taking care not to mention the fainting, and Jim gave her a smile and another of those grateful looks with those eyes of his so that Effie left the house feeling she was emotionally back in extremely choppy waters.

Ch. 11

The tube door slammed behind her and Effie took the only remaining seat. It was rush hour on Thursday and she had not finally made up her mind about Susie's plan. She'd left work promptly to meet up with Bea for a gallery private view in town, Bea having assured Effie that the young man concerned, unromantically named John Black, was one of the up-and-coming artists of the decade. Bea prided herself on being something of an art connoisseur and Effie was happy to go along and have her mind 'stretched', as Bea put it. The last time she had accompanied her friend to an art exhibition she came away wondering if Bea's judgement was quite as hot as she liked to think. In her quiet way, Effie had a well-tuned eye for good and bad art; her responses were unashamedly emotional and tended to be born out by a particular critic whose column she read every Sunday. His picture conveyed a rather plump man, not obviously good-looking, but she had developed a soft spot for him as she tended to do with cuddly men. Not that Jack had been at all cuddly.

As she sped along on her journey, however, it was not Jack she wanted to think about. She needed to make up her mind about Susie's suggestion. Could she face another encounter? She had left a message with Oliver thanking him for the lunch to which he had promptly replied expressing his desire to see her again soon. He even suggested going to an art gallery which surprised Effie since there had been no evidence from her observations that he had any interest in art. Sally, too, had left a message asking if she was all right and recommending a herbal tea 'for nerves' which had caused Effie to squeak with laughter. What a woman! So really what it added up to was a lack of urgency to do anything and her own good advice was to direct her emotional energy towards her family for the rest of the week. Cathy had rung her mother last night sounding perfectly cheerful reporting that all was well with the family, making no further reference to the weekend. None of which helped to resolve the question of Friday.

She had dug out her soduko puzzle for distraction. There was nothing like the 'fiendish' one to dispel troublesome thoughts. She loved the way it finally all fell into place. If only life were so accommodating. She raised her eyes from the paper, observing that the carriage had cleared a bit. A young girl was sitting opposite wearing an extremely short skirt and high heels that Effie could only marvel at. She had auburn hair arranged in a stark line across her brow and she was in the process of making up her eyes. In her left hand was a small pink mirror, raised close to her face while with the other hand she was carefully tracing a dark line across her eyelids. A mascara was produced from a vanity bag, pink of a different shade, and she proceeded to brush it on to her eyelashes, going from side to side, side to side again. Then came the lipstick and several minutes of applying a bright pink colour on to full lips that she pouted and pulled in alternately until she was satisfied that they looked sufficiently smooth or pink or whatever it was she was after. She paid no attention at all to Effie's hostile stare which expressed her indignation at this flagrant disregard of those around her. Like being invited into the bedroom she thought. Could she imagine Daisy and Rosie behaving like this in years to come? But the girl had coolly repacked her makeup and settled down to flicking through a magazine. The train stopped and she looked up, catching Effie's eye but this time she smiled and Effie smiled back despite herself, and she realised as she approached her own stop that she wanted to put a bit of lipstick on herself. But that's different, isn't it?

She left the train with relief, telling herself not to let such goings on with the younger generation spoil a potentially enjoyable evening. She arrived at the gallery to find that Bea was already there with a glass in hand and ready to sweep Effie off into the melee. Bea was in her element and Effie's spirits rose rapidly, buoyed up both by the party atmosphere but also by the paintings which were better than she had expected. The artist's style was semi-abstract, which appealed to Effie. She liked the process of searching out links and recognisable forms from the shapes and colours, which tied in with her interest in cryptic crosswords and detective stories.

One particular picture was attracting a small huddle. Effie joined the group, standing on tip toes so that she could see. It was a small painting of what she worked out was a figure, perhaps two figures entwined and staring away from the viewer. A swirl of colours both joined and separated them. Or so she heard someone saying, a gray-haired man with a prominent nose and striking brown eyes. Not English, she thought.

'You see, he's captured that essential tension between certainty – look, there, you can see a suggestion of a foot that has penetrated the earth, and there is also a tree whose roots intertwine with it... yes, certainty, solidity, rootedness, all those sort of things, and on the other hand, life's uncertainties, its caprices, its unpredictabilities. See how the colours fly off and suddenly change... even the brushstrokes do umpteen unexpected things. Quite thrilling' he intoned.

Effie became totally focussed as he spoke, as did several others, though it was not entirely clear if it was the painting and his enlightening words or his definitely handsome looks and air of authority that drew them in.

'Who's he' she whispered to Bea

'Whoever he is, he's worth knowing. Let's stick around.'

Which they did for a further happy half hour, shuffling along with a growing entourage of followers who seemed equally keen to catch the words of wisdom and something rather glamorous. Effie had taken a glass of red wine, not her usual choice because it tended to go to her head more quickly. The effects were pleasing; the man's charisma was powerful and Effie experienced a pang of excitement when he looked in her direction and smiled. She really was a soft touch for beautiful eyes.

Bea was chatting to a woman with long gray hair and a skirt down to the ground who she introduced as Shirley, her tutor from her art class.

'So who's the gorgeous guy we've all been following so adoringly?'

Shirley laughed. 'Oh that's Luca. He's an art historian/cum dealer, specialises in contemporary stuff. This is just the sort of thing he likes. Wants to be the first one to spot a new name. He's lucky enough to be rich so he can afford to take a gamble. He never quite took to my stuff, but can't blame him really.'

'Can't you?'

'Well, art is such a personal thing.' Shirley shrugged. 'I forgive him because he knows what he likes, which is fair enough, and also because he is so good looking.' She sighed. 'You can see what effect he has on people.'

The object in question had by now ceased his lecture tour and was resting a neat backside on the drinks table while he chatted to a woman who held his right arm firmly.

'Interesting,' mused Shirley, 'people can't keep their hands off him. Pity, really. I mean, it can be a bit of a distraction. Anyway, ladies, let's take a look at the rest of the show. And this is Peter...'

Effie and Bea were amongst the last to leave the party, departing in good spirits, enlivened and suddenly ravenously hungry. Even skinny Bea, who rarely admitted to experiencing this basic need, was keen to find somewhere to eat.

'It must be all that high culture or something' said Effie. 'but thank goodness you are actually hungry and we can go somewhere where we can get more than a lettuce leaf tonight.'

'Culture? Are you kidding. It was that gorgeous man. He just oozed sex.'

'Bea! I thought it was the art you were excited about, or at least the occasion.'

'It was, it was, but he was just such an unexpected bonus. Such a pity he's attached.'

'To whom? You mean that stringy woman who was clutching him at the bar?'

'I'd say so. She looked like a wife to me. Hey!,' Bea darted into a doorway as they walked. 'This looks good, let's try it'.

Twenty minutes later they were seated in an Italian restaurant eating ravioli stuffed with spinach and ricotta, one of Effie's favourites, and sipping chianti.

They ate silently for a while, concentrating on the food.

'I've never known you eat so much, Bea.'

'Well, it was a stimulating evening. You seem quite peckish yourself.'

'Yes, but I'm always hungry. You never are, or at least you never admit to it.'

'Oh I have my moments.'

Yes, I'm sure you do, Effie thought. She did not know Bea as well as she knew Susie, but the atmosphere of the party and the good food and drink were a heady combination so that she soon found herself chatting quite freely, telling her about her venture into the world of dating, skipping over Oliver for the moment, but presenting her with the possibility of the man in the dress shop. Bea, of course, was enthusiastic and encouraging.

'Look, a man who buys his daughters gorgeous dresses and actually accompanies them into the dress shop can't be bad.'

'Funny. That's just what Susie says.'

'She's right.' Bea was emphatic. 'Sounds like you've nothing to lose. I mean, if the worst comes to the worst, you can always walk out with a new dress.'

'But have you ever done anything like this? I mean I'm not exactly a spring chicken.'

'No, but you're still very attractive, a bit on the plump side, a few smile lines, but you've really worn extremely well.'

'Gee, thanks, Bea.'

And so with that vote of confidence Effie accepted her fate. After all, who was she to go against the opinions of two of her good friends?

Ch. 12

'I really think that suits you. It brings out your pale colouring beautifully and shows off that lovely neat waist.'

Susie was speaking in her professional voice. Effie was tempted to burst out laughing but didn't. The girl was far from funny. She really was a beauty with lovely straw-coloured hair, fine features and a slim figure. The sort of looks that were difficult to fault, if a little bland. Her father was sitting on one of Susie's delicate white chairs, tipping it back as he contemplated his daughter. Effie feared he would topple over. He, too, was good-looking and she could see where the daughter got it from. Thick gray hair, a strong nose and regular features, fashionable glasses and what looked like a well-honed figure. I bet he goes to the gym regularly. Can't be much less than 60.

It was 10 past 5 on Friday afternoon and Effie had been ensconced in Susie's boutique since 2.30 anticipating Kenneth's arrival so that she was by now filled to the brim with coffees and teas which were producing a strangely bouncy feeling. Indeed, as she watched Kenneth's chair momentarily teeter she found herself leaping up almost throwing herself at him.

'Oh do be careful - you'll fall.'

He turned and smiled benignly at Effie as the legs of the chair returned safely to the ground.

'Sorry. A bad habit of mine. Tilting chairs.'

'Oh, I tilt at lots of things... I mean lots of bad habits.' Effie felt awkward and knew her face was getting hot, damn it, which undoubtedly meant red. The parts of the body one can't control. But the dad was not looking at Effie for the moment. He was looking at his daughter who was posing for him in the dark green dress Susie had picked out for her. Susie was right: the colour suited her and she could carry off the neat fit. She twirled round for her father to admire: yes, she knew she looked good in it.

'Well, what do you think, Dad?'

'Oh, I think you look good in all of them.'

'So, why don't you try on the others, my dear,' suggested Susie. 'You might just prefer one of them when you see it on.'

The daughter, who to Effie seemed amazingly compliant, duly disappeared into the changing room with Susie who could be heard helping ease her out of the tight fitting outfit. Effie could not imagine either of her daughters caring a damn what she thought of their clothes, let alone their father, but this man was taking a kindly interest and clearly price was not the primary consideration, not for Kenneth Lennox. So far, they had exchanged very few words since the focus had been on the girl, Julie, and her dress search. Susie had introduced Effie as 'my colleague who has a designer's eye for what suits the young' so that Effie felt obliged to make some attempt to play the part of being in the know about design. She had heaved herself into a skin-tight pair of black trousers a size too small, supplied by Susie, with a fitting matching black top over which she wore a long loose emerald green cardigan in a fine silky material that flowed rather nicely when she moved, or so Susie assured her. Effie was grateful that it at least partially covered her thighs.

'Height of fashion,' asserted Susie.

'Height of agony!' complained Effie. 'I'll be lucky if I don't burst the seams in these things. Honestly, Susie, don't pretend you don't know my size.'

But that was a few hours earlier and Effie had both survived and adjusted somewhat to the constriction of her outfit which together with the thorough soaking in caffeine added to a sense of unusual lightness. Hence the leaping up to catch Kenneth Lennox as his chair tipped.

In the absence of his daughter - wasn't Susie taking a long time in the changing room? - he turned to Effie and smiled giving her a first proper glimpse of a pair of dark brown eyes behind the glasses. What did they convey? Interest? He appeared quite at ease, telling Effie about his daughters, joking about their predilection for shopping – 'probably worse since their mother died. I know I spoil them dreadfully.' Effie filled him in on her three, avoiding any reference to ages. He mentioned where he lived – not so far away - and obviously had a large house with a garden in which he took some pride. She told him about her house which she described as 'big enough for someone who's out a lot.' Was she apologising? The conversation moved on to food and favourite restaurants in the area, a topic dear to Effie's heart. 'Have you tried the Carping Cod in East Coresham? Best ever fish and chips' or 'the Gluttinous Pig in High Street Hennington? Fantastic roasts, lamb to die for.'

Julie appeared at this point as Effie's stomach began to rumble audibly at the consideration of all this tasty food which she realised was not surprising since she had eaten nothing since a small plate of cereal at breakfast. The girl twirled around to be admired, firstly in dark blue to be followed by an equally stunning pale pink, then a taupe, a beige and finally back to the dark green, or 'deep viridian', as Susie insisted on calling it, by which time it was after 7 o'clock and Effie caught Susie looking at her watch. Julie was humming and hawing between the pink and the green, unable to decide until her indulgent father resolved the issue by declaring that since she was being just like her mother, never able to make up her mind, he would solve the problem by buying them both, at which point Susie visibly relaxed, smiled broadly, and Effie gasped 'lucky girl'.

Still on something of a high from the caffeine and the empty stomach Effie's thoughts raced ahead inspired by this display of paternal generosity. She flew to an image of herself and Kenneth Lennox living together in blissful harmony, he, bringing her home bunches of flowers when it wasn't even her birthday, taking her out to dine, bringing her tea in bed. His world would be ordered but relaxed, a man at ease with himself. There would be no tension, no arguing about who took the rubbish out, no leaving greasy pans for her to wash up like Jack used to do, no carping at her predilection for double Devon cream...

'Well, I think we all deserve a drink after that' said Kenneth, getting up to insert his credit card in the slot of Susie's machine. Back to reality, Effie squinted to see what the total came to for not only the two dresses but a silk scarf and a darling little handbag the same shade as the green dress which were somehow neatly added by Susie at the last minute. She couldn't quite make out the total. Kenneth barely glimpsed at the bill before he tapped in his pin. Julie appeared in her jeans and sweater and popped a kiss on her father's cheek.' Thanks, Daddy, I love them.'

And well you might, young lady, thought Effie as she gathered her stuff together. But her mood was light, even excited. It all seemed so easy. The four of them left the shop with Julie clutching two smart bags tied together with Susie's exclusive black and gold ribbon.

Susie was purring to Kenneth like a contented cat. 'I think your daughter looks quite stunning in those outfits. A very good choice if I may say so, and I'd love to join you for a quick one – mustn't be long – Fred gets fretful if he's left on his own on a Friday night.'

'Fine, my dear lady. But I would like to show you my appreciation for all your help with my girls. They are not easy to please, I can assure you' he said as he patted his daughter's bottom affectionately. 'And Effie – I can call you that can't I? - I hope you can spare ten minutes or so.'

'I might just manage that.'

The ten minutes turned out to be twenty minutes, then forty minutes, when both Susie and Julie left leaving Effie and Kenneth, neither of whom seemed to want to or need to go. Kenneth sat back after kissing his daughter goodbye.

'Effie, I must say when Susie mentioned last week that she had a friend who was a clothes designer who might be helpful with the girls I had no idea she would turn out to be such an agreeable lady.'

'Well, I'm not actually a professional designer. More of an amateur' she lied.

For a moment Kenneth looked serious.

'You know, some of the best designers started up stitching things in their kitchens'.

'Kitchens?'

'Oh yes. My grandfather was actually a tailor in the East end. That's how he started, or so goes the family story' he laughed. 'My grandmother always complained that her husband couldn't boil an egg or roast a piece of meat but he could make mutton look damn like lamb in one of his creations. Not that she'd have said 'damn', being a bit proper. Suits too. He looked a bit of a scruff himself but could put together an extremely smart suit for rich city gents. 'Afraid it's a bit lost on me, but the girls certainly love clothes as you can see.'

Effie was curious and didn't want to distract to the girls. So how had he made his money? It didn't sound as though he had followed in his grandfather's footsteps and carried on the tailoring business. Was he Jewish with a story like that? He didn't sound or look it. Like the Irish, Effie had a bit of a soft spot for Jewish men, not that Jack was.

Kenneth was looking at his watch. 'Effie, I'm afraid I have to go. I've got a bit of business needs attending to. And you must be starving. But I wonder if you'd be up to trying one of those restaurants we were talking about? Another night?'

Her stomach contracted in excitement. 'Oh yes, very much.' Yes, she did want to see him again. She jotted down her 'phone number and he gave her his card.

'I'm away a couple of days next week, but how about next Friday? It seems like a good day for things to happen.'

So they parted with Kenneth promising to confirm time and place when he returned from whatever he had to do. Effie refused a lift, preferring to walk to her house which was not far away, wanting some fresh air and exercise to clear her mind. He gave her a peck on the cheek much as he had kissed his daughter earlier and he was off, waving cheerily. Effie took the path through the park and pulled out his card, smiling to herself. It was a smart business card which gave his name and that of what she presumed was a company, Lennox Enterprises, which didn't really tell her anything. Maybe Susie could fill her in. She could certainly tell her what the outfits had cost. Dear Susie. She mentally hugged her friend for having pushed her in to the meeting as she slipped Kenneth's card into her wallet. A smart card. A smart man.

Ch. 13

Tonight was the third meeting since the encounter in the shop. Effie was preparing to go out, perched on the edge of the bath easing on a pair of new tights that really were tight like everything else since that evening. She was wearing a skirt one size down from her normal one. 'Well, you made a hit in the shop, didn't you?' Susie had asserted in a tone of voice that brooked no dissent. Her feet were squeezed into high heels despite a warning spasm of pain from the bunion on her left foot. Not too much walking tonight she reckoned. Kenneth was picking her up and the rendezvous was a Japanese restaurant further into town. Twice they had been to local restaurants, both excellent, and Effie had gained an impression of a man with an easy manner that instilled confidence, clearly successful in his business, extremely fond of his girls and with a variety of cultural interests one of which was food from different countries, hence the Japanese restaurant tonight. Effie, in turn, had let him know she was divorced without going into any details about just how painful it had been. She had spoken about the children, her work and her own interests in art, theatre and cooking. 'A woman after my own heart' had been his reaction and music to Effie's ears.

Her thoughts lingered over her developing picture of Kenneth as she added the final touches to her makeup. She stared closely at her own gray eyes in the mirror. Hadn't they once been bluer? A spot of colour to the eyelids, brown mascara to the lashes which were annoyingly not as long as they used to be. Kenneth's eyes were delightfully warm and brown under his shaggy dark brows, brows that were still dark despite his gray hair. She could picture them now and found herself smiling until she realised that the eyes in her head were no longer brown but blue, a lovely soft blue.

There was a honk from outside. Effie thrust the image out of her head and her arms into her navy blue jacket. A smart new shiny black mini was drawn up outside the house, not quite what she had imagined, but there was Kenneth grinning at her cheerfully as he exited the driver's seat.

'Right, madam, your carriage awaits' he smiled as Effie with a girlish giggle allowed herself to be ushered into the front seat.

'Well thank you kind sir.'

They sped off at a pace that also surprised Effie whose last experience of a mini had been a model of twenty years ago and even then it had not been new. This was a different thing altogether and she decided she liked the fact that Kenneth did not have a big flashy car like Quentin, even if he could afford it. Not being ostentatious was a definite plus. She recognised radio 4 as she clicked herself into her seatbelt but Kenneth was quick to change it to classical music.

'Are you Ok on this?' he inquired,' my wife was fond of the classics. Not particularly my thing. More of a jazz man really, but I tolerate Beethoven, some Bach. Really prefer Brubeck. All the 'Bs'' he laughed, with Effie chiming in a second or two later as she grasped what he meant.

'Well, I guess I'm a bit of a 'B' person too: just love the Beatles. Bees too as a matter of fact. They were comparatively novel when I was young – the Beatles I mean.'

'Really?'

'Yes, I mean they weren't new but still very much around. I just liked them' she added, wondering if she had made herself sound too old. What age did he think she was? But Kenneth had moved on to another topic and was telling her about the restaurant, his love of Japanese food and a visit to that country some years before. He seemed in good spirits as they drew up at 'The Mount Fuji' which they entered through a bamboo gate hung with pretty lanterns to be greeted effusively in Japanese by the restaurateur with Kenneth responding in what sounded equally Japanese to Effie. She was impressed: so at ease with the world, polite and attentive. She experienced quite a thrill as they were taken to their table, to be in the company of this urbane, nice –looking man. He was definitely quite handsome tonight dressed in dark trousers and a smart casual jacket, his thick gray hair brushed back emphasising the dark eyebrows and the etched wrinkles on his face. It all added up to an image of a mature man, confident of his place in the world, at home equally behind the wheel of a Landrover or a mini, in a smart London restaurant or the local pub. Or such was Effie's impression.

She left the ordering to him accepting that he understood the menu better than she did and they were soon sipping warm saki and nibbling delicious morsels of exquisitely cut vegetables and raw fish - 'starters' - according to Kenneth, to be followed by a steady flow of delicate portions of meat, fish, and rice which continued at a gentle pace through the evening.

'So what took you to Japan? You seem to know a lot about it.'

'Japan? Yes, I've been there a few times. Business. It's a very advanced economy. Sophisticated engineering and such-like, sort of our area. But I took to the country It's so clean and well-organised and everyone's so polite. Never overstated. At least since the war'. He laughed. 'And I love these customs like the greeting from Yuko when we came in. I've picked up a smattering of words for greetings. I assure you that's all.'

'Well, it sounds very impressive to me. So where else has business taken you?

'Oh, most of Europe, the Middle East, Central America, bits of Africa.'

'Goodness, quite a list. Unfortunately my work keeps me on the whole stuck here in the home counties. Such a shame because I'd love to travel more. Jack wasn't much of a traveller. Our holidays when the kids were young were limited to England or Scotland. He liked fishing which bored me to tears, whereas I like walking which he didn't.'

Warming to the theme of her husband's incompatibility, Effie continued. 'When the children became more civilised and less of a nightmare to travel with we did venture across the channel a couple of times and once as far as Spain but he was always complaining about things: the food was no good and made you sick or the beer was too pricey or the signposting confusing. When I think about it now,' she said reflectively,' it just wasn't much fun'.

'Oh dear,' Kenneth laughed, 'it sounds as though you're a frustrated Dr Livingston. Maybe we need to give that side of things some thought.'

'Oh, I'm game' was Effie's impulsive response, and then, to lessen the impression of undue haste and a lack of moderation, she ventured to bring up the subject of his wife: 'so tell me about the girls' mother? Jenny, isn't it?.'

Kenneth sat back in his chair and looked away towards the window:

'Yes, Jenny. Not a bad marriage. We had our ups and downs. A good mother. She loved children and always regretted we only had the two girls. Quite enough for me,' he smiled looking back at Effie. 'She worked in a local nursery for years and was thinking of setting up her own little school when she got sick. 'Afraid it dragged on for a couple of years, quite tough on the girls even although they were quite grown up. But that was nearly four years ago and they're young. The young recover more quickly, don't they? Both have boyfriends now and I think the older one, Sara - you met Julie didn't you? - she's probably with the guy she's going to marry. They seem quite committed to each other. Still difficult though, I mean, not having their mother around. I'm sure I spoil them rotten, which Jenny never did.'

He shrugged. ` So what about you? How do you manage, or are you through with all that sort of thing now?'

It was an interesting question for Effie to consider: the idea of being 'through' with one's children. She understood what he meant, the hopeful idea, that once his daughters were safely married he'd not have to worry about them any more. She had believed that once upon a time, that marriage was the answer to all problems. Not that she didn't want all three of her children to eventually get married. She knew she used to think the umbilical cord would be cut once they left school, or university? Surely it wouldn't still be attached when they got married? The evidence from her one married child was that the ties were obstinately rooted. And then, her own marriage had ended in disaster.

Effie paused, chopsticks in hand, as she contemplated the couple next to them who were gazing into each other's eyes. Had she and Jack once been like that? She supposed they had although she could barely remember the good times, so powerful had been her reaction to his betrayal. There was a moment of sadness at the thought of the couple next to her and their inevitable descent into the pitfalls of human existence, like everyone else. As she watched them watching each other she noticed that the girl's sleeve was dipping in one of the dishes of sauce. A dark stain spread up the pale silky material.

Kenneth was looking at her, chopsticks also poised. 'So what are you saying? Don't have children, or don't get married?'

'Oh no, I love my children to bits, but I find I'm having to review my ideas all the time, that cord turns out to have roots like a vine that sink deep into the earth and twist around in one's emotional life. So here I am now into the next generation of worries.'

'I hadn't thought about grandchildren' said Kenneth looking quite downcast.

'Oh, it's mainly sheer pleasure, believe me. I adore my grandchildren. A huge responsibility but they make me laugh. It saved my life that Daisy appeared soon after Jack did his disappearing act. I guess it was quite tough for my kids too at that time. Not that it's like a death' she hastened to add, 'at least I imagine it's different. But, anyway, having a baby arrive when she did was wonderful. And now they're proper little people and we have lots of laughs. They're into jokes now, even Rosie the little one and Daisy's are sometimes mildly shocking. I mean what they seem to know about these days.'

'Oh I think you can't leave it like that. Can't you give me some idea what lies ahead?'

'Oh goodness, it's mainly scatological humour I'd say. Daisy's lot seem to think anything about down there - Effie indicated her lower regions - is hilariously funny. Rosie's jokes are much sweeter, sort of the 'what do you call stuff, like, what do you call a deer with no eyes?'

'So what do you call a deer with no eyes?' Kenneth was playing the game.

'No idea.'

He chuckled: 'I like that. Rather quirky. So perhaps you'll tell me some of Daisy's contributions another time. You've certainly opened my eyes to the possibility of joys ahead.'

The two of them clinked glasses and they sipped another jug of warm rice wine and generally mellowed into the soft atmosphere of the place allowing Effie to ponder the implications of his last remark so that she was not at all surprised when he put his hand on hers and told her that he was getting to like her a great deal and hoped that she too was happy they had met. Which she was. The bill arrived just as Effie stood up to visit the ladies' room so that she had no chance to see what the evening had cost. Kenneth, anyway, quickly picked it up, holding it in his hand without looking and Effie felt he was waiting for her to go. So be it, and curiosity would remain unsatisfied.

They took a taxi back to Effie's house. So far the meetings had taken place outside the house and Kenneth had picked her up twice now, so that he knew where she lived. Effie also knew that he lived in a rather nice street two or three miles away but had not yet been invited to see it. She was thinking about this as the taxi approached her address, beginning to feel she knew this man and yet had never set foot in his house. These cosy evenings in a good restaurant encouraged a sense of intimacy which was far from the whole story. As Effie struggled to push her feet back into the high-heeled shoes she had taken off with relief in the taxi she wondered how he would react if he saw her on an average work day sporting worn out flat shoes, clothes a size larger and no makeup. On the other hand, she was blessed with good skin which barely yet showed serious signs of aging. More immediately was the question forming in her mind of whether or not she should invite Kenneth in. Would it be too forward? Would it be seen as an invitation to stay the night? Her mind was rushing along.

The decision was effectively taken out of her hands when they stopped outside her house and Kenneth again took her hand and pressed it affectionately.

'You know I'd love to have a look at your house but I think better not tonight. I've got to go off on a trip tomorrow and need to get up early. But I'm back Thursday, so let's do something on Friday, can we? Why don't we meet at my house. Time you had a look at the family mansion' he said with a laugh, and proceeded to lean over and give Effie a kiss on the cheek causing her instinctively to shut her eyes.

'Yes, lovely. That'd be lovely. Next Friday then.' And as an after thought as she eased herself out of the cab. 'And are you on the end of a phone during the week? It'd be good to have a chat.'

'You can try but I'm in far distant lands and it might be tricky, time changes and reception, you know.'

He flashed her a smile and the taxi was off leaving Effie both excited, there was no doubt that she was thrilled at the idea of going to his house, but also bothered by the feeling that it was frustratingly hard work to get to know this man and there were more questions than answers. She embarked on her bedtime rituals as she mulled this over: brush teeth for two minutes, wash tights, open the window three inches for air, check the computer is off. Basically, though, she was in good spirits as she eventually laid her head down on the pillow. Tomorrow she could look forward to seeing the grandchildren. She was baby sitting for Cathy, and on Sunday she had a coffee and catch up with Susie in their favourite cafe. Meanwhile she set about soothing herself into sleep by going over in her mind the number and variety of dishes she had consumed during the course of the evening.

...

'"And so the sad old donkey nobody wanted, who had helped the old lady across the river and kicked away the wild wolf that tried to eat her up without thought for himself, was so admired by King Marvel for his bravery that he was turned into a handsome prince. When the King's daughter, the lovely Princess Peony, saw the prince she instantly fell in love with him and the two were married amidst much jubilation, defeating the plans of evil uncle Mortico who wanted to marry the princess himself."'

'What's evil?' piped up Rosie from her snuggled up position under her pink duvet.

'Evil? Oh, it's when you're really bad, very bad', replied Effie.

'You mean, like when Pedro weed in the playground and the teachers were cross.'

'Yes, well, that's not really evil, more sort of naughty. I wouldn't necessarily say Pedro's a bad boy for that.'

'I think the baddest thing I know is when Daddy shouts at Mummy. I think that must be evil' said Daisy from her bed which was covered with a duvet strewn with ballet dancers.

'Yes, well, I don't really know, Daisy, it depends...'

'What does it depend on?'

'It depends on if there's a good reason to shout. I mean we all get angry about things sometimes, don't we?'

'I didn't like it when teacher Pat was cross with me.'

'I'm sure you didn't, darling, but why was she cross? What had you done?'

'It was Celia's fault. She took my pencil sharpener and I prodded her with my pencil 'cos she wouldn't give it back.' Daisy was defiant.

'I hope you didn't hurt her, Daisy? Pencils can be sharp.'

'Well it wasn't sharp 'cos she wouldn't let me sharpen it!'

'Oh, you've got a point there, Daisy,' and the two of them laughed. Rosie, who had missed the joke, piped up from her pink corner in a plaintive voice, 'I don't think it's funny when people shout and I don't like it when Mummy and Daddy shout. It scares me.'

'Oh, sweetheart, you mustn't worry about that. It doesn't mean anything.' Effie tried to sound reassuring and was thinking that distraction was now the best policy. 'Look, I'll read you one more story'.

She flicked through the book. Choose something soothing. No monsters or witches. Hansel and Gretel? Far too scary for Rosie who could be anxious anyway when her parents were out at night. Jack and the Beanstalk? No, there was a scary giant who could eat you up and she herself thought Jack was a far from admirable character, getting up there and pinching things. And the name, Jack, was a sore point, and she had a sneaking sympathy with the giant. Little Red riding Hood? Absolutely not. The terrifying idea of a grandmother who is really a wolf in disguise. Oh dear.

She finally settled for The sleeping Beauty which the children knew well but it was about sleep and sleepiness and the story worked out all right in the end and so that was her choice. By the time she got to the bit where the daring young knight had hacked his way through the undergrowth of a hundred years and was moving in amazement from room to room of sleeping courtiers, Rosie's eyes were closed. Effie leaned over to check, pausing the story.

'Don't stop, Gran'ma, just when he's going to wake everyone up'.

'Sorry, Daisy. I thought you were asleep too.'

'No, I'm wide awake an' I can't go to sleep till I hear the end. That's the whole point.'

'Fair enough, "So the knight at last came to the small windy staircase that led up to the top of the turret where he found the princess lying there on soft cushions all covered in dust and spiders' webs. Through the webs he could see how beautiful she was and could not resist bending down to kiss her on her pale brow. His lips brushed away the cobwebs as he did so and as they touched her skin there was an immediate stirring. The princess was not dead. No, she woke up and so did all the people in the castle. And, of course, she fell instantly in love with the handsome young knight who had rescued her. They were soon married amidst great rejoicing and lived happily ever after."'

'I don't think I believe in happy ever after' said Daisy sleepily as she turned towards the wall, her eyes closing. Which left Effie feeling sad as she kissed the back of her granddaughter's head.

Ch. 14

Effie looked at her watch impatiently. It was nearly 4.45 and Susie was late. She was dying to tell her all about her Friday outing and benefit from her friend's considered and probably more sober opinion. She ordered herself a large cappuccino with 'plenty of chocolate'. The hot drink arrived a few moments later with a chocolaty heart-shaped pattern adorning its frothy top. Just what she loved, though she had to watch out she did not end up with a white moustache. Daisy and Rosie had made it very clear that this could turn her into an object of total hilarity. She had to watch that kind of thing in her new position of dating. A degree of self-consciousness was required if she was to make a good impression and that meant restraint. But Kenneth is worth it, she told herself as she stirred a large spoonful of brown sugar into her coffee. The clickety clack of high heels interrupted these ruminations and Susie sat down beside her.

It may have been Sunday and a day of rest but Susie was making no concessions. She wore a dark tight-fitted skirt with a silk shirt and on her feet a pair of bright red stiletto heels.

'Sorry, darling, we had people over for lunch-time drinks and they stayed and stayed. Then I had to give Fred something to eat or he'd've made a fuss about me going out. So anyway, here I am.'

Susie positioned herself elegantly on the plastic chair and hailed the waiter.

'I guess it had better be coffee, but not that calorie swimming bath you've got, Effie. Honestly!' She ordered black coffee. No milk.

'I need it' said Effie firmly 'and it's not everyone likes a skinny stick like you. Some men like a bit of flesh.'

'Now, now, don't be defensive' said Susie, stirring sweetener into her black coffee. 'So is this Kenneth guy one of those men who likes a lady with a bit of flesh? Come on. Do tell what's been going on.'

Effie leaned closer to her friend, aware of a young man at a table on her left who was lazily tapping on his I-phone and absolutely oozed cool. She had no desire for him to hear their conversation. *He probably thinks we're totally over the hill as far as anything vaguely sexual is concerned.* Even Dr Gordon had implied this crushing assessment. So how to account for the surges of excitement when she was with Kenneth?

Ignoring the young man, she gave Susie a broad grin. 'Well, I must say I feel a bit like an adolescent all over again. Quite disturbing.'

This was a realisation which only now crystallized for Effie. 'Yes, it really is rather disturbing if I think about it. I mean, I really want to hear from him and don't like it if I don't. God, I hope this isn't going to end in tears.'

'So why should it, darling? It's wonderful that someone you actually like's taken a shine to you. Don't go dragging in all the things that are wrong with it yet. Goodness!' Susie sighed 'there's plenty of time for that later.'

She stretched out her shapely 57 year-old leg, shook off the red shoe and bent down to massage her foot. 'My feet are killing me.'

The boy next to Effie was staring at Susie as she massaged her foot. His eyes followed down from her face to her leg, hesitating a moment to take in the glimpse of inner thigh which Susie was exposing. Effie instinctively moved her chair round a fraction in an attempt to block his view. She wanted her friend's full attention.

'This is serious, Susie. You're right, I do like him, but I'm not so sure if I like feeling like an adolescent when I'm sixty.'

'You don't look a day over fifty.'

'That's not the point. The point is I suddenly don't feel remotely sixty or even fifty. More like fifteen.'

'You're lucky, darling. Having spent four hours in these wretched shoes I feel about seventy' said Susie who was extracting her foot from the other shoe and in the process flipped it across the floor to land under the young man's table. 'Damn it.'

The youth, who had shifted his gaze from Susie's legs, was busily texting on his mobile phone and glimpsed up as the red shoe came to a halt beside his foot. He bent down to pick it up as Susie rose to retrieve it. He held it out as though presenting a precious gift. 'Yours I believe.'

'Sorry. Miscalculation.'

The youth stood for a moment, smirking, flirtatious.

'Any time.'

'Well thanks.'

'No problem.'

This stimulating conversation was interrupted by the arrival of a blond slip of a girl who sported a tiny pelmet of a skirt over a pair of long slim legs which ended in a pair of bright pink trainers. She kissed the boy on the lips and the two of them rapidly moved off linked together arm in arm. Without turning round the lad raised an arm in a farewell gesture as they disappeared through the door, laughing.

'Obviously a leg man' was Effie's comment. 'They say men view women like chickens, either leg or breast. Anyway, where were we before you made such a hit with the younger generation? I think I was trying to have a serious discussion about this situation I find myself in and whether I should give this one the go, or am I just crazy to even think about it?'

Intent on tackling this foregone conclusion, they ordered some more coffee and the two women spent a good hour reviewing Effie's progress, agreeing that of all the men she had met Kenneth was definitely the most hopeful and that there was no reason at all why she should not pursue the relationship. Susie's advice on the intriguing question of how he earned his money was to leave it for the moment – 'early days after all' - in the expectation that all would be revealed as they got to know each other.

'Talking of revealing all' said Effie as she emptied her third cup of coffee,' I think there's a distinct possibility that we could end up in bed together quite soon. I mean, I actually feel for the first time in years that I want to. Is that being adolescent or what?'

'Oh, I'd say that's a sign of just how adult you are.'

'It is?'

'Does it matter? Just go for it if you want it. What's to lose?'

'Dignity, for a start. I mean just look at me. I'm not exactly a model figure and there's no disguising things when your clothes are off.'

She stared down at the sugary remains at the bottom of her empty cup and leaned forward to her friend. 'Do you realise, Susie, it's about seven years since a man has seen me naked. I've got a spare tyre, varicose veins on my left thigh, skin which close up looks like the surface of the moon and too high blood pressure. God, I feel embarrassed just thinking about it.'

Susie put her cup down firmly. 'Now, Effie, this really won't do.' Sometimes her friend was trying. 'You, madam, have a pretty gorgeous body for your age. Plenty of flesh which you said Kenneth seems to like, even if it is a bit saggy, your skin is actually still nice and plump, not drawn like mine, and no one really looks at thighs, least not in the dark. I mean you aren't going to be subjected to a microscopic examination under the spotlight. Be pleased!'

Effie was silent.

'Look, darling, I do understand it's a big step after all this time, but, honestly, I think you'll find it just sort of happens and hopefully you'll enjoy it and you'll wonder what all the fuss was about.'

Effie glanced at her watch, still looking serious. 'It's 6.00 o'clock. I think we can open the bar. I could do with a glass of wine.'

She had a sudden urge to indulge herself in the luxury of confiding in a friend and the alcohol would facilitate the process. They ordered two proseccos, brought by a waitress whose fleshy thighs bulged in a pair of super- tight jeans that momentarily distracted Effie. Can't be good for the circulation she thought as her left hand stroked the area of her own varicose vein. Susie too was watching as the waitress moved off revealing the clearly moulded outlines of her plump buttocks. The two women looked at each other, eyebrows raise before they both burst out laughing and clinked glasses.

'It's all so flagrant, Susie, that's what scares me.'

'But you don't have to be like that. You, my dear, are the epitome of grace and discretion, you are not remotely vulgar and only display good taste.'

'Susie, flattery is not helpful in this case. I really do need to think seriously about all this. I'm not joking about the sex thing. I mean I'm

O. L.D. I haven't had anything inside me, you know, –' she waved her arm airily towards her lower regions 'not even a tampon, for years and, much as I like Kenneth, I guess I am a bit nervous.'

Susie just grinned and Effie pulled her chair in closer to the table, glimpsing round to make quite sure there were no youthful voyeurs in the vicinity. She sipped her drink pensively. 'Have you got to rush back for Fred?'

'No, no... Effie fire away, I've got bags of time.'

'Well, I suppose these recent developments in my life are making me think a bit about my marriage, you know? And I probably haven't wanted to think too much about it to be honest. I mean it doesn't exactly boost one's morale to have your husband of twenty plus years, the father of your three children, go off with one of your best friends.'

Susie tutted sympathetically.

'Anyway, that's nothing new, but probably what I never told you was that I wasn't actually totally surprised. Not that I suspected anything about Hilary but more that I knew things weren't as good as they should be.'

'Goodness, sometimes Fred bores me to bits. If I didn't have my work and a few good girl friends, like you my dear, I'd go spare and sex is almost bound to lose its excitement. I can tell you, Fred and I work hard at that one,' she said grinning.

'Yes, but it wasn't exactly that things in that department were dull, it was more that Jack wanted me to do things that I felt I didn't want to do. My tastes were different.'

'Different?'

'Yes, in fact far from dull. But contrived.'

"Contrived?'

'Yes.'

'Effie, if you don't want to tell me what you are talking about, fine, but please don't hint at things and then be evasive.'

Effie sighed and swallowed the remains of her prosecco.

'You see, I can't stand the idea that you have to create a sort of stage set in order to have decent sex. It shouldn't be necessary, and you're the one who keeps telling me it should all happen naturally...'

'Don't get ratty, now. Just go on with the story.'

'OK. So, we're going back a few years. Maybe Jack was a bit bored. The kids were off doing their own thing in the world. So we had more time. Just us. I missed the kids, but I was doing Ok at my work. That's when I moved to work for Toptravel. A lot more responsibility and I started to earn good money. I think I really enjoyed that and what I wonder now is if jack was actually a bit envious. I mean, he'd been in the same job for yonks. Well, you know he always liked shoes, always liked it if I got dressed up when we went out and put on a pair of high heels. God, I blame him for this damn bunion' she muttered, rubbing her foot. 'So this liking for high heels, me in high heels to be precise, gradually turned into me wearing the high heels and more - or do I mean less? - at the weekend which was set aside as our together time. But honestly, Susie, it's not my thing to prance around in nothing but a pair of skimpy high heels and wave whips around. I mean at fifty plus, god, I felt like an aged tart and I eventually told Jack it wasn't on and I guess it wasn't so long after that he started making eyes at Hilary. Not that I noticed anything. I just thought we'd gone back to normal and so it was a terrible shock when it all came out. But I suppose you could say I was the mistress of my own downfall. Who knows what would have happened if I'd just gone along with it, even if I did think it was a bit pervy.'

'Oh Effie, what a bastard. And to think of stodgy old Jack being vaguely a sexual pervert and you in the altogether tottering around – or crawling around in those shoes!' she cackled.

Effie stared at her friend for a moment, grim faced, before she too burst out laughing, laughing loudly from her belly so that her eyes watered, attracting the attention of a couple of bored-looking youths who were slumped over a couple of cans of coke at a nearby table, causing them to grimace at each other and move their fingers in screwing motion to their foreheads. 'Crazy. y. y...'

Effie didn't care and merely wiped her eyes with a Kleenex as the laughter calmed. 'But seriously, I've got to think about this. I mean, What if he turns out to be like Jack with kinky tastes?'

'You should be so lucky!'

'Susie, it's not my thing!'

'OK, OK, only joking. But let's think, darling, here he is, a highly eligible man who seems to like you, nothing obviously wrong with him, perhaps it's time to broaden your tastes, be a bit experimental. He's new and better looking than Jack, he's got hair for a start.'

'That's true'. Effie sounded more confident. ` I say, shall we have another prosecco? The thought of all this is making me feel quite hot.'

She had gone a shade pinker.

'Maybe some cold water, my dear' from the suddenly responsible Susie.

'OK, but I'm going to have another glass as well' she asserted as she hailed the waitress.

A few minutes later the two women were clinking glasses with Effie toasting 'sex and the older woman' and Susie raising her glass to 'the older man, and long may he love that sexy older woman, even if she does go on a bit.'

'Go on a bit?'

'You know you do' said Susie dismissively 'but, if I might say so without offending you, darling, I think you've been a bit more like that since the business with Jack, which is quite understandable. What it all adds up to, though, is that Kenneth's arrival on the scene is timely. You need to have your attention taken up with something other than your job and your children.'

Effie considered this. 'The family are absolutely my nearest and dearest. But you're probably right. It's a gamble, though, isn't it? And you know how I feel about gambling.'

Susie only vaguely knew that Effie had a thing about gambling which was connected to her father in some way, but she spoke with conviction nevertheless, 'Of course I know that. But almost anything you do has an element of risk about it. Anyway, I think you've made up your mind and what you want from me this afternoon is encouragement to keep going, not advice to stop.'

Effie emptied her second glass and smiled. 'I think I feel better.'

'Me too. And while we're on the subject, did I ever tell you...' Susie gaily plunged into her store of stories about early affairs in her life, whispering loudly, about 'the youth with the rosebud penis –'a darling little bud of a prick' - and 'the hairy gorilla man' - 'the hairiest guy I've ever come across - it was like hugging a fur coat – a bit hot for July', at which point the waitress banged the bill down on the table, the two sobered up, paid the bill and exited, in good spirits.

Ch. 15

'I'm sorry, darling. I'm afraid I'm going out on Friday.'

Cathy pursed her lips and surveyed her mother with raised eyebrows.

'That's a pity, Mum. I was rather relying on you. It's quite difficult to get baby sitters at the moment, as you know. Exams and things not finished yet.'

Effie winced. Had she done something wrong?

'I'm sorry, Cathy. Perhaps if you'd asked me earlier. I do get booked up sometimes, you know.'

'So what is it? Your latest beau?'

'Well, I'm not sure if I'd describe him quite like that, but, yes, I've been invited out for dinner and I'd rather not cancel it.'

'So, what's this then? Effie's got an admirer?.'

Jim had returned from work and was hanging up his jacket. Effie shifted uneasily in her chair. She was not at all sure if she felt ready for enquiries about her social life. Leave it alone, Cathy. She had no desire to talk about it in front of Jim, nor the children who she knew would pester her with questions if they got wind of anything exciting in their grandmother's normally uneventful life. She realised that since the episode with Oliver, she hadn't told Cathy anything about her social life, nothing about Kenneth, and this unwelcome scrutiny left her wishing that she had.

Cathy, clearly oblivious to her mother's discomfort, pushed on.

'Oh, come on then, Mum, tell us who he is. I think I'd like to know who my competitor is.'

'That's not how I'd put it, Cathy.'

'What's a competitor?' piped up Rosie who had also just entered the kitchen where Effie was now helping to clear up the children's tea.

101

'I know' shouted Daisy who was pirouetting round the table in her ballet shoes, 'competitor is when you want to beat someone.'

'Something like that' said Cathy' though in this case it is us having to get in first to get grandma's time so she can look after you when Mum and Dad go out.'

'Don't you want to look after us, grandma?' Rosie's little face was crestfallen.

'Of course I do, poppet, it's just that sometimes I have other things to do.'

'Like what?' persisted Rosie.

'Well, I've already arranged to do something and Mummy only just asked me and when you've said you'll do something to someone, it's important that you do it. I mean' Effie added, aware that she seemed to be tying herself up in knots 'if I'd said I'd baby sit for you two on Friday I'd not have let anything else get in the way, I promise.'

Daisy had stopped pirouetting and the two little girls were looking seriously at their grandmother. It was Jim's turn to comment.

'So what's this then, Effie? Are you being a dark horse?'

'Why is grandma a dark horse?'

'It's a figure of speech, Daisy' snapped Cathy.' So, come on, Mum, don't keep us all in suspense.'

'Honestly, Cathy, don't make such a big thing of it. It's nothing really.' Effie was turning to the sink, pushing her hands into a pair of rubber gloves and grabbing a brillo pad with which she proceeded to scrub the nearest saucepan with a great deal of force.

'Well, come on, Mum, it is a big thing if you've met someone you like and I can't think why you don't want to fill us in.'

'Why does Grandma need to fill us in?'

'It's another figure of speech, Daisy. Just be quiet a minute.'

Effie continued her energetic pan scouring, studiously ignoring the family that had formed itself into a crescent shape behind her back. After a few moments when the only noise was the sound of scrubbing, she turned off the tap and tugged off the marigolds which she arranged neatly beside the sink before turning to face her expectant family.

'I'm sorry Cathy, and Jim, if you think I've been secretive. Anyway, if you really want to know, my dinner date is with a man called Kenneth who lives in West Langdon, he's about my age, looks nice, runs a business and lost his wife a few years ago. He's got two grown-up daughters, one of whom I've met, and he likes things like food and eating out, modern art and going to the movies. He seems kind and rather generous in his outlook. And really, that's about as much as I know.'

Four pairs of eyes were staring at Effie whose colour had livened up a couple of shades as she spoke. Jim was the first to speak.

'Hey, that's great, Effie. I thought there was something different about you recently, a certain, je ne sais quoi?'

'Who's Jenny Saykwa, Daddy?'

'What?'

'Jim, must you confuse the child.'

'I think, Cathy, I am just trying to clarify things and say something nice about your mother's news' he sighed, flashing Effie a smile: 'so, keep us posted won't you, Effie. I'd no idea you were expanding your social life like that, and wish you luck with it.' Then as an afterthought he added 'I mean he is OK I suppose?'

'You mean, is he after my money?' Effie laughed. 'Oh that I had some for someone to chase me for.'

'But you do have a house and a reasonable income, mum.'

'Thank you for reminding me, Cathy, but I can assure you that it is very unlikely that Kenneth's interest in me is financial. He's obviously much better off than me anyway, lives in a big house and doesn't seem to be short of funds. We've been to some rather nice restaurants together and he always pays the bill. Doesn't even let me get a glimpse of it.'

'So long as he's not just putting on a show to impress you. I mean don't let him go to your head.'

'Cathy really! I am not a silly teenager and I can look after myself. I can see I should have told you about him before but I was waiting to see how things go. I mean' she added 'I am entitled to a private life I think.'

'Oh of course you are, Mum'. Cathy's voice softened. ` But it is a bit of a surprise. I thought you'd given up dating since your experience with that man Oliver who sounded quite an odd-ball.'

The still attentive Daisy was about to ask what an odd-ball was but was pre-empted by her grandmother who found herself coming to Oliver's defence. 'No he wasn't odd, just not properly recovered from his wife's death and a bit distracted. I can't really blame him for what happened.'

'Happened...?' Jim's eyebrows rose quizzically.

'Look, I'd rather not go into that now. Shall we get back to the question of who's going to baby sit for you on Friday?'

'Fair enough' said Jim. 'So what about Lauren from round the corner? Maybe she's finished her exams and could help out.'

'I don't like Lauren' complained Daisy, ` she 's not any fun. She only wants to do things on her mobile. She doesn't play games like grandma.'

Cathy now turned to her husband: 'this whole thing would not be a problem if you'd given us a bit more warning, Jim. You just sprung it on me this morning.'

'No, Cathy, I told you about it last week. Work things I always tell you about.'

'Well, I don't remember, but then I'm so busy I may have missed it. You have to make sure I hear you when you tell me things like that. You know how much I've got to cope with.'

'Yes, I know, but all I can say is I did tell you. It's been a busy week for me too.'

'But it doesn't take much effort just to make sure your wife has absorbed a bit of information if it's so important, which you always tell me work things are.'

'Cathy, I don't say that just to be awkward - it really is important.'

The temperature between husband and wife was clearly rising while the two girls were standing there listening, looking unhappy, and Effie had the uncomfortable feeling that she was the cause of it all. Should she cancel her rendezvous with Kenneth? She hated bad feelings and felt taken back at the turn of events, an unpleasant twist to what had so far seemed an exciting and enjoyable prospect. She also felt a degree of pique at her daughter's response and found herself comparing her unfavourably to her sister who she was sure would not have reacted like this. No, she was not going to give up her evening that she was looking forward to.

'Look, I'm really sorry I can't baby sit but I'm happy to help you find someone else. Even if Lauren can't do it, surely she's got a friend and she'd know who's finished exams. Why don't you call her now, Cathy?'

'But it's all very well, Mum, just anyone won't do. The children need to know who it is... but I guess we haven't much choice' Cathy protested as she marched off to make the phone call to Lauren.

An hour later, after half a dozen calls, a lot of irritable waiting and a general deterioration in the atmosphere, the matter was finally settled. A girl from Lauren's class, Jasmine, who had just finished her exams and had met Daisy once or twice at the dance studio agreed to baby-sit on condition that she didn't have to cook any meat for the girls. 'I've recently become a vegetarian' she pronounced 'and I don't like to contaminate myself by touching meat.'

'No problem' responded Cathy tersely 'the children will be watered, fed and in their night clothes. You don't have to touch anything or anybody except the light switch, to put it off.'

'Not put it off!' yelled Rosie who had been listening intently to the conversation 'not put it off. I don't like the dark!'

'Don't worry, darling' Cathy addressed her youngest daughter, her voice at last softer, 'of course I won't leave you in the dark. You'll have your Hello Kitty light on as usual and I'll give Jasmine strict instructions not to shut the door and Daisy will be with you.' She hugged her daughter to her and Rosie, who looked on the point of tears, buried her face in her mother's chest. Effie surveyed the scene soberly. Should she stay and try and sort things out before leaving? She wasn't sure if she felt guilty or annoyed or both. Jim was looking serious too, sitting at the table with Daisy now on his lap, and she wished someone would speak to her.

No one did. And so it was Effie herself who spoke up 'well, would anyone like a cup of tea, now we've got Friday sorted?'

Cathy ignored her mother. Jim was rocking Daisy in his arms but looked towards his mother-in-law and smiled. 'Yes, that would be nice. I think we could all do with some tea.'

'Ooh, can I have some' perked up Daisy 'I like tea'.

'Too late,' said Cathy as she put the now-recovered Rosie down. 'It'll keep you awake and it's nearly your bedtime.'

Daisy grimaced but did not protest. She slid off her father's lap, grabbed her sister's hand and the two girls hurried off.

'Fifteen minutes!' shouted Cathy after them.

Effie poured out three cups of tea and sat down with the still serious –looking parents. Cathy exuded tension into the atmosphere and was not looking either at her husband or her mother.

'Come on, Cathy' coaxed her husband 'I think it's fine now.'

'Only because I spent hours on the phone' she protested, banging her tea cup down. 'It wouldn't've been such a business if you'd only let me know earlier. I just hate doing things at the last minute, you know I do.'

'But I did tell you Cathy. I distinctly remember telling you, and you muttered something.'

'Muttered, probably means I didn' t hear... I mean does it never occur to you that I am so busy that I may have other things on my mind.'

'I know, I know... anyway I don't think we should go on with this while your mother is here and the children are not in bed,' he said, rising.

Effie, with her inbuilt abhorrence of leaving a troubled ship, in a last ditch attempt to improve the atmosphere, offered to help Cathy put the children to bed.

'No, it's all right, Mum. It's Jim's turn to do the bed-time reading' said Cathy firmly.

'Well, if you're sure?'

'Quite sure thanks, Mum.'

'I'll be off then.'

Effie picked up her bag, leaving her unwashed teacup on the table, anxious now to get going. The bus journey home gave her a chance to consider the situation which had taken her by surprise, both her daughter's display of ill humour towards her and also the obvious tension between Cathy and Jim which was new to her. Or was it? She gazed out of the window from the top of the bus as it sped down the High Street and remembered Daisy's remark the other week about Mummy and Daddy shouting, which she had rather dismissed. And as for Cathy's mood this evening, it had also not occurred to Effie that her children would be other than delighted if she found herself a new partner. And was that what it was about anyway?

She put her ruminations on hold as the bus reached her stop. It was a fine evening, almost the longest day and still clear light at a little after eight o'clock. People were sitting outside in the garden of the King's Head enjoying the evening warmth. Effie was briefly tempted to join them but pushed on homewards driven by a desire to offload her troubling thoughts by some other means. En route, she nipped into her local Tesco, exiting with a bottle of Pinot grigio, some milk and a packet of salted peanuts.

Fifteen minutes later she was ensconced in her favourite armchair with a bowl of peanuts and a glass in hand. She wasn't sure whether she wanted to speak to Susie or run things by her older daughter Jane whose approach to life was considerably more laid back than her sister's. Not for the first time she thought the girls had been given the wrong names, Cathy, with references to the wildness of Wuthering Heights, and Jane with its suggestions of plainness. They really ought to be reversed. But, yes, she needed to speak to her older daughter and see if she could help her comprehend the situation.

Jane answered promptly and sounded cheerful.

'Hi, Mum. How's things?'

'To be frank, darling, a bit bothersome' Effie confided and proceeded to give an account of events, emphasizing Cathy's reaction to the information about Kenneth as the source of the baby sitting problem.

'I mean, I did tell you children that I was going to develop my social life, and I thought you were all OK about it.'

'Well, I certainly am. I think it's great, and so does Leo...'

'Does he?... He hasn't said anything..'

'Oh, you know Leo. It's not his style to let on about things. He's fine but just doesn't want to know too much about it. I mean you don't really want to have to think about your sixty-year old mother having sex, do you?' Jane tittered on the other end of the phone.

'Jane, I certainly haven't said anything remotely about that to anyone as far as I know.'

'Yes, but you can't stop people thinking things, Mum. When it was just you and Dad, well, we didn't have to think about it. Children don't think of their parents like that. Then you two split up and we had to get used to the idea of Dad and Helen which wasn't easy since she used to be your best friend. We were used to you and Helen sitting in the kitchen having a cup of tea together and gossiping. So now, if you have a man friend – a boy friend - it's something else to have to get used to.'

Effie considered this silently and took a large sip of Pinot before replying.

'I think I do understand that but you know, the thing is,...I've been so close to Cathy since the kids and to be honest, I've done a lot for them. I'm usually very happy to baby sit. I adore those two. So it's a bit hurtful that Cathy should so quickly get so – well – so ungrateful and almost accusing..'

'Mum, come on, I'm sure she's not. I'm sure she didn't mean to hurt your feelings, she's just a bit up tight, as always' Jane laughed. 'I must say I sometimes wonder how Jim puts up with her.'

'Now don't start having a go at her in order to defend me. But I can see I'll have to think carefully about things.'

'Don't be too careful, Mum. So aren't you going to tell me something about this young man who seems to like you? I think I could stand a bit more information, so long as there is definitely no S. E. X' she chuckled. 'I mean don't forget I'm in one of my 'resting' phases as far as men are concerned. Ian and I didn't really hit it off, so I don't want to have to be jealous of my own mother having a gorgeous man.'

'Oh, Jane, don't remotely think it, please darling. Look he's just a nice, ordinary guy,..'

'Don't worry, Mum. I'm only joking. I've got my eye on someone new at work anyway... another Scotsman as it happens but a more relaxed model. So tell me about this Kenneth.'

Which Effie did. Her daughter listened and made the occasional clucking noise, like a parent listening to a small child, thought Effie, but she was more relaxed by the end of the conversation and finished the evening feeling very good about one daughter, a little better about the other, and more than usually conscious of uncertainties ahead.

Ch. 16

Effie had not slept well. She woke on Friday morning at 5.17 and could not go back to sleep. She wondered if it was excitement about seeing Kenneth that evening. The date had been confirmed: he would pick her up from her house, they would go for a drink at Kenneth's favourite local pub and they would then have dinner at his house with Kenneth acting as chef. All Effie's offers to bring something and help with preparation were turned down and she was politely forbidden from bringing or doing anything. She had to admit she rather liked this assertive side to his personality which suggested confidence, a feeling that surprised her when she remembered how irritated she had felt when Jack tried to exercise his authority over her. In post-divorce mode she considered him just a bully. But somehow Kenneth was different.

She found herself pondering this at 5.17 that morning, trying to understand what it was that felt so different. Such ruminations, however, encouraged not sleep but dark circles under her eyes, with which realisation Effie hauled herself out of bed and staggered to the kitchen. She rummaged in the fridge salad drawer for the cucumber she knew was there and sliced off two pieces which she placed over her tired eyes as she laid her head back on the pillow, praying for sleep and a more youthful skin. The feeling of damp cucumber on her eyelids was mildly distracting from the racing thoughts. The next thing she was conscious of was waking in a bit of a sweat to find her ear pressed to the now warmly damp piece of limp vegetable matter which she shook off with a 'yuck!'. Sitting straight up in bed she waited while the fragments of a dream came to mind in which the cucumber transformed into first blue then purple, growing larger and larger as she ran from it, her mouth open as though to scream but with no sound coming out. It was scary but also exciting. She could see the children in the distance but they seemed quite unconcerned, far off and insubstantial.

The digital clock by her bed showed 6.30; she might as well get up. She made herself a cup of tea which she took back to bed, feeling faintly disturbed but not unhappy. She sipped the hot tea and considered the dream, unsure if the picture of her children in the distance was reassuring. They're not involved and shouldn't be, or was it concerning that they were not taking more notice? The upset with Cathy needed thinking about, but where to go with it? She switched on the radio for the 7 o'clock news, an essential part of her morning routine, tutted at the usual saga of frightful events taking place throughout the world and in relief turned her attention to the more superficial question of what she was going to wear that evening.

She mentally counted out the possible combinations of skirts, tops and shoes, having decided that a dress was too dressy and trousers were too casual. Having honed it down to a red pencil skirt with a black top and black heels - not too high – she was five foot five as it was - and a fitted gray jacket she swallowed the last of her tea and made for the bathroom to survey the damage from a restless night. What she also saw as she slipped off her nightdress to step into the shower, emphasised by the harsh bathroom strip lights, was a deal of sagging flesh which, of course was nothing new, but which this morning greeted her like a wet cod. Clearly two days of missing lunch had done nothing to improve matters.

The fact was that whereas when she had gone out with Quentin or Oliver the emphasis had been on giving herself a smart covering, this evening she suspected was going to be different. She dared to hope it would be, and with this thought came the realisation that she would have to think not just about the covering of her not so young body but about the underneath too. There, hanging uninvitingly on the towel, rail were a pair of once white grey pants and a drab cotton bra. It was definitely time to dig out the Halter and Gusset undies.

And so 8 o'clock that evening found Effie in the black skirt with the red top, her hair freshly washed and blow-dried by Toni, a touch of make –up to cover her undoubtedly dark-circled eyes, a brush of mascara and a dash of soft pink lipstick to complete the picture and she was ready.

Kenneth's mini drew up outside her house with impressive punctuality at 8.01. Effie had been waiting expectantly like a green teenager for a good half hour already and so she was grateful that he had not extended her agony by being late. She watched him come up the short path in front of her house. He looked good, a slim, distinguished figure, with his gray hair swept back, sporting a casual but smart navy jacket over a pale blue shirt which showed off his mildly tanned complexion. Effie clenched her stomach muscles as she opened the door in a desperate attempt to disguise that unbudging roll round her midriff. But Kenneth was all smiles when he saw her and gave her a friendly kiss on the cheek.

'You look nice.'

With relief, Effie stopped the clenching and smiled too.

'Right' he said with pleasing firmness 'now, first stop the pub and then dinner to be served at the family residence.'

He ushered her into the front seat of the car and tucked himself in beside her. The word 'coincé' came to Effie's mind. Definitely cosy. She noticed her neighbour's face pull back from the window of the house next door and allowed herself a brief moment of pleasure at having succeeded in whetting her curiosity after the long arid period of the last few years.

Kenneth was in good humour and chatted easily. 'We're going to a pub near my house, kind of traditional in that you can still get decent beer but they also cater for sophisticated tastes in wine which I think is more your thing? It's called the Coach and Pumpkin.'

Effie laughed out loud as the image of another giant vegetable loomed into mind. 'Sounds lovely, and makes a change from horses - pumpkins, I mean.'

Kenneth laughed too and swore under his breath at a passing cyclist.

'I think the owner was rather taken with the Cinderella story, so we have to watch it around midnight. Need to make sure we're safely elsewhere by then.'

Effie's imagination fast forwarded to midnight.

'You know, I've always had a sneaking sympathy with the ugly sisters, I mean, not much fun having a gorgeous young half sister if you know you look like the backend of a bus. And the father didn't help did he?'

'I must admit I hadn't thought of it like that. Though, I suppose I'm glad my two girls are both good-lookers. Less room for jealousy, is that what you're implying? How about your two?'

'Oh, they're very different and I'd say they're attractive rather than pretty or beautiful, and I don't think they're particularly rivalrous, at least not about looks. As far as character is concerned I think they're sufficiently different not to clash too much. Or does that make sense?'

This contemplation of respective daughters was cut short as the Coach and Pumpkin loomed into view:

'Here we are. Let's see what they've got to offer this evening.'

The pub was jam packed with Friday night revellers who spilled out noisily on to the pavement. Kenneth propelled a mildly anxious Effie through the melee to the bar as a shift in the throng opened up a small space and an empty barstool which he grabbed.

'Right, what'll it be? Have whatever you'd like, please. I'm sticking to beer because I know in a minute I'm going to be hot and I need a long drink, and it's got the brand I like.'

'Well....' Effie had to lean close to his ear to make herself heard... 'I think I'll stick to wine. Sauvignon please.'

'I hope you're all right with it being so busy; I thought we'd start noisy. I promise you it'll be peaceful at my house. Here we are' he raised his glass and gave Effie a warm smile. 'You know, I've been looking forward to tonight.'

'Me too' she shouted in his ear.

'Shall we try and find somewhere a bit quieter – maybe outside?'

They eased themselves through the obstacle course of the throng towards the garden door passing a row of fruit machines on the way. A couple of youngsters were busy pulling handles and giggling.

'Want to have a go?' Kenneth called over the racket.

'Oh no thanks. I've a horror of gambling.'

'Yeh?'

They pushed through the door and breathed more freely in the fresh air.

'Perhaps pubs aren't your scene?'

'No, I like them. Just don't go very often I suppose. So tell me a bit more about it. You say it's your local.'

'Well, it's Victorian, I know that and did used to be called something different - maybe it was the coach and horses. The road used to be quite a major thoroughfare. Still quite busy as you can see. I like it, as I said, because it caters for all tastes and seems to attract lots of different people. There are still a few old- timers, like Bill over there –' he indicated an elderly man with straggly gray hair sitting on a bench by the open door – 'he's been coming ever since we moved to the area.'

'When was that then?'

'Oh about seventeen years ago. My oldest daughter was just starting secondary and my wife liked this area which is near a good school.' Effie was struck by the formality of 'wife' and 'daughter'. 'So we settled here and the girls spent all their teenage years here. We used to come to this pub now and then, though probably more my thing than my wife's.'

'Your wife?' Effie had almost to shout.

He looked pensive for a moment. 'Sorry, yes, my wife was called Ann and my eldest daughter is Janet - you met Julie - two 'Js' I'm afraid'.

Effie sipped her wine which was beginning to ease any remaining nervousness. The noise level in the pub was rising even outside but it was lively and she realised she was enjoying the proximity to Kenneth which was required if she wished to hear what he was saying.

'I can see why you like it. I mean this pub is like a country pub although it's in the city. 'afraid I'm more of a cafe person than a pub person, or maybe a wine bar' she grimaced. 'Does that reveal my solid middle class origins, or just getting a bit old?'

'Nothing wrong with the first and not much sign of the second' was Kenneth's gallant response. 'But come on, drink up. Aren't you starving? I want to impress you yet with my culinary skills.'

Which he did.

The kitchen was modern and looked as though it had recently been decorated. There was plenty of stainless steel, shiny work surfaces and an array of modern equipment. There was a breakfast bar which served as a drinks bar and this was the first port of call for Kenneth as he ushered her in. He produced a bottle of champagne from a discretely hidden fridge and filled two beautiful cut-glass champagne flutes before toasting Effie and suggesting a quick tour of the house while the oven warmed up.

It was basically a Victorian end-of-terrace house that had been extensively modernised inside They started with the living room which was spacious, if a little sparse. Perhaps not used a great deal, was Effie's thought. There were one or two wedding photos of Kenneth with a pretty young woman with fair hair, both smiling happily. 'Ann?' she queeried.

'Yes, and there're the girls as babies. God, they were angelic then,' he laughed: 'have no control over them now, particularly since their mother died, but I guess they're grown up anyway.'

Effie peered at a picture of a group picking out Kenneth, sporting shorts and a broad grin and an Ann looking older but still attractive in a yellow sundress against a background of what looked like Nice or Monte Carlo. There were further pictures of the girls at varying stages of development but Kenneth did not seem keen to linger on the photos and was already in the next room, a small 'study' which had a more homely feel. This was clearly his office with computer, filing cabinets and shelves of books and papers but there was also a large and extremely slim television plus a couple of comfy chairs so that Effie could imagine this was the room where he spent most of his time. She curiously inspected the shelves, plenty of books on travel, France, Spain, the USA, the Far East, and business tomes:'How to succeed in business without losing sleep', and another one that grabbed her attention:'The risks of risk-taking'.

'That's all rather boring business stuff' said Kenneth from the doorway, 'but I like this room and you've probably guessed I don't only work here. It's a good spot to become a couch potato from time to time. I do like the sport at weekends. Sometimes saves my life.'

Effie had been going to ask something about the books and his last comment but did neither as Kenneth sped on with his tour. The bathroom attached to the main bedroom was ultra modern with lots of glistening tiles and shiny chrome with a shallow trough of a basin running the whole length of the bathroom while the loo was surrounded by an array of buttons and levers.

'That's the latest Japanese way of cleaning yourself up which if you don't mind I won't go into but the girls think it's fabulous and funny. Personally, I prefer the old-fashioned methods but this is what the designer gave us.'

Effie wasn't quite sure if she followed this but had a feeling some humorous comment was called for and in fact she felt mildly hilarious as the champagne began to lighten her mood to find herself standing in this futuristic bathroom discussing the facilities with an attractive man she didn't know that well. Inevitably there was a flash-back to her incarceration in Oliver's awful bathroom. 'You know, I never realised dating could be so exciting on the bathroom front' she quipped and was pleased that Kenneth laughed so that they were both in fairly jolly spirits as they entered his bedroom which emanated a very faint odour of what she recognised now was Kenneth's smell – not unpleasant. The room was filled by an enormous double bed, a couple of arm chairs and a chest of drawers on which were the only real signs of male mess, a pile of brushes, boxes, aerosol cans, papers and bibs and bobs. Kenneth apologised in a cheerful fashion:

'Sorry about the mess. House stuff not exactly my thing. But come and look at the view '. He placed his hand on her arm to usher her towards the bay window and Effie's heart picked up a pace. 'See, being at the end of the terrace we get all the neighbours gardens and it's quite an open feel.'

'Yes, a marvellous view.'

He stood beside her still holding her arm while leaning forward to point. 'Look, you can just see the spire of St Peter's.'

'So you can' said Effie whose heart by now was racing so fast that she would have found a view of the local refuse dump entrancing. 'Splendid view.'

It was at this point that the phone rang and Effie suffered another flash back to the dreadful dinner with Quentin and his telephone. Kenneth, however, was not put out and merely tutted as he went to pick up the receiver. Not a daughter, was Effie's thought; they would never ring on the landline. It sounded like a work arrangement which was quickly dealt with.

'Well, Effie, I think that's our cue to go downstairs and have something to eat. I'd be most upset if it got overcooked.'

So they returned to the shiny kitchen where Kenneth topped up their glasses, put on an apron and transformed himself into a chef. Effie was directed to sit on an elegant looking stool by the breakfast bar where she perched a little precariously, acutely aware of her weight and everything feeling tight or bulgy but was soon caught up in Kenneth's obvious enjoyment in what he was doing as he spun the handle of the egg whisk with considerable flair. Within minutes he had whipped up an impressive mound of thick white froth which he carefully folded into a pale green mixture which he had already prepared. The mixture was poured into small ramekins, sprinkled lightly with grated cheese and placed in the hot oven with a satisfied 'voila!' from the master chef.

It was quite a performance and Effie burst into applause and laughter.

'Now all we have to do is wait precisely 21 minutes, just long enough for us to have another glass and me to put the final touches to the sea bass which is going to go in when the soufflés are done. Baby new potatoes – I hope you're not on a diet - and a little wilted spinach and that's the main course.'

'Terrific!'

'Yes, but that's not all. There will be dessert to follow which..' he added momentarily serious.. 'which I haven't yet decided, but, do not fear, there will be sweet to follow in some form.'

And sweet there was after the delicious courgette soufflés that rose like a dream and melted in the mouth and the succulent sea bass browned to perfection on the griddle with just a butter and dill sauce accompanied by tiny new potatoes and tender strands of spinach. It was all so easy, so heady, that Effie's resistance to the 'sweet', had it been there at all, simply faded away and she could have been any age - eighteen, forty two, seventy – she experienced a deep longing that she hadn't felt in years that simply surged over her so that as Kenneth moved closer and closer to her as he presented each lovely dish they moved seamlessly together into an embrace that moved inevitably to touching, grasping and kissing, to fumbling and tottering upstairs amidst much laughter and groping, Effie finding herself in some way or other on the divan with a half-clad Kenneth passionately kissing her and caressing her and loving her, tugging on buttons and pulling on zips, throwing off garments, kicking off shoes until the two of them were able to grasp each other in a sort of frantic embrace. Effie opened herself up to him, encircling her man with arms and legs, gasping in pain as he penetrated her but the hurt quickly merging into the marvellous sensuality of it all and she grasped fiercely at his thigh, pulling him round the way she wanted it, working him, determined to achieve a climax which she did with an expulsion of breath and a gale of laughter, holding him tight as he, too, strained and gasped, whispering in her ear 'take my seed, take my seed' and fell back exhausted onto the pillow.

'My god' said Effie.

'Phew!' said Kenneth.

They lay there for a while like a couple of star-struck lovers, each with their own thoughts. Effie felt good. She'd almost forgotten what it was like. She liked Kenneth. He liked her. She couldn't have asked for anything more of the evening and dared to hope she had found herself a relationship that would work. There was just one little niggle in her euphoria. A fantasy had appeared in her mind's eye as the two of them had writhed together: it was an image of a strong shapely leg and a pair of soft blue eyes, and she knew they were not Kenneth's.

Ch. 17

She simply had to get home. The whole experience was so exciting, so marvellous and so terribly disturbing that she had to get back to her own territory, despite Kenneth's protestations. The thought of spending the night in this strange house with her excited and troubled thoughts, not to mention not having a tooth brush, night clothes or makeup did not appeal. And then there was the Japanese loo. Kenneth had discreetly taken himself off downstairs to bring up a couple of brandies leaving Effie free to use the bathroom. He had fished out a white bathrobe which he assured her was 'quite clean'. Effie wondered whose it was.

In the bathroom was a bidet as well as the loo, equally adorned with buttons and levers. She hesitated between the two and plumped for the loo. She did need to relieve herself. Now that the excitement had died down she felt a little tender in her lower regions and looked forward to bathing herself in some warm water. But how to flush the loo? She squinted at the buttons beside her on the wall and pressed one which she thought said 'heated'. Nothing immediately happened and she was just about to get up when a powerful shot of hot water spurted onto her backside startling her into a shriek. She hastily pressed the next button to stop it which only had the effect of changing the hot spout to cold which poured out even more fiercely before gradually slowing down and completing the process with a final loud sucking sound as the contents of the bowl disappeared down the hole and the air was filled with a fine jasmine-scented vapour.

Effie waited a moment, not daring to raise herself from her sitting position, but her backside was now freezing cold and she wanted to warm herself up. She eased herself over to the bidet, sitting astride like a horse. This time she took more time to consider the labelling and went for a button that promised 'heated massage: gentle' which proved to be a good choice. A warm shower sprayed her from below moving in a wave motion backwards and forwards so that her frozen bottom was soon thawed and soothed and she was beginning to enjoy this pleasant increasingly stimulating sensation, curious about the next button which described 'heated massage: vigorous' when Kenneth's voice came through the door.

'You all right?'

Effie pulled herself up. Enough stimulus for one night. She really did need to have a bit of quiet time to herself to digest the events of the evening. So she thanked him profusely and sincerely, arranged to call the next day and meet the following Friday - 'seems to be our day' - and gratefully sank back in the seat of the mini cab which Kenneth had ordered.

She slept fitfully and dreamt of another giant vegetable which she was devouring hungrily making lots of holes where she took large bites which seemed to wink at her like eyes as she chewed on the flesh. Next morning, in the bathroom she stared at herself in the mirror: her eyes were blue-grey, not as clear as they used to be and those lines etched round them which looked particularly deep today. But what did she see in them? Warmth? Compassion? Intelligence? and... she moved closer to the glass, peering, guilt? Yes, definitely guilt, and they seemed greyer as she stared. Perhaps that was the colour of guilt, a dull grey like heavy metal. If envy is green then guilt is grey. Yes, guilt grey sounded right, but no point in dwelling on it. It was best to get on with normal morning rituals, a cup of tea, radio 4, breakfast, a shower. She felt a need to get on with familiar things while some part of her was insisting that her world today was different from the one of yesterday, and it wasn't just that she had experienced intense physical desire, even lust, for the first time in many years. She needed to speak to Susie.

'Susie, are you up? Can I talk?'

'Effie?,'

'You know it's me'

'Hold your horses. What's up? Don't tell me the lovely Kenneth and you have finally mixed your DNA together!'

'Never let it be said you aren't quick to cotton on! So, yes, as a matter of fact we have, but, honestly Susie, I don't know what to think, I mean it all seems so...' Effie's voice tailed off. Did she want to tell Susie what was really disturbing her? Susie was speaking:

'I'm delighted, darling. Aren't you pleased? Or was it all a frightful disappointment?'

'No, no,... not at all. It was fine, actually pretty good. Quite amazing really that it's all still working.'

Susie laughed.. `so can we give him an A+ for sexual congress?'

'I guess so.'

'So?'

'I'm just not used to being so stirred up. I just hope it doesn't all end up in tears.'

Susie expostulated `but why should it? You're both adults and free agents, you've no ties that you need to worry about. Honestly, Effie, I don't know why you aren't dancing in the aisle.'

'You don't?'

'No I don't. Or is there something about him: he has BO, a wart on his penis, lousy politics?'

'No, no, nothing like that. Can't really fault him, though I wish I knew him better. The house didn't really give much away, all very modern inside and a hugely smart kitchen and an excellent cook.' The grey feeling was beginning to mellow as she chatted, warming to the familiar engagement with her friend, and she was soon laughing as she described the bathroom with all its technological gadgets.

'Sounds a bit kinky to me.'

'Actually it was quite soothing.'

'You realise you haven't said anything about what actually happened, though I've got a pretty good picture of your Kenneth's plumbing facilities.'

'Well, you'll just have to sit on your curiosity, Susie. I am entitled to a private life you know.'

'Since when?'

'Since last night' was what she said, while to herself she thought, since I started having secrets.

Susie had moved on. 'I've got to go, darling, some of us have to work on a Saturday. What are you up to this weekend? You're very welcome to join me and Fred tomorrow evening for a bite, or are you meeting your lovely beau?'

'Tomorrow? No. I'm not seeing Kenneth till next Friday. But glad you asked me that. I said I'd baby sit for Cathy. To make up for my errant behaviour last night.'

'But you always enjoy that, don't you? Roll on the day when I have grandmotherly duties to perform. You realise, Effie, you're my shining example of the ideal grandmother.'

'I am?'

...

The conversation with Susie left Effie only partially reassured, as she mulled over the evening: was there something 'kinky' about Kenneth's tastes or was it her? She felt her body was still tingling with both pleasure and pain and it was all rather overwhelming. And then there was that image, which she simply had no idea what to do with other than try and push it aside which she attempted to do by throwing herself into some quite unnecessary housecleaning. Having exhausted herself in this pursuit she was about to settle down to tackle the Saturday 'fiendish' soduku with a cup of coffee when the phone rang and a cheerful Kenneth greeted her. She felt he meant it when he told her how much he had enjoyed the evening. She could respond equally sincerely that she had too. He had a busy week ahead but looked forward to seeing her on Friday again for a movie and a meal out.

Effie perked up after this conversation. The joy of feeling someone liked her and having something to look forward to. She hummed to herself as she went about her domestic tasks. Determined to tackle that bulging midriff that Kenneth's culinary skills were clearly not going to help, she subjected herself to an hour of torture at the gym followed by a skinny latte and a mini croissant with one of her gym mates who to Effie's annoyance wolfed down a huge slice of chocolate brownie while not showing an ounce of spare flesh.

Sunday evening found her at Cathy's house. The girls were in the garden when she arrived and Cathy was busy preparing their supper. She looked up as her mother came in.

'You look well, Mum. Been to the gym?'

'Yes, I'm glad you noticed. I needed it after a late night out on Friday.'

Cathy raised her eyebrows. 'Oh yes, you and your young man. So how did it go?' She sliced into a carrot, chopping off the green top.

'Fine. Yes, very nice. How about your evening?'

Cathy banged the lid on a saucepan. 'Oh, it was the usual rather tedious work do. Lots of people yattering on about their children's schools and having their kitchens refurbished and stuff, and everyone eating and drinking too much and really not worth the bother of all that fuss to find a baby sitter on Friday.'

'Oh dear, sorry about that. It's a pity, darling. I thought actually that Jasmine was quite a good find. I mean she seemed willing and the kids liked her. I'm sure you could use her again.'

'At this rate, we may have to.'

'Cathy, what do you mean – 'at this rate'?'

'Well, if gadding about with young men is going to be a regular occurrence.'

'I wouldn't call it 'gadding about', Cathy, and Kenneth is not young.'

A burning smell was coming from the cooker and Cathy hastily pulled out the grill pan to reveal six shrivelled black fish fingers. 'Damn it! Oh really that's the last straw.'

'Here, Cathy,' Effie touched her daughter's arm 'come, let me help. There are some more in the packet.'

Cathy sniffed, tossing her hair back, 'Well, if you really want to help you can get the girls in to wash their hands and lay the table, thank you. We're trying to get out to a 6.40 at the Cornerhouse. There's a French film about a man who's been having an affair for years and finds out that his wife's been doing the same thing. Meant to be a comedy' she laughed.

The girls were eventually brought in from the garden, seated with clean hands in front of plates of fish fingers, carrots and over-cooked chips about which Daisy started to complain until she noticed her mother's steely expression.

'I know they're a bit burnt but you're lucky to be offered decent food. There are hungry children in other parts of the world who would be grateful...'

'Hi, there.' Jim appeared, 'what's up?' he enquired looking towards his wife till he noticed Effie whom he greeted cheerfully. He had a paint brush and glass jar in hand. 'Been doing a bit of DIY in the girls' room. We've got time for a quick cup of tea, haven't we, Cathy?'

'I'll do it' Effie leapt up.

'No, you sit down, Mum, and keep an eye on the children. I'll make a pot.'

Tea cups and spoons clattered. 'Here, Jim, give this to Mum.'

Jim took the cup and placed it carefully in front of Effie, catching her eye and holding her gaze with a warm smile. 'Hey, Effie, you're looking great. This new man of yours must be doing you good.'

Effie's face immediately warmed up and she knew she must be scarlet.

'Why is grandma's face all red' piped up Rosie, darling Rosie.

The two girls giggled, Cathy stared while Jim continued to smile and look at her with his blue eyes. Effie shut her own briefly.

'Well, I'm glad you find someone attractive.' Cathy was addressing Jim. He sighed and went over to his wife giving her a hug and a peck on the cheek.

'Come on,Cathy, you look great and you'd look even nicer if you didn't look so fierce.'

'Fierce?' Cathy's tone was angry. 'I didn't know I inspired fear and trepidation, and...' she turned to the children who were sitting watching, no longer giggling...`don't ask what that means, Daisy, because I have no idea' with which she marched out of the kitchen.

'Oh dear' said Effie `I do hope that wasn't my fault.'

'No, no, not your fault, Effie. Cathy's just a bit up tight at the moment. I think she's finding working and looking after the children and everything quite tiring. She'll be OK after we've been out. I'd better go and see if I can calm her down.'

The children were quiet after that and still subdued at bedtime despite Effie doing her best to be cheerful.

'So what does 'trepidation' mean, grandma' asked Daisy as Effie tucked her into bed.

'Well, if you are in trepidation, it suggests you are sort of frightened of someone, darling, but I don't think Mummy really meant it. She was just a bit tired. Come on, I want to read to you.'

'I was frightened when Mummy was cross' said Rosie.

'Oh, you're just a scaredy' Daisy dismissed her sister.

'We all get scared sometimes' said Effie a bit sadly as she opened a book she had brought. 'I'm going to read to you about a very brave Greek hero called Theseus who was so brave he was ready to fight the fearsome minotaur, a kind of huge dangerous bull, in order to save the people of Crete. He was lucky in that he got the assistance of a beautiful maiden who used her intelligence to help him. So...' she read on.

Ch. 18

From Monday to Thursday evening Effie buried herself in work, excelled herself on the 'fiendish' sodukus, stretched and pushed her body to unaccustomed extremes at the gym and resisted the urge to call Cathy. By the Thursday evening she could not stop herself from phoning first Jane and then Leo.

'Just wondered if you've spoken to your sister this week?'

'No. Should I have?'

'No, I suppose not, but' and in a sudden burst of confidence 'she really was in quite a mood on Sunday, Jane, annoyed with everyone. I wasn't sure if it was the children or Jim.. or me. And I haven't seen or heard from her this week so far. Normally at half term I take the children out for a day, but Cathy didn't ask me. Do you think it's me?'

'Most likely Jim. They've been married now just long enough to find each other responsible for everything that's wrong in their lives and you are part of the collateral damage. I fear, mother, you are just an easy target.'

'Oh, Jane, you are sometimes just a bit too cynical.'

'I don't think so at all' her daughter replied breezily 'I'd say I'm just being realistic. Which is precisely why I do not intend ever to get married or live permanently with a man. It's going to be two residences or nothing.'

Effie sighed: 'so do I have to worry about both my daughters?'

'No, Mum, that is exactly what you do not have to do. You may want to go on fretting about Cathy but, honestly, don't waste any sleep over me. I have every intention of being fine, just fine.'

'So how are things going with the nice Scotsman?' Effie ventured to ask.

'Actually,' Jane's voice softened by several tones, 'rather well. With luck we're going to avoid Cathy's mistakes, and yours and Dad's, even Leo's, though he hasn't really made any yet I guess. But, hey, I've got to go, Mum. My date with my personal trainer. Now that makes me feel better. You should try it. It'll help you forget those knotty family problems.'

'It will? But I spend enough time at the gym. It just exhausts me.'

'Keep at it, Mum, you look great for your age. You should be enjoying your life not worrying about all of us. Must go.'

And so saying she was off, leaving Effie far from reassured about Cathy. The call to Leo followed. He was not answering and so Effie left a message, trying to sound perky and unconcerned. By 11 o'clock she was in bed with the times crossword, determined to get some beauty sleep this week before the Friday outing. She was about to put her light out when the phone rang and it was Leo.

'Hi, Mum. What's up?'

'Up?' Effie hesitated. She had a mother's soft spot for her only son who seemed somehow to have escaped the worst characteristics of his father, Jack's bullying quality, and was in many ways the easiest of the three. Tonight she found herself confiding in him: 'Cathy never used to be quite so touchy, and I'd never dreamed that she and Jim might not be getting on.'

Leo was more reassuring than his sister. 'Come on, Mum, one evening when she's a bit irritable. Looking after those two kids and a husband and running a house and having a job: of course she's ratty. It just gets too much sometimes but I'm sure she'd basically fine. Don't let it get to you so much.'

Effie mulled over these two conversations knowing that she had been looking for reassurance which was not going to come easily since she had not and could not tell the whole story. Nevertheless, life somehow felt a bit more normal and she was able to drift off to dreamless sleep to be woken at 7.15 by the thunk of the paper landing on the doormat.

It was Friday. Kenneth in the evening, 6.30 at the cinema. She was looking forward to it. The morning off and so she was able to take her cup of tea back to bed with the paper. She scanned the domestic news coverage, lingered a while on the latest turmoil in the middle east and settled down to the business pages which always fascinated her. She amused herself by calculating the likely gains if she switched her energy provider, concluding that it wasn't worth the hassle, checked the stock market reports to see if her last week's predictions had materialised and took mild satisfaction in finding that she was largely right. I can't understand why I'm not richer, she thought as she heaved herself out of bed and made for the kitchen. She was buttering a piece of toast for breakfast when the phone rang and it was Cathy who sounded quite her normal self and made no reference to the previous Sunday.

'You've been very quiet this week, Mum. What have you been up to?'

They chatted like old times, much to Effie's relief, so that when she put the phone down, having promised to do some baby sitting the following week, she could convince herself that all really was well and that she had no reason not to look forward to her coming evening out with Kenneth. A niggling voice, however, insisted on pointing out to her that it was a bit odd – wasn't it? - that Cathy not only said nothing about the Sunday display of temper but also omitted to ask anything about Kenneth.

With a shrug, Effie gathered herself together and sat down to write her list of things to do for the day, a list which she reckoned helped to keep her blood pressure down by encouraging her to believe she was in control of her life.

'So who wants to be so controlled?' had been Susie's blunt response to discovering her friend's penchant for listing things. 'I spent a lot of my life fighting for freedom from control. My parents were awful control-freaks.'

Effie had protested 'but really you were fighting to control things yourself, and you didn't have my Dad who couldn't control himself at all. It led to a lot of unnecessary misery' she had added darkly.

The list so far contained two items - 'ring hairdresser', and 'wash undies'. She was contemplating the day ahead, pencil poised, when the phone rang again.

'Hello, Effie?' It's Sally.'

'Sally?'

'Yes, you remember. You had lunch with us that time you got stuck in the lavatory.'

'Oh gracious! Yes, Oliver's... Sorry, I just didn't connect.'

'Don't worry. But how are you? It's been ages.'

Effie had two reactions: one was to glimpse the terrible turd bobbing away in the loo, which was rapidly followed by an image of Oliver's bald head covered in the wisps of orange hair.

'I'm fine, just fine. Busy, you know?'

'Look, Effie, I didn' t ring up just for a polite chat '- ever the direct Sally - 'I'm looking for support for this charity I'm involved in. You know Oliver's wife died of cancer. Well, there's a bazaar and we've organised a cooking competition to raise money. It's both a competition and a lottery - you buy a ticket and you can come along and watch and the winning tickets get to eat the prize dishes - plus a bottle or two of champers. Do you fancy coming along? All in a good cause.'

'Right, well, when is it happening?'

'Saturday week – 5.0'clock in the town hall annex. Tickets are £5 each. Can I put you down for a couple?'

'Well, I guess so. I'll need to check my diary, perhaps Susie'll come.'

'Great. I'll put you down for two tickets. Must go. Masses to do. Oh, and by the way, Oliver'll be manning the tea urn.'

Oliver. Effie had managed to put Oliver firmly in a drawer in her head marked 'do not open for fear of food poisoning and unexpected consequences'. The idea of meeting him again, particularly behind a tea trolly or anything to do with food left her feeling decidedly unenthusiastic. But she'd said she would go and she reminded herself of Sally's excellent meal and wondered if she would be competing herself in which case, if she won, the prize meal would be a good one. She thus convinced herself she was neither a sucker nor a sado-masochist and proceeded to get on with her day and the much more important task of getting ready for her evening out.

Ch. 19

Effie was wearing dark glasses and a light jacket with the collar turned up even though it was a warm August evening. Her loose skirt was well below the knees and on her feet she wore rubber-soled pumps. She made her way through the open gate towards the building, a single-storey brick structure with a small neat garden in front and a path flanked by regimented borders of pink geraniums leading up to a swing door. A sign to the left of the door was decorated with blossoming fruit trees and announced a cheerful 'Welcome to the Orchard Clinic'. She hesitated on the threshold, scanning her surroundings before following a sign to 'reception', moving instinctively quietly.

A large lady of uncertain years was sitting at a desk behind a glass window with her head down busy with a mobile telephone. She did not immediately look up so that Effie coughed, whereupon the woman jumped in her seat, exclaiming 'oh goodness - I didn't hear you come in.'

Effie laughed nervously: 'sorry. I was a bit quiet.'

'So have you got an appointment?'

'Appointment? Well, no - I thought you could just drop in.'

The woman regarded Effie, sizing her up, causing Effie to clutch every muscle in her body and pray, pray that she could control the blood flow to her cheeks.

'This is the Orchard Clinic?'

It was said in a questioning tone which had the instant effect of triggering a tsunami-like blood surge to her face and a prickling of sweat under her arms. She knew only too well where she was. If only the ground would swallow her up. The woman was waiting, still looking at her, making no effort to help. So far, every hideous thing that she had imagined could happen on this visit had happened, but there was no going back. Through gritted teeth she spoke up:

'Yes I do know this is the Orchard Clinic and I understood I could see one of the doctors here without having made an appointment..'

Relenting her bluntness the woman suddenly smiled and reached for a clip board which she held out to Effie.

'You haven't been here before...? Just fill in some details, your GP and so on.'

'Do I have to do that? I'd really rather keep this to myself and the doctor here.'

'All right, but it means you'll have to call yourself for the results of any tests we do. Anyway you can discuss it with the doctor. But without an appointment you'll have to wait a bit, maybe more than half an hour. I think Dr Brown should be able to see you after his last appointment.'

'Did you say his last appointment?'

'Yes I did. If you want a female doctor you'll have to come back tomorrow morning. Sorry about that.'

The idea of returning the next day was such a hideous thought that Effie decided to swallow her embarrassment and sit it out there and then. She was beginning to feel the whole venture was such an odd experience, so far from her normal everyday existence, that it was becoming quite unreal. Perhaps she could just switch off her feelings for the next hour.

'I'd rather wait, thank you' she said politely as she took the clip-board and sat down to fill it in. Name, address, date of birth. She wanted to lie, but did not. 'When did you first notice symptoms?' Good question, and one which she could answer although she had not known at the time that the agonising pain she had felt when she and Kenneth had had sex was a symptom of disease. That was at least two weeks ago and, knowing she was still not right, she had eventually confessed to Susie.

'But, darling, you poor thing, I hate to upset you with a dreaded word but I think you've got an STD.'

'A what!' squeaked Effie.

'An STD, you know, a sexually transmitted disease.'

'That's an acronym, not a word' had been Effie's defensive response.

That was a few frantic days ago when Effie had spent hours on the internet reading articles and scaring herself silly with frightful pictures of enflamed and terrifying genitals, both male and female until sanity had at last prevailed and a degree of calmness that had enabled her to venture forth to the Orchard Clinic, a building she had never noticed before, tucked away as it was behind the main hospital.

She handed over the form which she had filled in as best she could and was handed a pink ticket with a number on it.

'People usually prefer a number rather than a name' the receptionist confided in her. 'If you go along to the waiting area someone'll come for you there.'

'Oh thanks, yes, good idea' Effie agreed, gratefully taking the ticket, conjuring up a picture of a Heinz can of beans as she noticed her number was 37.

The next obstacle was the waiting area where Effie knew she would have to wait feeling exposed and awkward. Anticipating that wearing her dark glasses would attract more attention than not she headed for a corner of the room, casting a suspicious eye on the upholstered chair as she sat down, watchful for stains or other signs of infection. From behind her newspaper she surveyed the room. There were two other people already waiting, both at least half her age, one a young red-headed man wearing headphones who was chewing gum and staring hard at Effie, the other a young girl whose plump legs oozed out from the edge of a tiny skirt, her head down and fingers busy with a mobile phone. The room itself was pleasant enough with potted plants and bright posters on the wall, some proclaiming the joys of 'protected sex'.

Behind her newspaper Effie tried to relax and while away the half hour or so by doing the crossword but her mind would not settle to the task, flying backwards and forwards like a yo-yo: how had this happened, what if, and the uncomfortable knowledge that she had not broached the subject yet with Kenneth, having ascribed her sexual reluctance on their last date to the traditional female dampener of desire, the headache.

'Number 35, please' called out a pretty young woman in nurses uniform, whereupon the plump girl raised her head from her phone and disappeared through one of the doors, leaving Effie alone with the insolent youth who continued periodically to stare in Effie's direction, smirking and tapping his foot to the beat which reverberated from his headphones.

Ten more minutes passed during which time Effie filled in just two answers in her 'easy' crossword, and then another nurse appeared, who looked neither pretty nor young nor happy, to call out 'number 37.'

She ushered Effie into a small room to be greeted by a schoolboy with a choirboy haircut and round glasses. He greeted her 'I'm Dr Brown, do sit down.' He shuffled some papers on his desk and retrieved Effie's form which he inspected through the circles of the glasses. 'So how can I help?' he looked enquiringly at her and Effie realised that she was going to have to spell it out. There was no getting away from it.

Dr Brown turned out to be tactful, sympathetic and gentle when it came to the examination, while the unhappy-looking assistant mellowed and gave Effie a cheerful smile and a nod as the examination came to an end, patting her reassuringly on the arm as she helped her up. She could hear the doctor tapping away at his keyboard as she pulled her clothes together behind the screen.

'Right, Mrs McIver', he spoke seriously. Oh god, the verdict, thought Effie.

'I'm pretty sure you've got the herpes simplex virus' he said 'though I'll need to send off the swabs for analysis. I understand it's the first time this has happened, and the first time is always the worst. You've just been unlucky, I mean for this to crop up at a - well, mature age. But it can happen to anyone, really, at any time and a huge percentage of the population are carriers, have the virus without knowing it and never having any symptoms. But you really should discuss it with your partner and it is definitely advised not to have intercourse while you have any symptoms.'

Effie's heart thumped. She knew it was what she'd half expected but it still came as a shock.

'So what do I do?'

Dr Brown immediately smiled. 'Oh there's not much to do. Just abstain for a bit, and if it ever recurs again which it might, it shouldn't be quite so painful. I really think you can be relieved it's not something worse.'

And with an angelic beam, he held out his hand to shake Effie's. She took it in a sort of daze, unsure whether to feel relieved or fearful, stammered her farewells and blundered towards the door which the nurse opened for her, leaning in to whisper in her ear, 'don't worry, my dear, you're certainly not the oldest we've had here.' Most reassuring, Effie muttered to herself as she exited the building, smarting like a piece of raw garlic.

Ch. 20

Effie had found her way home like an automaton, oblivious to her surroundings, her mind in a turmoil. In the house she dropped her bags and jacket on the floor, making straight for the fridge to open a bottle of her favourite chardonnay. She sank back on the couch and audibly breathed out. Well, at least she wasn't going to die, although that moment when she had stepped into the waiting room had brought her close to understanding the meaning of the phrase about 'dying of shame'. Utterly mortifying. So now she knew what was the matter there remained the vexing question of what to do next which was linked to the other question of how the hell this had happened to her and who was responsible?

Assisted by a glass or two of the Chardonnay, she did a pretty good job on working herself up into a lather of indignation at the very idea of having a sexually transmitted disease, she, a senior lady with a far from adventurous record sexually. Admittedly a bit wild in her youth, but having spent over twenty years faithfully in a marriage that had ended badly and never having had any problems physically in that department, and she couldn't even blame Jack, who until his moment of betrayal when he walked off with her best friend had been a nice clean boy. Here the thought of Jack and Helen together stirred a vengeful image in her febrile imagination of the two of them spatchcocked on a bed displaying hideously infected genitalia with supturating sores. She hated them, she hated her situation and she felt thoroughly sorry for herself. The disease had not come from Jack, nor from her: no, the obvious culprit was Kenneth.

Having satisfactorily come to this conclusion Effie felt a little better, topped up her glass and went to phone Susie who was suitably sympathetic even impressed.

'My god, Effie, I wonder if you could get in the Guiness Book of Records as the oldest person to catch an STD?'

'You may laugh, Susie, but I've got to tackle this with Kenneth. Any suggestions welcome.'

The conclusion of a further half hour on this topic was that the subject would best be broached at the start of their next meeting on the coming Friday rather than over the phone and that Effie should do her best not to make it sound like an accusation.

'Approach it gently' Susie advised.

'But I don't feel gentle. I feel bloody furious.'

In fact the conversation with Susie succeeded in calming Effie sufficiently so that she could pay some attention to soothing her suffering body. A long hot bath followed, then a shower with plenty of soaping and rinsing, not to mention finishing off the bottle on an empty stomach. Next was a clinical inspection of the offending area - she had to see – in the spirit of science, to make sure she didn't look like one of those frightful pictures. She took her mother's silver hand mirror and crouched down trying to angle it so that she could see, but it was awkward, everything in shadow, everything felt wobbly. The final indignity, as she shifted uneasily to get more light on the subject was to topple right over and end the day flat on the bathroom floor like a splayed cat.

She had no memory of how she got into bed but woke early the next morning with a headache and the tail end of a dream in which wild creatures, all spotted and striped in garish colours, romped around a jungle landscape which metamorphosed into her childhood house. A couple of cups of coffee and toast and honey improved the headache and put Effie in a better frame of mind. It was a work day and she was grateful to be able to focus on other things. The prospect of some light-hearted chat with the girls in the office appealed and in the evening she would drop in on Cathy. The family had just returned from a camping holiday in France and Effie looked forward to seeing them after two weeks away.

It was another warm evening with late summer flowers blooming in front gardens as Effie walked from the bus stop towards Cathy's house. The sight and scent of them succeeded in driving away the last of her heady feeling and she was in better spirits as she opened their garden gate. She had had a quick conversation with Kenneth, who sounded in a hurry, about what they were going to do on Friday - go to a pub by the river if the weather held - and had said nothing about the clinic visit as she and Susie had agreed.

When she pressed the doorbell she could hear two sets of feet come running and the familiar girlish chatter as Daisy and Rosie opened the door. They greeted their grandmother noisily, hugging and pulling her in, chatting excitedly about their holiday. They looked tanned and healthy, their hair was lighter and Effie was sure they were taller.

'So you obviously had a good time' she laughed' and looks like you had good weather, you're so brown. Just look at you.'

'I can speak French' boasted Daisy 'I can say 'bonjour' and 'come on ali view' which means 'hello and how are you'' she trilled.

'And I know that 'sank' means my age and it also means a boat got lost in the sea' said Rosie, not to be outdone.

Cathy's voice came from the kitchen:

'Hi, Mum, come on in the kitchen. Kids, tea's ready.'

She was standing with her back to the door dishing up a pan of peas and carrots so that Effie caught sight first of her daughter's rear view, a bit heavier she thought. The old jeans Cathy was wearing were stretched tightly across her backside and an ancient t-shirt flopped off her shoulder. Her hair was strewn around her face, half screwed up in a clip. Effie resisted the temptation to pull her comb out of her bag and offer it to her daughter.

Instead she said: 'You look great, darling, and the girls - they look so well. You obviously had a nice time.'

Cathy clattered the pan in the sink, turning the tap on full-force so that hot water splattered around. Sausages were spitting under the grill.

'Come and sit down, you two' she called to the girls. 'Now let's not have any fuss tonight. Just tell grandma all the super things we did and, Daisy, please eat your carrots.'

Daisy screwed up her face in protest and Effie sat next to her, anxious to prevent her granddaughter from provoking an argument.

'Come on, girls, you can talk to me while you eat. I want to hear what you ate in France. Did you have lots of pastries. I love them.'

The girls finally settled and with mouths full of sausage and peas chattered on about their time away. Effie joined in with enthusiasm but Cathy was noticeably quiet, occupying herself with clearing up. After a while Effie got up.

'Come on, Cathy, leave that. I'll do it in a minute. Let me make a cup of tea and you come and sit down. It's so lovely to see you all again. I missed you. Two weeks is a long time to be away.'

'A bit too long if you ask me' was Cathy's glum response.

'Oh, why? What happened?'

'Nothing 'happened', Mum, but it was just a bit too long to be with the Williams and two demanding children and Jim. He didn't help half the time. I can see why the divorce rate goes up in the autumn. Anyway, I think the children enjoyed it. They got on with the other kids most of the time,but the little William's girl: god, was she a little princess. She couldn't do anything wrong in her parents' eyes and she moaned half the time. Wouldn't share and screamed when she didn't get her own way. Then of course Daisy and Rosie started complaining that it wasn't fair to them, so, yup, I think I had just about enough of children by the end of two weeks.'

She stirred her tea forcefully.

'Well, I'm certainly glad to see you, and you do all look well.'

'I do? I wish you'd tell that to my husband. Jim was crass enough to comment on my eating too many pain au chocolat in front of Val who, of course, is skinny as a rake and she just said something stupid about being lucky that she didn't put on weight, which I don't believe anyway. I think she just starves herself secretly and then eats like a pig. Might even be bulimic.'

'Cathy, come on. You're looking great. Really.'

Cathy pushed away the biscuit tin as Rosie stretched out her hand.

'No, Rosie, you may not have a biscuit. You haven't eaten your carrots.'

'But you've had two!' Rosie protested.

'Carrots first!'

Cathy turned to her mother 'thing is, Mum, you <u>would</u> say I look nice. You're my mother. I need to hear it from my husband occasionally.'

This comment was the cue to the sound of a key turning in the lock and all four females turned their eyes in his direction as Jim entered the kitchen.

'Hi everyone. Hello Effie, you're looking good. Great to see you. So what's been going on since we were away?'

'Oh, not much. But I want to hear about you. I was saying to Cathy how well you all look' said Effie, praying that he'd say something complimentary about Cathy.

'Oh sure, the kids look great, don't they? I think they had a good time despite having to live alongside a bit of a spoiled brat of a child. We didn't realise just how tiresome the William's daughter could be. Odd really when you think you know people. I mean the parents are decent and good fun but they've no idea about discipline, how to manage a group of children. The older boy was OK though, wasn't he, girls?'

Rosie, who had finally swallowed two small bits of carrot, perked up.

'Daisy likes Johnie' sang Rosie in a high pitched voice. 'She thinks he's funny 'cos he's got a funny willie, 'cos he showed us his willie when he peed.'

'For goodness sake, Rosie' Cathy spoke firmly' and Daisy, do not kick your sister.'

Rosie began crying and rubbing her leg.

'Well, Rosie, if you insist on saying stupid things'

Which made her cry even more and the kitchen was filled with discordant sounds until harmony was finally restored by Effie producing two chocolate mice from her bag, a treat that seldom failed with her two granddaughters. Rosie still sniffed periodically but was soon munching away on the mouse while Jim held her on his knee, rubbing the injured leg.

'So what do you say to grandma? And haven't we got something from France for her? Daisy, go and fetch the bag with the picture of a vineyard on it. See if you can carry it, it's quite heavy.'

Daisy staggered back with the said bag which contained four bottles of chateaux wine which Effie received with unfeigned delight. With peace restored and checking her watch, Effie suggested it was opening time and they might as well get on and sample her present right then and there. Which they did. Cathy mellowed a little as she sipped the rich red burgundy and the whole family relaxed. Daisy disappeared briefly and returned with a postcard picturing the village where they had stayed on holiday.

'Well done for remembering, darling. Yes, sorry, Mum, we didn't get round to posting any cards but the girls chose this one for you.'

'I wanted to give it to you yesterday when we saw you but I didn't have it with me' said Daisy as she handed over the card.

'Saw me?'

'Yea, we saw you, didn't we Daddy?'

Jim flashed one of his engaging smiles. 'Yes, we saw you outside the hospital. We were coming back from the library..You looked like you were in a hurry.'

Effie swallowed a mouthful of wine before replying, half-registering that it didn't taste as good as it had a few seconds ago.

'Oh yes, I was visiting a friend. She had to stay in overnight.'

'Not your Susie I hope' said Cathy as she topped up the glasses round her. 'I've always thought Susie was a candidate for health problems one of these days.'

'No it wasn't Susie and I don't know what you mean by health problems, Cathy?'

'Ok, OK... I just meant she looks thin, so thin that she might snap in two one day.'

Aware that she was feeling both defensive and bothered by the turn of the conversation Effie decided on a timely exit and rose to leave.

'Anyway, darlings, time I was off. Marvellous to have you all back, and school must be starting soon? Perhaps I can have the girls for an outing before that happens?'

'Great idea, Mum, I'll call.'

'Here let me help you with the bag, Effie.' Jim was picking up the wine and making for the door. ` Your car outside?'

Effie's blue Fiat was parked by the house under a tree and a large dollop of pigeon dropping could be seen to adorn the windscreen. Effie exclaimed in disgust as she edged herself into the driver's seat.

'Supposed to be good luck' Jim chuckled as he wedged the bag of bottles behind the front seat. Effie had started the engine and was pressing the wipers to try and wash off the offending muck but only succeeded in smearing it all over the screen.

'Hang on, I'll get some water.'

He returned a few minutes later with bucket and cloth and proceeded to wash the screen, bending across Effie's open window, wiping vigorously with the cloth so that she noticed the muscles flex on his strong brown arms. Once he was satisfied he bent down to speak through the open window.

'That's better.'

He leaned in a bit, looking straight into her eyes and lowering his voice.

'Effie, you are all right aren't you? When we saw you at the hospital you did look extremely worried. I mean you would tell us if anything was wrong?'

Effie let out a small gasp and spoke almost without thinking with the strong urge to get away.

'Well there was a little problem, but it's fine, quite fine, and please, Jim, for heaven's sake don't say anything to Cathy, or the others. I just don't want Cathy fussing over things. She's got enough on her plate anyway.'

Jim placed his hand briefly on Effie's arm, patting it gently.

'OK, if you'd rather keep it between me and you, so long as you're sure you're all right. I'm quite capable of being discreet, as you are, I know.'

He withdrew his hand and leaned in to kiss her on the cheek. Effie sped off as the blood predictably rose to her cheeks and she turned the radio on loud to drown out any possibility of thinking about the unthinkable.

Ch. 21

Effie sat gazing at the river which flowed peacefully past quite unconcerned about her inner ruminations. Kenneth was fetching drinks. She had ordered a spritzer which she felt was a nice balance between staying sober, so that she could tackle the issue, and needing a drink to help her cope with that very problem. The dry spell had lasted and it was a fine evening, the pub throbbing with Friday-night revellers and Effie had spread herself out at a picnic table in the garden which she shared with a group of noisy youngsters. Kenneth had turned up in a t-shirt and jeans and looked relaxed. Effie had noticed that the barman greeted him like a friend as they passed on their way out to the garden. She watched him depart towards the bar, stopping to chat to some young man on the way as though he knew him: how at ease with the world he appeared, how people seemed to like him. She reflected that there were people that he obviously cared about, his daughters, his wife, and he even seemed to be attached to the local pub, but she still felt she didn't know him well and the business with the herpes was still rankling. The symptoms had gone and she was back to normal, but it felt like unfinished business. She had to tell him and the sooner the better.

He was handing her a tall bubbling glass and easing himself into the seat opposite her.

'Kenneth.'

He raise his own glass of beer, smiling and clinking glasses.

'Yes, my dear? So what's been going on for you this week? This, by the way...' and he waved an arm airily in the direction of the young man Effie had noticed earlier.. 'is Alexander. He's the star of the darts team.'

Effie nodded. It was a far from ideal setting for an intimate conversation, but she pressed on.

'Kenneth?'

'Effie?'

'Look, I wanted to talk to you about something.'

'Goodness, that sounds serious.'

Kenneth in fact looked far from serious and Effie wondered if he wasn't already a bit drunk while Alexander had squeezed himself into a tiny space opposite her.

'Good to meet you, Effie.' He raised his glass in her direction. 'Kenneth tells me you are a lady of many talents' he grinned.

'I am?'

It was no good. Alexander had clearly settled himself down. 'Waiting for the lads to join me later' and Kenneth was making no move to move, so that all Effie could do was finish her spritzer, accept a glass of Chardonnay and try and put her prepared speech on hold. An hour later, having been joined by the whole darts team, a group of hearty young men, Kenneth suddenly looked at his watch and announced they had to be at the restaurant precisely ten minutes ago and so finally off they set, Kenneth wrapping his arm around Effie's waist as they walked the couple of streets to La Fontana, an Italian restaurant 'of some repute', according to Kenneth.

He was clearly in good spirits and kept telling Effie how delighted he was to be with her, what a hard week he'd had and how he had been looking forward to their meeting. The jovial mood persisted during the ordering process with Kenneth showing off his limited Italian, addressing Effie as 'mia amore' They both ordered pasta and a bottle of red wine. The good mood was catching. She didn't want to spoil it by having to raise the subject of 'down there'. She inwardly chuckled to note her own euphemism. Why was it so difficult to name things for what they were? Could it really be so difficult to discuss this with Kenneth?

There was a lull in Kenneth's rhetoric as he dug into his fettucini with porcini mushrooms and truffle sauce, so that Effie was finally able to gather what was left of her resolve. She swallowed a large mouthful of Sicilian red:

'Kenneth, look, I need to talk to you about something.'

Kenneth paused, his arm half-way to his mouth.

'That sounds serious?'

'Well, it is and it isn't.'

'My dear Effie, you're not ill are you? You haven't got cancer or something?'

'No, no – nothing like that – and I'm fine, at least, I'm not entirely fine, but it's not cancer.'

'Well, thank god for that. Here, let's drink to that.' He raised his glass: 'to not having cancer. You realise I couldn't stand someone else dying on me. No, that I couldn't stand.'

This was not the direction Effie had expected the conversation to go.

'Kenneth, I need to be frank. I know it's nothing like cancer but I found out last week that I was suffering from a sexually transmitted disease – herpes to be precise, and it was quite a shock.'

'Herpes!' boomed Kenneth.

Effie was sure, correctly, that everyone in the restaurant was looking in her direction. And then he burst out laughing

'Well, you didn't get it from me, my darling. I am symptom free, clean as a baby...'

'You mean, a whistle. Clean as a whistle' said Effie irritably 'and I can tell you that I have never had anything of that kind in my whole married life..'

'And out of it? Out of your married life?'

'Kenneth, I am not in the habit of sleeping around. I am sixty years old, was married for over twenty years to a man I was faithful to and you are the only man I have had sex with since Jack left me eight years ago.'

'Am I really?' Kenneth's tone softened. 'Am I really your first lover in eight years?'

'As a matter of fact, yes, you are.'

'Effie, I feel highly flattered.'

'You do?'

'Well, of course I do. You are a very attractive woman, you know.'

'Kenneth, nice as that is to hear, I am really bothered by this situation; to find myself suffering from something I associate with promiscuous behaviour, to go through the indignities of the GUM clinic..'

Kenneth burst out laughing again, 'You poor thing, Effie. Did you really have to do that?'

'Yes I did, and I haven't felt so humiliated in a long time, waiting there with kids still in their teens. It was awful. And I really don't know what there is to laugh about.'

'Oh please don't be cròss, Effie. I am sorry you had to go through that, but it isn't such a terrible disease, is it? I mean, I may have had something like that when I was younger. Things happen, but it's not worth us falling out about, is it?'

Effie considered this, unsure quite how angry she still was, partly mollified, partly even more infuriated by his nonchalant manner. He topped up their glasses and lent his arms on the table, looking at her.

'I'd be really sorry if this gets in the way.'

'I have to say that for the moment it does. I mean, suppose my children found out? They nearly did. The grandchildren saw me coming out of the clinic.'

'Look, all I can say about that is that they can be grateful that their grandmother has a lively sex life and that she hasn't got cancer. And now' Kenneth hailed the waiter 'how about a pudding? You will have one won't you, Effie? They do a delicious tiramisu.'

'Yes, it's marvellous. One of the best I've tasted'.

This remark came from a middle-aged woman sitting at the next table, part of a couple Effie had barely noticed, but who clearly had been listening in to their conversation. Effie glared at her but Kenneth smiled benignly and was soon engaged in conversation on the subject of Italian desserts.

So subject closed for the evening? Not on your Nellie, was Effie's immediate response, but it was all so difficult. All her overt and covert attempts to get Kenneth's serious attention to the matter failed dismally: he was far too busy with the boring couple whose fascination Effie failed to comprehend. Two heaped portions of tiramisu arrived topped precariously with thick chocolatey cream which triggered further exclamations of admiration from 'Janet and John', as Kenneth introduced them, names which caused Effie to burst out with uncharacteristic lack of restraint 'you must be joking'.

Far from taking offense, the said Janet and John were soon tucking in themselves to the creamy dessert in obvious good spirits which only added to Effie's growing frustration and fury that the evening was not going according to plan, that she was surrounded by people with skins as thick as rhino hide. She plunged her spoon broad-side into the pudding spattering flecks of coffee and cream over not only herself but Janet's pale pink trousers.

'Oh god, I'm terribly sorry' Effie lied 'here, let me help.' She plunged her napkin into her water glass and began to rub furiously at Janet's trousers, spreading the brown colouring across the rosy stretch of her ample thigh.

'Oh don't worry, my dear. It's all artificial fibres, it'll come out in the wash.'

She smiled in an annoyingly friendly way leaving Effie feeling angrier than ever as she rubbed at the spatters on her own trousers which she knew would not wash out so easily. Wouldn't anyone this evening react in the way she wanted? Kenneth just seemed to find everything amusing including the discovery of a creamy splodge on his shirt which John, not to be left out, echoed as he licked something off his cuff.

'Good shot' chortled Kenneth 'you couldn't have hit so many targets if you'd tried.'

What makes him think I didn't? thought Effie angrily as she conjured up the image of the four of them as children in the nursery throwing their food around when mummy's back was turned. A trip to the ladies' room was needed to gather together more adult resources. She was not entirely surprised to find that even this did not go according to plan: Janet followed close on her heels intent on a bit of female bonding in the 'powder room' as she quaintly called it.

A long pee and plenty of hand washing did relieve Effie sufficiently to allow herself to be at least civil to Janet, who she knew very well was not responsible for her feelings, she just happened to be in the wrong place at the wrong time, and her main fault was to be a bit too friendly. As Janet powdered her nose she chattered excitedly about how nice Kenneth seemed 'such a lovely sense of humour' and how she wished her John could laugh at things the way Kenneth did.

'You're very lucky, I think.'

None of this really helped Effie who was not feeling lucky at all. She was left at the end of the evening in a state of considerable indecision, if not confusion, and the immediate issue was whether she would go back to Kenneth's and spend the night in his bed, or whether she would insist on going back to her own, to nurse hurt feelings and anger.

Ch. 22

'Compromise: isn't that what those of us who don't like conflicts do?'

Effie was on the phone to Susie, telling her about the outcome of her meeting with Kenneth. 'Yes, we went back to his house but I said I didn't feel like sex after what had happened. He said he was totally surprised and didn't understand, but he was sorry and he liked me a lot and didn't want to hurt me and all that, and so I just sort of stayed...'

'What do you mean 'sort of stayed', Effie?'

'I stayed and we went to bed together like an old married couple and watched a movie. It was really quite pleasant in the end. He made me breakfast in bed in the morning and we went for a nice walk by the river...'

'But do you mean he denied any responsibility for what happened?'

'I guess he did. He claimed that he was symptom-free and hadn't had any trouble with anyone else...'

'Anyone else? I thought he was meant to be the grieving widower.'

'Yes, well, I think he was very fond of his wife...'

'So?'

'.. I don't know... he's good fun and nice looking for a man of his age and he has been kind.' Effie tailed off, aware that she was manoeuvring herself into a position where she was defending Kenneth against Susie's scrutiny and perhaps her own. She sighed. 'Why can't it be simpler? I thought this one was a good one.'

'Maybe still is, but the fact is his response to you, Effie, was not a kind one. Still' and she sounded more encouraging 'men are never at their best when they feel they are being criticised on matters which even remotely touch on their sexuality. He's a proud guy: remember how he was when he was buying that dress for his daughter. Proud as a peacock.'

'I do remember and I thought it was rather touching. I mean I do like a man who's a good father. I like the idea of a family man.'

'Well, see how things go for a bit. Can't do any harm, can it?'

Effie put the phone down and sat for a while, knitting her brow and sipping the remains of a now cold cup of coffee. Her thoughts wandered back to an image of her own 'family man', Jack, together with his children, her children, the five of them sitting on a beach in the south of France. He'd seemed such a good father, teaching Leo to play cricket, putting Cathy on a pony and reassuring the child that she'd be all right. Cathy, always the most anxious of the children, so different from her younger sister Jane who from early on relished a challenge and hated to have to depend on her parents. It was through Cathy that Helen had come into their lives. She remembered meeting her at the school gate when Cathy was about 8 or 9. Helen's daughter, Amy, was in the same class as Cathy and the two girls had hit it off. The two mums were soon seeing a lot of each other's children and gradually a lot of each other. Their friendship had deepened during the girls' progress through secondary school, university and into adult life. Amy had gone into publishing and Cathy had tried her hand at social work. It was around this time that Cathy met Jim, both of them fresh from college and enthusiastic about doing something worthwhile in the world. Amy, too, had a boyfriend and the two families had been delighted when both daughters, within six months of each other, announced their intention to get married. There had been a subsequent summer holiday when Jack and Effie had shared a villa in the south of France with Helen and Tim and there had been much talk of wedding plans for the girls. Cathy was hoping to marry in the early spring and Effie remembered how preoccupied she had been with the arrangements on that holiday. She and Helen had whiled away many a happy hour lounging by the pool discussing the relative merits of venues, menus and outfits.. On the last night Jack had made a special toast to the daughters and their coming marriages: 'may they both have as long and happy a marriage as mine has been.'

And then had come the crash, and in retrospect the dedication sounded more like a memoriam than a wish for the future - a 'has been' marriage.

A week after they got back Jack had announced his intention to leave Effie and go and live with Helen.

Effie was roused from her ruminations by the door bell. Archie, the gardener, liked to work on a Sunday. A man of the old school but clear that 'the Lord would'na have given us gardens if he hadn'a wanted us to cultivate them' he 'd assured her in his Scottish drawl. He was older than Effie and she liked him for his solidity, his rootedness, his good common sense. Today she felt like hugging him when her own thoughts were wandering all over the place. The ritual of making two mugs of tea was also settling and this morning Effie had time to wander round the small garden with Archie, letting him take the lead as to what needed doing.

'This un's nae good' he intoned as he kicked at a small flowering shrub which to Effie looked perfectly flourishing. 'Look'. He folded up the lower leaves to display some yellowing on the otherwise dark green stem.

'Summit's eating the roots. Might be vine weevil and that you can'na see:it's all hidden under the ground.'

'Oh dear, Archie..'

'Aye, and there's no much else you can do but dig it out. It may still look all pretty but it's what's underneath that counts.'

'I know what you mean' said Effie with feeling.' I guess you'd better take it out. I just hope it hasn't spread.'

Ch. 23

Effie had last seen Kenneth three weeks ago and it seemed an achingly long time, even though it had been her decision to end the relationship. Or had it? Whichever way, she felt relief but also regret at what had started out so well and had ended badly: the business with the herpes, together with discovering evidence that he had a roving eye. He had been driving her home when his phone rang and she felt he was just a bit too quick to grab it as she made a move to pick it up. Something similar happened a few days later as they sipped gin and tonics before a movie and this time Effie caught sight of a name, Fiona. 'Just an old friend' he had protested when confronted, but Effie was not convinced. To cap it all she also discovered, thanks to a chance remark made by his secretary, that the nature of his business was gaming and gambling with an interest in casinos in far flung parts of the world. Her experience of having a father who was unable to keep away from the gaming tables and had ended up bankrupting the family as a result of his addiction, had left Effie instinctively wary of anything to do with gambling. Her rational self told her she should cut her losses and get out before she got so entangled that it really hurt. The fact was, however, that it did hurt. It was painful that he so readily agreed that they were not suited after all and his persistent refusal to understand why she was so upset by his attitude to the herpes, revealed an unpleasant side to his character.

'He told me I wasn't street-wise' Effie complained to Susie.

'Sounds too adolescent for words!'

'But, you know, I did feel rather adolescent at times and quite enjoyed it.'

'Darling, you'll enjoy yourself again.'

'Will I?'

'Definitely. I know it's a cliché, but there are other fish in the sea.'

'I don't want a fish' said Effie, petulantly stabbing at a sugar cube she had dropped into her coffee, 'I want a proper, grown up relationship with a decent man.'

'Well, aren't you going to your friend Sally's charity bazaar this weekend? You told me Oliver might be there and you could do worse. I mean, if you want a decent man, doesn't he fit the bill?'

It was true that Sally had been in touch, reminding Effie about the bazaar. Her confident assumption that Effie would not only come but that she would bake a cake for the occasion was hard to resist. The prospect of meeting up again with Oliver, however, did not produced any exciting response in Effie. If anything, she felt more interested in getting to know his sister-in-law rather better and resolved that she would put in an appearance. She would buy a cake from Marks and Spencer and present it as home made. She just didn't have enthusiasm for baking and on Friday she had booked herself a hairdo after work with the express intention of cheering herself up. That, and a movie with one of the girl's in the office was Effie's Friday plan.

The hairdresser always made Effie feel better. She generally came out looking good – lucky with her sleek grey hair - and feeling good, having engaged for an hour or so in an intense conversation with the hairdresser which ranged from the superficial to the personally intimate. 'Coiffeur therapy' was what Effie called it. This Friday was no exception and the movie was amusing, so that as she made her way home she was in better spirits, chuckling to herself at a scene from the film as she put her key in the lock and opened the door, to find that the light did not come on when she pressed the switch. She tutted with annoyance and fumbled for the other switch.

Something didn't look right. What was it? She moved from the hallway to the living room. Again the main light did not go on and she tried a table lamp which lit up instantly to reveal a room in chaos. She gasped. Books on the floor, a broken lamp, chairs upturned, cupboard doors open, stuff spewing from drawers. She stared. For a moment that was all she could do. She listened, holding her breath. Not a sound. She slowly exhaled. She felt sure whoever it was had gone. The kitchen door was open and she saw immediately that the window was broken.

'Bastards!'

A wave of anger swept over her. 'the bastards! The fucking bastards!'

She didn't even want to know what they had taken: she was simply overwhelmed with a sense of outrage at the break-in, the intrusion, the assault on her home, her personal space.

So what to do? Her thumping heart settled a bit and she managed to pull her thoughts into practical mode. Ring someone?– yes – ring the police. Which she did and had no memory of how long they took to arrive but arrive they did, a policewoman and a lugubrious looking constable who produced the proverbial notebook and stood silently as though waiting for instructions. The policewoman, who said her name was constable Warren, was more efficient and soon had Effie sitting down with a cup of tea, giving details of what had happened and eventually getting her to walk round the house to check what had been taken. Her bedroom was a complete tip, and Effie gasped again as they opened the door. Every drawer had been pulled out, cupboard emptied, bedding turned over, dressing table ransacked, clothing everywhere.

'Looking for cash and jewellery' said the policeman morosely.

Effie was by now searching frantically through the debris by her dressing table.

'My necklace. The only decent thing Jack ever gave me. Where the hell is it?' But after a few more minutes of fruitless searching, she sat back on her haunches, the hot fury surging over her again: 'the fucking, cuntish, shitty bastards.'

It wasn't entirely clear to Effie herself who she was cursing.The burglars obviously, perhaps also Jack. 'So what happens now? she enquired of constable Warren who was inspecting the window frame.

'No doubt they got in downstairs. We'll send forensics around tomorrow morning to check for fingerprints. Unlikely we'll find anything but you never know. It doesn't look like a particularly professional job. And we need a list of everything that's missing' she added, giving Effie a quick efficient smile. 'Now once we've checked the other rooms I think we can get going.'

The three of them descended to the kitchen which felt chilly from the draft from the smashed window.

'So what do I do about that? I'm not going to be able to sleep with that gaping hole – they might come back.' Effie shivered.

Constable Warren agreed that it was not ideal, remarking that it was also a bit late to get anyone out to fix it. Her helpful suggestions were that Effie could either batten it down with some boards, if she had some, or spend the night with a friend, if not.

'I don't and I can't' was Effie's curt reply: 'never mind, I'll ring my daughter, see if she's got any suggestions.'

A few minutes later Cathy picked up the phone: 'Mum? What is it? It's late.'

'I know – sorry, darling, but...'

'Mum, what's up?'

'Nothing, Cathy, at least, actually, something. Yes, I've been burgled, broken in and there's a huge great open window in the kitchen. They smashed it..'

'Christ! Mum, poor you. So are you OK?'

The result of this conversation was that some twenty minutes later the door bell rang and there was Jim clutching a couple of sheets of old hardboard under his arm and a bag of tools. He set to work without delay, rapidly roping in the lugubrious-looking PC to hold the boards in position while he hammered them home. The gaping hole disappeared behind Jim's not-so-deft handiwork.

'Well, I think we'd better get back to the station. I think you should be all right now, Mrs McIver. So, don't forget, there'll be a couple of our forensics team call round tomorrow morning. Don't touch anything, of course, if you can help it.'

And with that, the two officers left. Effie stood by the door for a few minutes after they'd gone, listening as the squad car roared off. Can't wait to get back, she thought. And suddenly she felt as though her whole insides released, the tight grip she'd been holding herself together with since she stepped through the door earlier simply dropped away and she almost collapsed onto the kitchen floor, just managing to grasp a chair to catch her fall. She felt the colour drain away from her face as she let out a gasp of air, at which point Jim, still busy with the window, turned round.

'Effie? Are you all right?'

Effie's head was down. For a moment she thought she would faint as her head buzzed and something was thumping through her body.

'Here –' Jim hurried straight to one of the kitchen cupboards 'you need some of this.'

He extracted a large bottle of scotch and poured out a sizeable quantity into a wineglass he grabbed from the draining board. Effie took it, swallowed two or three mouthfuls. The cool liquid slid down her throat, hitting her stomach with a blast of an impact which made her shudder but enabled her to sit back and breath more freely. Jim was watching her intently, standing with the bottle in hand.

'Better?'

She nodded. Jim moved to find another glass and poured himself a large tot. He pulled up a chair close to her.

'You've had quite a shock. I guess it's only hitting you now.'

Effie still found it difficult to speak, continued to sip her whisky which was rapidly going to her head, attempted to get her breathing under control, and tried hard to keep back an urge to cry. She closed her eyes and shook her head, as though to banish the experience, the effect of which was to set her head spinning again so that she had to open her eyes, to find another pair of eyes very close to her own, those lovely soft blue eyes, Jim's eyes.

He was bending down, looking at her with concern, but didn't speak. He put out his hand to touch her thigh, caressing it gently. 'Poor Effie, such a shock.' Effie nodded, not moving away but closing her eyes, letting her head ease closer to Jim who made no attempt to move away. He continued to stroke her thigh and murmur 'poor Effie, poor Effie, lovely kind Effie' which shifted into a sort of whispered rhythm as his hand moved up from her thigh to her arm, her shoulder and her sleek grey hair. 'A horrible thing to happen, such a horrible thing' he was stroking her hair. 'Such a lovely person, such lovely hair'. And the fiery feeling in her stomach was now a fiery feeling lighting up her whole body so that there was absolutely no resistance, no murmur of protest, only wonderful electricity as she gave way to the thrill of feeling his lips on hers.

Ch. 24

Cathy rang early, waking Effie, who stretched a weary arm out to pick up the receiver. She had a dreadful premonition that it was her daughter. Who else would ring that early on a Saturday?

'Mum, are you all right then? Jim said you were quite upset. He was back very late.'

'Yes, darling, I'm sorry about that, but I <u>was</u> upset. It suddenly hit me. He was incredibly helpful, Jim I mean, really helpful and I've got to get that window properly fixed, but he did a good job.'

'Glad to hear he's doing something useful somewhere. Anyway, if you really are OK I'm just checking whether you are still 'on' to baby sit tonight. We've got one of Jim's boring dinners. A three-line whip, and I hate work stuff getting into the weekend, <u>and</u> they're a boozy lot his work mates, and not so easy to get another babysitter this late on a Saturday.'

Effie was aware that she hesitated for a moment before replying:

'Of course, darling. I'm fine. I'll see you at 7 then. Must get going now and ring that glazier.'

She put the phone down in a cold sweat, her daughter's voice ringing in her ears. Her mind was going to explode any minute and her stomach turned like a butter churn. What had she done? What had Jim done? What actually happened? Think! Don't think! Where to go with those thoughts? You are a train careering out of control?

Now this really won't do. Effie pulled herself out of bed with a degree of resolve, showered and swallowed a strong cup of coffee. The main thing, she told herself, was to get through the day in as calm a fashion as possible so that she would be fit to baby sit in the evening. She didn't even want to ring Susie to tell her about the break-in because

155

she knew she would not be able to hide her disturbed state of mind from her friend's sharp scrutiny. And right now, she felt so utterly shamed about what had happened that she could not acknowledge it to anyone. Distraction was the answer and a good start was to check last week's forecast for the stock market. She did this every Saturday, was rarely far out and this Saturday was no exception. Thus armed with some evidence that life was not totally random, that she was not solely subject to her most basic animal instincts, she set off to the shops with a long list of items to purchase which included a Marks and Spencer cake – she would still go to the bazaar - sweets for the children and flowers for Cathy. It was normally some fruit for the kids and a packet of herbal tea for Cathy but today felt different. Doesn't the guilty man come bearing gifts? said a voice in her head. The guilty woman too, or the guilty mother? Hideous thought!

However, the steel grey sky was beginning to shift, shafts of sunlight were breaking through and Effie's volatile mood gradually settled as she immersed herself in the hurly burly of the high street. She arrived home laden with groceries and a large bouquet of sweet-scented lilies as the glazier's van drew up. The window was soon replaced by the young man who assured her that 'that'll keep 'em out' as he gave her a rather too friendly pat on her arm.

The bazaar was being held in the grounds of the town hall and by the time Effie arrived there was quite a throng. She wove her way through the stalls of jams, honey, fruit and bric-a-brac until she spotted Sally standing tall over a stall laden with a colourful display of cakes and biscuits. She was busy with a batch of small chattering youngsters who were drawn with big eyes to the display of top-heavy cup cakes iced in garish pink and blue. Sally noticed Effie as she hovered, cake platter in hand.

'Ah, hi, Effie. Great. You made it' she said taking the cake from her 'but not the cake I see.'

Effie grimaced. Did this woman know everything?

'Sorry, Sally, I just didn't have time for baking. Anyway, how are you?'

'Oh absolutely fine. Now hang on, keep your fingers out, please' she addressed a small red-haired child. 'Frank's here somewhere. In charge of the treasure hunt and I think Oliver's manning the tea stand. Sure he'd like to see you. Can't talk now. No, Sasha, you can't have another one when you've bitten into one already.'

Effie left Sally to it. She had to admire her competence, her confident certainty while she was feeling bowled over by self-doubt and guilt. She couldn't imagine Sally being so weak as to allow herself to get into such a tangled situation and she had a brief fantasy of telling her all about it, of sitting in a chair and having Sally sit opposite listening and giving her clear expert advice. But the atmosphere of the afternoon was cheerful and she soon relaxed into the festive mood. She wandered through the crowd, letting the autumn sunshine warm her, greeting a couple of people she knew, stopping to buy a pot of honey for Cathy, more sweets for the children. She had a go at the tombola, throwing with unusual accuracy so that she found herself walking off clutching the prize of a huge bright pink teddy bear.

By now Effie was dying for a cup of tea and a sit down so that any reservations she had about meeting Oliver again were overruled and she wended her way towards the tea tent. At first she did not recognise him. He was standing behind a large urn filling and handing out cups of tea and slices of cake. There was definitely something different about him. He looked less scruffy and all over the place. She realised that it was his hair: the awful wispy bits had been cut and his balding head now looked neater, he looked younger, surprisingly modern.

'Effie! Sally told me you might be here. What a pleasure. So how are you? Tea?'

'Yes, thanks.' She took a plastic cup from his eager hands. 'So....? How have you been?'

'Good. Better, yes, in fact, very well. Sal's been taking me in hand and I really do think life looks good. I've joined the local history club and getting involved in it and it really has opened things up for me. I think I was needing something to focus on, you know. But what about you? You know I felt after our last meeting that perhaps I needed to apologise to you for something but I wasn't quite sure what.'

'Really? That's funny because that's exactly what I felt. I don't think I left your house with much glory. And Sally is such an amazingly competent woman. She's quite hard to live up to.'

157

Oliver laughed. 'Oh Sal's certainly a super-woman, but hugely nice with it. She and Alice used to get on well although they were very different. But how are <u>you</u>? It's so nice to see you, I can't tell you' he beamed.

A couple of hours later Effie was staggering off the bus laden with bags and clutching the pink teddy. In her enthusiasm to come bearing gifts she had forgotten that her car was at the garage and she would have to carry her shopping. Not the only weight I'm carrying, was her thought as she pressed the bell which was opened promptly by Cathy.

'Good god, Mum, what on earth's that?'

'What?'

'That hideous pink thing you're carrying. You're not thinking of giving that to the girls are you?'

At that moment Daisy and Rosie appeared and promptly began to squabble over who should have ownership of the furry beast so that Effie felt compelled to dig into the bag for the sweets and also to offer the bunch of slightly sagging lilies to her daughter.

'I thought you might like these, darling, they smell nice, and sorry about the teddy. I won it this afternoon.'

Cathy took the proffered flowers, frowning and holding them away from her.

'They may smell nice but the pollen is a nightmare if you get it on your clothes. It never comes off. I mean, Mum, this is my best dress.'

'Oh dear, well, let me put them in some water. There's some honey and things for you too.'

'Mum, it's all very lovely but, honestly, you know I don't like the kids having too many sweets and just look at them, listen to them. Sugar goes straight to their heads. You'll be lucky if you get them settled for a few hours and that pink thing is quite gross, totally tasteless like processed cheese. Yuck.'

Cathy was warming to her task of having a go at her mother as she jammed the lilies into a vase. 'Anyway, I'm happy to leave those two in your capable hands while Jim and I go off and have a marvellous time with his oh so exciting work-mates. And where is he? That man's never around when I need him. Seems to spend his time helping other people.'

Effie said nothing. She had very little defence and her daughter's ill-humour seemed quite justified and appropriate, even quite a relief. But she had little time to reflect on this as the noise coming from the direction of the girls was increasing exponentially and Cathy was clearly in no mood to intervene.

'Your call, I think, Mum' she said turning to leave the kitchen as Jim entered.

'Ah, there you are. Come on, Mum's arrived as you can hear and if we're going I'd rather not be late.'

So saying, Cathy swept out of the kitchen, Effie headed for the noise and Jim followed his wife, turning as he reached the door to call a goodbye to the girls. Effie looked round as he did so, catching his eye in a moment of hesitation when he smiled at her briefly before disappearing, with the result that Effie had to tackle her over-excited grandchildren with a bright red face and thumping heart.

The process of calming them down, however, had the effect of settling her own feelings so that by the time the girls were tucked up in bed Effie could tell herself that there was at least a semblance of normality and she was ready to throw herself into the bedtime story. 'So what's it to be tonight? Rosie, I think it's your turn to choose.'

Rosie chose a book of 'modern-day fables for young people', a tome which Effie picked up doubtfully, but which she couldn't resist faced with the child's insistence that she was definitely a 'young people'. The story was the tale of how 'Awful Andrew' sends a text message to 'Cool Carol' pretending to be her boyfriend Johnnie, setting up a date to meet after school, so that Awful Andrew can turn up at the rendezvous ready to step in when she finds out that her boyfriend has let her down.

'But what Awful Andrew does not know' read Effie 'was that Cool Carol has checked the message with Johnnie, realises that it is a trick and the two of them decide to teach Awful Andrew a lesson. So Cool Carol arrives on time whereupon Awful Andrew appears from the bushes where he has been lying in wait, only to be confronted by Johnnie who has been filming the whole thing on his I-Pad including a shot of the hoax message. Johnnie wants to take his mobile phone off him but Cool Carol persuades him that he has had punishment enough and the two of them go off arm in arm to get a coke, leaving Awful Andrew skulking in the bushes, wondering how he is going to face everyone at school the next day.'

The two girls listened intently to the story with only one interruption from Rosie who asked what 'skulking' meant.

'So there we are' said Effie closing the book and mentally telling herself she wasn't going to read one of those again. 'Time to go to sleep.'

'They were doing a lot of pretending' said Daisy as she snuggled herself down under the duvet. 'I don't see why Awful Andrew had to pretend he wanted to see Cool Carol, I mean, what was wrong with him?'

'Darling, I don't know. Maybe he didn't think she'd like him.'

'But she didn't like him when he played a trick' protested Daisy.

'Yes, I think that's the point of the story, it's helping us to see that it's better not to pretend things, to be as open and honest as we can'.

'Mummy says I can pretend if it's a game' piped up Rosie 'and I like when we play 'let's pretend I've got two pounds to spend... I'd spend one pound on sweets and one pound on colour pens and one pound on buying Mummy a bag of crisps.. and..'

'That's more than two pounds, silly' interrupted a sleepy Daisy 'and I don't like it when people don't tell truthful things. Big people shouldn't do that, should they, Grandma?'

'No, poppet, they shouldn't' said Effie as she tucked the little girl in, willing herself not to think about the mammoth-sized lump of guilt that was pressing hard inside, at least not until she'd settled the children for the night and she could escape downstairs to pour herself a stiff drink.

By the time Cathy and Jim returned Effie had consumed a considerable quantity of Scotch, not having found any open bottle of wine in the fridge and not wanting to appear too eager by opening a new one. It felt, anyway, as though it was spirits that would do the trick, if anything, tonight. And do what exactly? The sense that a clash of titanic proportions was engulfing her between her desire and her worst fear was only partially ameliorated by the Scotch and a couple of hours spent watching trivia on the television.

Around 11 o'clock she heard the key in the door. Cathy threw her bag down on the sofa.

'Well, that was a waste of a Saturday evening. The food! I'm always telling you there's no such thing as a little garlic. I must be reeking.'

'I thought the food was rather good' Jim shrugged 'you were determined not to enjoy yourself.'

'No! I was sitting next to a man who quite honestly had nothing to say and just kept on saying it. Bo. o.o..ring.'

Neither had yet looked in Effie's direction.

'Well, I guess I'd better get going. The girls are fine. They settled OK' said Effie rising and suddenly a bit dizzy as she searched in her bag: 'where's that umbrella, it's raining, isn't it?'

'You mean you haven't got your car, Mum?'

'No, it's at the garage, what with the break-in and everything, I haven't been able to pick it up. Drunk a bit much, anyway. Sorry, darling, don't worry. I'll get the bus.' There was definitely some relief in being able to apologise for something openly.

'Oh don't be silly, Mum' said Cathy irritably 'Jim'll take you home, won't you?' She glowered at her husband. 'He's happy to take you and I'm grateful for the baby sitting, so everyone's happy, and I'm off to bed 'perchance to dream' – as Macbeth or someone said.'

As though to take up the theatrical reference, or soften the mood, Jim swung his coat round his shoulders, bowed to Effie like one of the musketeers and fixing on her with his blue eyes assured her that he would be 'honoured' to take her home. It was a request Effie could not refuse.

Ch. 25

They were silent for a few minutes as Jim drove off. In fact Effie was aware of two noises: one was the sound of the windscreen wipers working away with a steady - thump – thump; the other was a thump in her own body which was probably her heart. She didn't dare look at Jim. She was light-headed. She had no idea what he was thinking or what he might say, what to expect. What he did eventually say was

'Another successful evening with my wife' and proceeded to stretch out his left hand which he rested on Effie's thigh causing her heart to race even faster and her eyes to close involuntarily. They drove on. Thump, thump - don't think - don't speak. But Jim was saying something again and she opened her eyes to find him looking at her as they waited at a traffic light.

'You know, I do think you're terrific, I really do. You're such a sexy woman and so kind, so soft. I just wish that Cathy...'

'Jim, please don't say anything about Cathy...'

Jim laughed but took his hand off her thigh as they moved off again.

'Of course. So what about us? I need to know how you are feeling after last night.'

'Feeling? I wish I knew. I've hardly dared think about it. I mean less than a year ago I was a single divorcee living quietly on my own and the big excitement in my life was when the guy who came to fix my washing machine gave me a wink as he left. So far this year I've been out with half a dozen more or less eligible men, had an affair with a bit of a rogue, suffered a couple of indignities and now find myself kissing my own son-in-law, the father of my grandchildren.'

'Quite an impressive record for a lady of mature years, I agree.' Jim sounded cheerful as he swung the car to a halt outside Effie's house, switching off and turning towards her.

'Well, here we are then: back at the scene of the crime.'

'God, don't say things like that, it terrifies me.' But she made no move to open the door. Jim had put his hand back on her thigh and was looking at her without speaking. The rain had stopped and the streetlight cast a shaft of light across his face so that she could see right into his blue eyes and the thumping heart started again. He leaned closer and took her chin in his hand raising her head so that he, too, could see into her eyes. 'Such lovely blue eyes, Effie, I never realised how beautiful they are.'

'I always thought I had grey eyes, that's what my mother always told me.'

'Let's keep your mother out of this.'

He moved his hand on her thigh and Effie did not resist.

'No, you have lovely eyes and they are full of kindness. They are soft and blue and intelligent' and so saying, he deposited a gentle kiss on her closed eyelids.

As her heart raced she had a momentary flash of panic about her blood pressure, but she ached to respond, to lie back and let it all happen. She opened her eyes and there was Jim, lovely Jim, gently stroking her face and smiling. She closed her eyes and there was just a wonderful rush of feeling.

'Jim...' she registered a faint protest as his hand stroked her hair.

'Don't say anything.'

'Yes, yes, I won't... say anything I mean' she whispered as he sought out her mouth and closed it with a kiss.

And for a while, a moment, or was it an hour? with her lips pressed to his and his tongue seeking her mouth, when she closed her eyes there was nothing, nothing but a lovely blue and an excited, pulsing heat that spread through her whole body, urging her, wanting him to go on. He was leaning across her now, fumbling with something and Effie felt herself go down as the seat fell back. His hand was back on her thigh, moving up to reach for the zip on her trousers and she willed him to go on, reaching herself to feel for him, to grip the round of his firm buttock, to let her hand explore, lusting for him to touch her, not to stop, touch me anywhere. Go on.

A vague sound. A flash of light penetrated Effie's eyelids.

'Effie, Effie' Jim was whispering in her ear and letting his busy mouth explore her face, her neck, her chest while she was willing him to loosen the buttons of her shirt, don't stop, don't stop. She had no idea if she said it or thought it but she opened her eyes and found herself looking across the top of Jim's curly brown hair, as he rooted around in her shirt and underwear, into the bright lights of a car which had parked in front of them.

She froze. Jim continued. 'Effie, darling, don't stop...'

'Jim, it's my neighbours.'

'What?' He raised his head, to be caught momentarily in the glare of headlamps before they were switched off.

'Keep your head down, for god's sake' hissed Effie.

Jim ducked his head and buried his face in Effie's chest while she tried to hide her own face under her raised arm which she half-clasped around his head. No more frenzied activity. They lay still, listening. There were footsteps and two or three people talking, laughing. They seemed to stop right beside the car, chatting. Effie hardly dared breath. She recognised the voice of her neighbour, Val, a bossy, self-important woman and her husband, John, a swanky lawyer and there was another voice, a woman's voice, she did not recognise, and then a man's chuckle. Another couple? An age seemed to pass as the group chatted, laughed and she was aware that Jim was becoming adventurous again, his hand slowly moving down her body. 'They'll just think we're a couple of young lovers' he whispered.

'Wait, Jim, just wait.'

Wouldn't they ever go? The voices continued and Effie could feel Jim nibbling at her ear, whispering more loudly 'lovely ear, lovely eyes' and then nuzzling into her hair which had the effect of making him sneeze, a sort of muffled sneeze, which somehow released the tension so that they both burst into a fit of stifled giggles like a couple of adolescents. Once this had subsided there seemed to be silence and Effie dared to raise her head sufficiently to peep out of the window. She saw the back view of her neighbour and another woman who turned to wave, staring in Effie's direction as she bobbed down. 'Shit!' 'What?' 'Still there' she hissed, but the sound of footsteps was retreating. She waited, tense like a taught spring, before daring to peek again.

There was no one there. She could see lights were on through drawn curtains in her neighbour's house.

'Phew! They've gone' she exclaimed. 'That was a near shave. Do you think they saw us? And the car? Jim, they might recognise your car.'

'Effie, don't panic, please don't panic' he spoke calmly and firmly 'I'm sure they were not the least bit interested in the car or who was in it.'

'I hope so.'

She suddenly felt deflated and exhausted. The thrill had quite gone. Her head ached and she felt old. 'It's all a bit much, it's too difficult, Jim, it's just too risky, and' she added, looking straight into his eyes, 'it's just wrong.'

Jim held her gaze, saying nothing for a while, stroking her hair and face without smiling, serious, thoughtful.

'You're right' he said finally 'yes, of course, you're right' and he sighed a little as he gently, efficiently, did up the top button on her shirt.

'Come, I'll see you to the door and make sure there haven't been any more break-ins.'

Did Effie see a tweak of the curtain next door as she walked up the path? Jim was adamant that she had not, but the whole venture had taken on a dimension that she knew she simply could not cope with. It had to stop.

'This won't happen again, Jim.'

'No, it won't.'

He hesitated: 'perhaps I should apologise... I mean...'

'No, don't. We're both to blame. I was as mad as you, and it was mad, I got carried away. You seem to have hit a weak spot.' she gave a sharp laugh 'but just now, having to hide like a guilty teenager, and all behind Cathy's back. I can't do it. So...' she paused 'I guess we both need to do a bit of heart-searching. I mean, whatever my behaviour might suggest to the contrary, I'd be devastated if Cathy and you split up, and you may think that's rich coming from someone who's divorced but I often think that if Jack and I had tried a bit harder, paid more attention to each other, maybe we might have stuck together.'

Jim said nothing for a few minutes, then patted her on the arm.

'Well, I can try I suppose. But Cathy has to do her bit and...anyway, let's leave that now. Talking of Cathy, she'll be wondering where on earth I am.' He turned to go and then turned back.

'You know, I don't regret what happened. I know it was wrong, but I really do like you and think you're a terrific person. You may be a lot older than me but you're hell of a sexy' he laughed and gave her an innocent peck on the cheek.

'I'll stay out of your way for a bit, perhaps. Let things simmer down.'

And he was off, leaving Effie feeling sober and definitely old. All excitement had passed. She wandered round her living room, touching the family photos, pressing a couple of keys on the piano, stopping in front of the drinks cabinet but not opening it, moving instead into the kitchen to put on the kettle. She poured herself a strong cup of tea and took it back to the living room. She didn't want to look at the sparkling new glass panel in the kitchen window. She had to stop looking at things as though they were shiny and glittery. They were not. Life was grey, dull, hard work. Time for 'some work on yourself', as the Americans would say, she told herself firmly. For some reason this thought made her laugh out loud. Or was she crying? She instinctively hated anything remotely to do with soul searching but she had to admit that her present position did need some scrutiny. How could she understand what had happened and how could she face her daughter, her grandchildren, Jim. She couldn't just dismiss it as meaningless. The sense of guilt was acute and a deep pain.

The tea was calming but she was exhausted. Her leg ached and she bent to massage it, the leg which had varicose veins behind the knee, laughing ironically to herself: she bet Jim didn't see that, nor did he know she was the carrier of a dread disease. But as for going any further with such thoughts, she could not. The best she could do was to gather herself together, drag herself up off the sofa and make tracks for the stairs, noticing as she passed the phone that a light was winking. Like many things, that was for tomorrow.

Ch. 26

There were two messages: one was from Cathy who sounded irritated because Jim's mobile was off and she wondered where on earth he'd got to; the other was from Sally who in clipped but encouraging tones was inviting Effie for drinks the following weekend –'Sunday about 6.00. We'd like you to see where <u>we</u> live.'

Effie deleted her daughter's message and attempted to put all thoughts about her firmly into a mental drawer marked 'later'. She re-played Sally's invitation with some relief, something to take her mind off the still swirling confusion of her mind which a large cafetiere of coffee and two almond croissants had done nothing to settle. She had tossed and turned half the night, gone in and out of at least three bad dreams which she now could not remember but which had left her feeling like scrambled eggs. She longed to speak to someone and the prospect of hearing Sally's clear confident voice was just what she needed. Having gauged that 10.30 was too early to ring on a Sunday morning she resorted to the usually foolproof method of calming herself down with the 'fiendish' soduku. She impressed herself by completing it through sheer willpower in 17 minutes flat before she picked up the phone to call Sally.

'Effie? Delighted to hear from you. I imagine you got my message.'

'Yes, lovely to hear from you too. I'm sure I'd love to come.'

'Just a few people from around and about. I didn't have time to really talk to you at the bazaar, and thought you might be interested in seeing our house. Rather different from Oliver's.'

Effie had no doubt that it would be. 'So will he be there?'

'Oliver? Oh yes, he'll be there. That's OK isn't it? I think he's got himself together a lot since that last time. Just takes time, I guess.'

Does it? Effie was thinking as she put the phone down. Right now she could not imagine how the next few days would work out, let alone a period of years. But the prospect of next Sunday was something to focus on and she was aware that the idea of seeing Oliver again, while not exciting, was not unpleasing. Meanwhile she had to speak to her daughter.

She scrolled through her address list, skimming past 'Cathy', on to 'Jane' hesitated at 'Leo' and went back to 'Jane', who sounded surprised to be called by her mother. 'Hi, Mum, not like you to rouse me from my slumbers on a Sunday morning, what's up?'

'Oh, nothing darling, really. Just thought I'd say hello, see how your week's been?'

'Since you ask, as a matter of fact, not bad at all. My Scotsman is really becoming increasingly interesting. I think it might even be time to risk an introduction to the family.'

'Risk?' Effie felt a stab of alarm.

'Oh, don't worry, I have every faith you won't subject him to a cross-examination about his education or job or something. In fact, he and Jim might get on rather well.'

Feeling only partially reassured by the call to Jane, Effie pressed the 'call' button for Cathy, praying that she wouldn't answer so that she could leave a message. Cathy picked up. Her tone was irritable.

'Hi, Mum, it's not a good time, the kids are driving me mad. They keep squabbling and Jim's just hopeless:let's them get away with blue murder, then he's bloody awful to me, and I'm just fed up with being treated like the doormat around here. Anyway, how are you? I guess I ought to say thanks for baby sitting last night. Just sometimes doesn't seem worth going out with Jim. I don't enjoy it, he never enjoys it, he seems to get on better with you than me... and what <u>was</u> he messing around with last night? He told me he'd to do something with your back door, and I just wish he took as much care with his wife and...' a loud yell pierced Effie's eardrum. 'Daisy! Just stop that. You'll make yourself sick! Look, Mum, I've gotta go... 'bye.'

Her daughter's unhappy tone was to reverberate through the week for Effie. Despite her best efforts to keep calm and return her life to a degree of normality her insides continued to circulate an alarming array of emotions ranging from intense guilt to manic excitement, occasional waves of denial and some half-hearted soul-searching. On the Thursday Susie rang, demanding to know what was going on since she had been incommunicado for an unheard of two weeks and insisted on fixing a coffee date for the Saturday morning. By the time Saturday arrived Effie was exhausted from lack of sleep and bursting like an overripe tomato to unburden herself. She had little doubt that her blood pressure was oscillating wildly so that out of a sense of sheer self-preservation she decided that she would have to tell Susie something or she would die. The final straw was to find that her last week's stock market predictions, for the first time in years, were completely off the mark. She was devastated: her very own Black Wednesday.

'You look awful' was Susie's stark comment as Effie sat down next to her at their favourite table in Marco's.... 'What <u>have</u> you been doing?'

'Before you say anything else, I need a coffee, strong, black and lots of sugar.'

Susie, for once, was silent, waiting while her friend settled herself, drank some coffee, blew her nose.

'Effie, for god's sake, what's up? Are you ill?'

'Well, I feel as though I'm going mad if that counts' and she leaned in closer to her friend. 'Susie, have you ever wanted someone who you know you ought not to? I mean desired someone who's just not possible.'

'Oh lots,' was Susie's breezy reply, 'I was always lusting after Fred's work colleagues. He happened to work with some rather good looking, charming men. All a bit long in the tooth now, I guess. But who's tickled your fancy then? Don't tell me one of your dates has done something illicit?'

'Not a date. I wish it was.' Effie hesitated, absent-mindedly stirring sugar into her now empty cup. 'Oh dear, Susie, I fear I've done something...' she shook her head silently.

Susie, suddenly alarmed by her friend's inability to speak, hailed Antonio and ordered two more coffees and a couple of almond croissants. 'I think this calls for drastic action.' She pulled her chair in closer to Effie and patted her arm comfortingly 'darling, can it really be that bad?'

Effie mumbled, still looking down, slowly nodding, 'yes, I think it is pretty bad, and I don't think there's anything you can do but I simply must tell someone other wise I'll burst, and I'm terrified you're going to think me so awful you won't want to speak to me ever again.'

'For god's sake, Effie, that is highly unlikely, but it doesn't help you spinning it out like this.'

'No, you're right, it's just so shaming, so unexpected...' she tailed off.

'Effie, I can't help you if you keep talking in innuendos, and, believe it or not, I can be discrete, if that's what you're worried about. I really think you'd better tell me who you are talking about, this forbidden fruit?'

'You wanna the fruit tarta?' Antonio, was hovering, a plate with almond croissants in hand.

'No, that's fine.' The interruption seemed to jolt Effie back into speech.

'You're right, Susie. Well, it's not a date, and it's not that I've suddenly discovered I like women or something... it's Jim' she blurted the word out.

'Ah...' Susie lowered her carefully manicured hand.

'Yes. Jim.'

'I see.'

'You do?'

'Well, I can see it's awkward. Yes, very awkward.' She stirred her cup thoughtfully. 'I mean, when you say you 'desired' someone – Jim - am I right in thinking that you wouldn't be in quite such a state about it if nothing had actually happened?'

'It did and it didn't. But you'll be glad to know that I am not totally without boundaries. Having said that, it did go further than it should and I've now got to try and clear up the mess.'

'Mess? You mean Cathy knows?'

'Good god, no. At least I don't think she does, though she's always sniping at me and she and Jim don't seem to be getting on very well and I worry, of course, I've made it all worse....'

'Yes, I can see that. But you're telling me this because nothing further is going to happen, right?'

'Right. Nothing ever again.'

'And the lovely Jim?'

'Of course I worry about him, but I can't get beyond thinking about me and my part, that I could have been so weak, so susceptible and I'd be devastated if Cathy's marriage broke up. So I've got to try and do something, I've got to be able to face my daughter with at least half a clean conscience... I mean she and the kids are my nearest and dearest...'

Susie frowned as she brushed flakes of pastry on to the floor. 'All a bit too near, by the sound of it, but let's think. God, Effie, I'm not sure what I can do to help.'

'Oh I don't expect you to <u>do</u> anything, but it already feels a bit less dire having been able to tell you about it. This last week has been too awful. I haven't known what to think and I desperately want to see Daisy and Rosie later. I need to go and make sure they're all right. Does that sound crazy?'

'No crazier than anything else you've told me this morning. Fact is, darling, you've got yourself into a not so pretty pickle and I honestly don't think I've got any useful advice other than to be careful. I mean my area of expertise in terms of relationships is a bit more prosaic.'

'I'd hardly call three marriages prosaic.'

'But none of them were forbidden. They were all hugely available to my charms without strings. But, look, on a serious note, talking of marriages' she leaned in again, pausing as Antonio swept down to retrieve the empty cups. 'Effie, did I ever tell you about my six months on the couch?'

'The couch?'

'The analytic couch, though in fact I wasn't actually <u>on</u> the couch. I felt I wanted to keep my feet firmly on the ground..'

'You mean you submitted yourself to a shrink?'

'You needn't sound quite so bouleversee' said Susie haughtily.

'Right now I'm totally stunned.'

'I think you're stunned at your own behaviour' retorted Susie with a flash of insight 'but sounds like you could do with a dispassionate look. I went when my second marriage was on the rocks and it certainly helped me not to make exactly the same mistake again. I mean, Fred is by far the best.'

'Best?'

'Best marriage. That six months of searching in the deeper crevasses of my mind was quite an eye-opener.'

'But isn't it just a lot of psycho-babble?'

'Whatever it is it worked for me, and, honestly, I don't know what else to suggest.'

'I hear what you say, but I have to deal with my instinctive response which is to steer clear of all such stuff. Probably my parents' fault. They instilled in me a deep-rooted distrust of anything that smelt of the confessional which they saw as mumbo-jumbo, like selling pardons in the middle-ages.'

'Actually, it was more like struggling to untangle a huge knot of backcombed hair with a very small comb: all that twisted knotty stuff in the head.'

'My mother always said it was Freud needed his head examined, but then, she wasn't the most sane individual on the planet and certainly didn't seem to have much idea about how to bring up children. I've told you how she openly favoured my brother.' An image of a triumphant Victor came to Effie's mind, weeping crocodile tears in his mother's arms after an incident when they had both fallen off the toy cart that he had sent hurtling down a hill, she to be told to stop crying even though her knees were grazed and raw while his minor scratches were the object of devoted attention.

'No, my mother didn't help and I suspect I'm not going to risk relying on some other person to sort me out' she added angrily 'sometimes wish I'd never started this dating lark, it's stirred everything up...'

'Sounds to me as though you are sitting on a lot of unresolved suppressed anger.'

'Susie!' Effie almost shrieked 'don't <u>you</u> start trying to analyse me.'

The young couple at the adjoining table looked curiously in Effie's direction. A hot sensation filled her eyes so that for a moment she thought she would cry. Susie put out a comforting hand to touch her friend's.

'Sorry, Susie,' Effie whispered 'I didn't mean to embarrass you.'

'So what are friends for?' Susie quipped with the lightness of touch that was her forte. 'Actually, you know I've got a bit of a thick hide:

all the time I spend being nice to difficult clients. But let's think what you're going to do, if you really are determined to resist shrinking.'

'At the rate of all these almond croissants we've been devouring there's very little chance of shrinking' Effie laughed, relieved that at last she could use her humour to defuse her feelings.

'So if counsellors and therapists are beyond the pale, I think at least a visit to the lovely Dr Gordon would be a good idea. You quite alarmed me just now. You're the one with the high blood pressure.'

'But I couldn't possibly tell Dr Gordon something like this. He'd send me to the nearest loony-bin.'

'Aren't you getting this a bit out of proportion?'

'Right now, no. I think I'm seeing it in exactly the correct way. The only question is how to put it right. I can't un-think my thoughts or undo my actions.'

Susie tutted. 'Effie, I've gotta go in a minute. My parting shot is to encourage you to go to Dr G. He could at least check your BP. You realise you are worrying me. I mean to say for you to get the stock market <u>that</u> wrong is truly concerning.'

Effie could laugh at this too and gave Susie a big hug. 'What would I do without you? If you can bear to listen to me a bit over the next few weeks I think I can manage this thing myself. Starting with trying to smooth the waters with Cathy. Yes,' Effie spoke with new-found determination 'I'm going over there later. I promised the kids a cake. Jim won't be there. Just Cathy and the girls.'

'Into the lion's den, eh?'

Ch. 27

Jim, she knew, was almost certainly out at a football match. She had taken trouble over the cake, a Victoria sponge with a white iced topping on which she had piped in pink the outlines of the girl's favourite cartoon characters, Petula Panda and Felicity the Flower Fairy. She called Cathy before leaving, really to check that Jim was out. Cathy sounded less irritable on the phone.

'Yes, come on round if you like just me and the kids. Oh, and Margie and her little girl Hannah may be here.'

As Effie stood on the doorstep, cake platter in hand, she had a brief flashback to the time only not long ago when she had arrived with all the bazaar gifts and Cathy had been less than welcoming. Was this another assuagement of guilt? The door opened and she was instantly engulfed by three excited children who danced around her, almost knocking the cake off its plate. There followed a chaotic five minutes or so as the three girls leaped around Effie or, more particularly, the cake, screaming and shouting as they tried to grab a piece with the favoured icing, until Cathy bellowed so loudly that the little friend sank back in terror, retreating to her mother's lap. Effie, too, felt definitely alarmed at her daughter's volume. Another present backfiring?

'For heaven's sake, Mum, couldn't you bring something that doesn't cause a riot?' she snapped 'and Rosie and Daisy, just calm down or no one gets any cake at all. Do you understand that?' and addressing Hannah who was staring wide-eyed from the safety of her mother's arms at the monster mummy Cathy had become 'it's all right, Hannah, there's no need to worry. Here, I'll cut you all a bit.'

The three girls, now quite subdued, each took the portion of cake Cathy offered them wrapped in a piece of kitchen roll and sat quietly.

Margie, who had so far said very little except to comfort Hannah, eased the child off her lap and stood up. 'We must go as soon as Hannah's finished her cake.'

'Oh, let's have some fresh tea before you go. Mum, now that you're here you might as well try your own cake' said Cathy rattling china mugs and pressing the kettle button. 'So, Margie, have you met my Mum who has the knack of causing instant typhoons when she brings presents?'

Margie laughed and Effie hesitated, fearing her face was flushing. Cathy went on 'you may well know each other from Milton Road. Margie's just the other side from you, Mum.'

'Oh yes? I'm 22.'

'Well, we're practically neighbours. Yes, we have met here, I think. I remember your hair. It looks so good that grey on you. I mean lots of older women would have coloured it but I think it suits you very well. So shiny.'

Cathy crashed a mug of hot tea down in front of her mother. ` There you go, Mum, you do seem to invite lots of compliments.'

Effie was not at all sure if it was a compliment and was already feeling nervous at the revelation that Margie lived so close, just a few doors down. Was her voice familiar? She flashed back to the groping in the dark with Jim and the sound of those voices. Could Margie and her husband have been the other couple?

Margie was speaking: 'I expect you know the Chisholms, Val and John? They live at 24, right next to you. Nice couple, good friends of ours really. We sometimes go out with them when we can get a baby sitter.. saw them last week, actually.'

'Oh yes? Yes, I know them, though wouldn't say they're friends exactly.'

Margie was biting into a piece of the Victoria sponge: 'so wasn't it you, then, who had the police round not so long ago?'

'Goodness, how the word gets around. Yes, I had a break in. It was quite upsetting.'

'Oh poor you. Val and John mentioned there were goings on in their street. Funny, I didn't connect to Cathy.'

'No reason to, I'm sure' said Effie as she rose from the table to grab the broom from the corner of the kitchen, and started to sweep up the cake crumbs strewn across the floor. Anything to get away from Margie's inquisitive stare. She bent to her task, working the brush energetically around the children's feet. Daisy, as often the first to recover her spirits, leapt up and started dancing around the flailing broom as the door opened and Jim walked in.

'You're back early' said Cathy without enthusiasm.

'Yeh, well, the match was a washout. We didn't hang around.'

Effie kept her back turned, unsure if he had noticed her as he pulled out a chair and sat at the table. She continued to sweep, sweep everything into the corner, crumbs, bits of old vegetable peelings, mud, sweetie wrappers, bending down to gather it all into a pile, searching noisily under the sink for the dustpan and depositing the collected trash into the nearest container, whereupon Rosie let out a loud cry – 'gran'ma! That's Kitty's bowl.'

All eyes turned on Effie who stood, broom in hand, staring down at the overflowing object, feeling that all too familiar hot flush creeping up from her throat.

'Mum, what are you doing <u>now</u>?'

'Oh sorry, dear, I didn't realise it was the cat's' mumbled Effie not looking up, her colour turning like a traffic light to brilliant red. 'I was just going anyway. Didn't mean to stay.'

The girls were giggling and Jim stood up. He moved towards Effie.

'Here, let me help,' and he gently took the broom from her hand, bent down to pick up Kitty's bowl, tipped the contents into the swing bin and replaced the brush in the corner. 'And you girls stop that giggling. Your grandmother is only trying to help. And aren't you going to introduce me to your friend, Rosie?'

'Oh, I thought you'd met' said Cathy, pre-empting her daughter as she poured Jim a cup of tea. 'This is Margie, who lives near Mum and the girl with the golden giggle is Hannah.'

'Oh, I think we have met' said Margie as she gathered her things together 'least, your face does look familiar, and I remember that curly hair from somewhere. Now come on, Hannah, time we went. Your Dad'll be wondering where we are.'

Effie followed close on the heels of the departing mother and daughter, barely able to raise her eyes to Jim as she made her farewells, wanting to tell him about her suspicions but not knowing how to and on this occasion Jim did not offer to see her to her car. At home, she dropped exhausted into bed, praying for the relief of sleep but fearing a fitful night. The better feelings from talking to Susie had taken a battering from her perhaps ill-judged visit to Cathy and the encounter with Margie. Margie. There was something just a bit too shrewd about Margie. Why did Cathy have to choose such friends? And on this unhappy note she finally dropped off.

Ch. 28

Effie was writing in her diary. This was a new routine she was trying to put into practice at the suggestion of Dr Gordon who she had visited under a three line whip from Susie: 'no more cappuccinos at Marco's with me until you go.' She had gone so far as to admit to the doctor that the fluctuations in her blood pressure were at least partially accounted for by the fact of having 'something on my mind'. He did not press her to elaborate but delved in his desk drawer to produce a pamphlet entitled 'Counselling for the emotionally challenged' which Effie politely accepted while insisting that it was not for her. 'So, if you don't want to go the counselling route, some people find keeping an account of their thoughts and events of the day can improve things' he had advised, adding, to Effie's surprise, as she rose to leave, 'you might even find recording dreams is helpful.'

The idea of keeping a record appealed to Effie's belief that order in a quite concrete sense was her best defence against the chaos of emotional disorder. Hence Sunday morning found her seated at her computer, mouse in hand, ready to start on the business of sorting herself out, which she abbreviated to SOP: sorting out process.

Where to start? Start at the beginning, she told herself and the obvious beginning was her own childhood. Half an hour later she had laid out a series of headings going from 'childhood' to 'adolescence', 'adulthood' and 'marriage'. There was plenty to write about her childhood she found as she got going. She described it as 'happy' but then changed it to 'happy enough' and soon found herself writing about Victor, lovely brother Victor. He had been so handsome with his dark curly hair and athletic body and his confident personality. She let her mind drift back to a time when the two of them were young, running along a beach in Cornwall on a hot summer's day. Victor charged ahead away from their parents, disappearing among the sand dunes, playing hide and seek, both of them excited and laughing, till eventually he threw himself down exhausted on the sand, flat on his back. The sun was blisteringly hot and Victor stripped off his bathing trunks, twirling them around in his hand, teasing Effie that she wouldn't dare take hers off. She remembered her defiant 'oh yes I will!' and seconds later jumping on top of him quite naked still laughing and suddenly quiet because it was the first time she had seen an erection, and the first time she noticed that he had black hairs growing round his penis and that he had gone silent too. She pondered it now: how old was she? Perhaps ten and Victor thirteen? She hadn't thought about it in years. How she had adored him, unable to resist his charms even when he was mean.

'Mother adored him too' she wrote 'and made no bones about the fact that he was the favoured child. Father was always busy and didn't know what to do with us.' But then she remembered that her father had played cricket with Victor, a game Effie was quite hopeless at and there had been nothing equivalent with her mother, no alternative activity for mother and daughter. 'The first person to tell me I was fat was my mother' she tapped out forcefully on her keyboard. This was getting interesting. 'She never told me I was pretty, nor did my father. But Victor was told he was handsome, which he was.' Effie's fingers flew over the keyboard as she registered a surge of feeling, anger at her parents or was it Victor? Were they to blame for her current situation, her failed marriage? Another dead end, and she had a fair idea that this exercise was meant to move her forward, not bring her to a halt.

She shifted to her 'adolescence' heading where she instantly wrote 'bloody awful time' without elaboration, not wishing at this first attempt to prolong the agony, and then there was 'marriage' which she did not find so easy to describe, feeling that 'not sure' sounded utterly feeble, finally opting for 'started Ok and thought it was mellowing in middle age when actually it was stagnating. Jack's departure experienced as a total betrayal - the most painful event of my life.' Yes, it had been and the memory of it now was still so sharp that Effie had to get up and replenish her resources with a cafetiere of coffee and a few ginger nuts. She pictured Jack as she dunked the biscuits in the steaming coffee. She'd thought he was soft but he'd revealed this steely hard indifference to her fate by going off with Hilary, her best friend. She snapped a biscuit in two as she pictured Jack walking down the garden path, suitcase in hand, getting in his car, driving off. Yes, Jack needed a heading all of his own, and she typed his name in huge bold letters. That was as far as she could go tonight with him. Then there were the children, and she tried to gather some thoughts together about them, registering them chronologically:

Leo – the first one and delighted to have a boy. He always strove for independence and think he's basically Ok.

Jane – argumentative and adventurous from birth. No problems about being the middle child. Never felt I had to worry about her. She can look after herself.

Cathy - the baby of the family, and a difficult baby, cried a lot, clingy and disliked change. Not adventurous, anxious about small things, quite messy but conventional. We haven't got on well for some time.

She paused waiting to see where her thoughts went. One obvious route was to Jim. She did not feel ready for that but added to her comments on Cathy that she had been delighted, possibly a bit surprised, that Jim had chosen her and that she had been the first of her children to get married. They had met at college and been together ever since, a happy couple, or so she had thought. And now?

Having asked herself this question Effie stopped. Again, she had no idea where to go from there. She had a sneaking suspicion that a counsellor would know what to do with it, whereas the best she could do was to resolve to keep regular diary entries during the week and make use of her friend's counsel at the weekend. At the thought of the weekend she remembered Sally's invitation and her fingers tapped out 'Oliver', but again she did not know where to go with it. Was he about to re-enter her life? With this simmering thought she closed down the computer, resolving to seek out the calming atmosphere of the library during the week. It would be a chance to do some research in the area of psychology away from the distractions of telephone and the temptations of coffee and biscuits

The experience turned out to be heavy going and far from reassuring. If Effie had wanted relief from her anxiety what she found was like reading the 'possible side effects' on a medication slip: she had everything. From a tome entitled 'psychoanalysis for the layman in ten easy stages' she gathered that she should take her dreams very seriously, that she was likely to be harbouring suppressed desires for her father and that she was doomed to repeat unresolved emotional issues relating to childhood traumas. The idea that she had ever been attracted to her father felt so alien to Effie that she decided to go no further with that one. The thought of her quiet, faintly distant father with his fringe of mousy hair round a plain face, filled her if anything with pity rather than desire. He had allowed her mother to dominate and mother had made it clear that the only man worth giving attention to was Victor, her one and only son.

An article entitled 'thinking about the unthinkable' caught her eye. That sounded more like it, and she plunged in. Half an hour later she was both aghast and relieved: she felt as though she had plumbed the dark recesses of the human psyche where incestuous thoughts, violent imagery, bestial desire were the stuff of everyday fantasy. Effie glanced round at the motley assembly of the library. Most people looked incredibly ordinary with admittedly one or two odd-balls which the library seemed to attract, as she knew to her cost. She had a momentary vision of the tramp with his trolley who had taken a fancy to her. And as if to emphasise the point, as Effie contemplated her fellow students, wondering if their ordinary looks belied an inner world of hideous fantasy, a middle-aged man hovered at the bay next to hers. He fussily dusted the chair with a wad of paper towels and spread out a layer before depositing his bottom on what now looked like a pile of nappies. Either incontinent or obsessive compulsive. Effie was beginning to get the jargon. She also had a flashback to the STD clinic and of placing her own bum gingerly on the chairs. But that was just normal caution, wasn't it? After reading this article it seemed that almost anything extreme or grim could be considered as normal and lusting after your son-in-law was on the mild side. So long as it stays a thought rather than a deed was the crucial point. And on that one, she knew she had gone over the mark; perhaps not very far, but she had certainly strayed.

She glimpsed at her watch. Her neighbour was now blowing his nose into a carefully folded handkerchief the contents of which he inspected minutely, which Effie took as her cue to leave. She looked forward to her rendezvous with Susie in a few days and to her friend's down to earth approach to life. In the meantime there was the distraction of Sally's drinks party and Oliver.

Ch. 29

Sally and Frank's house was as expected, smart, tidy and extremely nice to be in. The drinks were champagne cocktails and the canapés deliciously different and mouth-watering. Effie's moment of jealousy at how perfect everything was was short-lived as Sally gathered her up in a warmly welcoming embrace. She seemed genuinely pleased to see Effie and swept her along enthusiastically into the neat back garden where people were standing around, bunched in small groups. 'Right, Effie,' she trilled as she piloted Effie across the velvety green lawn towards a small huddle, 'guys, this is Effie, a friend of Oliver's. And where is he, by the way?'

A grinning face popped up from behind a rose bush: 'I was just admiring your Pink Dawn, Sal. Simply gorgeous...'

'Yes, she is, isn't she? I must say, Effie, you are looking particularly super tonight. But, Oliver, for god's sake get the lady a drink. I must see whether Frank's coping with the oven.' And off she went clicking a pair of elegant heels that somehow managed not to get stuck in the lawn.

Oliver beamed as he placed a bubbling flute into Effie's hand. 'Good to see you, Effie. I was too busy at the bazaar to really talk. So how are you? You're looking well.'

What Effie would like to have said was that she was feeling utterly churned up inside, that she was wracked with guilt about her daughter, disturbed by intrusive images of her 'ex', and generally feeling a bit of a mess. What she said was 'I'm good', proceeding to chatter about the last few days, her work, her family and a lot about the grandchildren, her tongue loosening as the champagne cocktails went to her head so that she had little memory of what she had actually said. She was aware, however, that Oliver was looking much tidier than at their first meeting as though something of Sally's neatness had rubbed off on him. She registered that he was wearing a pair of smart but casual trousers that showed off a slim waist and a pale blue shirt open at the neck which gave him a nautical air. The main improvement, as she had noted at the bazaar, was that his hair no longer looked ridiculous with the brushed over wisp. Now, with it close-cropped round clear-cut features, he looked surprisingly modern.

'You're obviously an excellent mother and so lucky to have grandchildren' he was saying. 'They clearly give you a lot of pleasure.'

'Oh they do, yes. I am lucky and I've got a most charming son-in-law too' Effie blundered on, finding that it was surprisingly easy to talk to Oliver. He seemed to be genuinely interested in her and her family and the words just slipped out. Perhaps that was how the confessional worked, a terrible urge to tell. The conversation was interrupted, however, by Frank who was doing the rounds with a bottle of champagne and a middle-aged couple who were introduced as 'old neighbours'. The man proceeded to regale Effie with stories of someone called Nancy who she thought sounded most odd until she realised he was talking about his pet terrier. He bored her for a further ten minutes or so while she searched for escape, scanning the assembled company. She couldn't help noticing that Oliver was engaged in an intense discussion with a woman who did not take her eyes off him. She had hair that looked too black and a nose that looked a bit too sharp. She instinctively did not like this woman's proprietorial attitude towards Oliver.

With an effort she dragged herself back to the terrier man and made her excuses to move on. She didn't know any of the other people but headed for a small group that clustered round the drinks table. She knew she shouldn't but she held out her glass for a re-fill. The mixture of boredom, guilt and some unidentified tension was quite a cocktail. The man pouring the drinks was jolly and soon Effie recovered her spirits enough to join in the chat. She calculated she'd stay another ten minutes before making her exit. She was aware that she wanted to be able to speak to Oliver before she went and had half an eye open in his direction. The intense engagement with the black- head continued. Effie sipped back another mouthful or two. The barman was joking and noisy but Effie didn't mind, and she was just about to put her glass down when someone touched her arm and it was Oliver.

'Effie, so glad you're still here. I got trapped by an ardent conservationist. I didn't think I'd ever get away. Not that I'm not in favour of conservation, I mean I belong to the National Trust and all that. What about you? Are you interested in historic buildings?'

A brief image of Oliver's definitely not-so –modern house flashed into Effie's view. She also thought of Jack, that they had been members of the National Trust until the children, wasn't it Cathy?, started to complain that they didn't like old buildings. 'Well, my membership lapsed after Jack left, like a lot of things. My house now has very little old in it which, come to think of it, is probably something to do with his departure. I mean I got rid of a lot of stuff when he went, quite cathartic I suppose.' Oliver was nodding which encouraged Effie to forge on with her revelations about her marriage. 'Yes, actually Jack liked antique stuff but I don't think what we had was much good, probably second rate, knowing Jack. The joy is that my house now is furnished with flat pack products, things I can put up myself and dispose of when I get fed up.'

'Oh that makes enormous sense. I suppose it's the difference between a death and a divorce. I mean I've probably held on to things a bit too long. Didn't want to change anything I guess, but...' he added cheerfully, looking at Effie, 'I think that's changed recently'.

'I'm so glad' said Effie, and she really meant it.

This moment of contact with Oliver was not to last, however, as the black-haired woman bore down on them. She was obviously not going to let Oliver go so easily. 'Ah, Oliver, there you are. I just want to make sure that you will sign the protest about the new cinema scheme the council is proposing.' She turned to Effie 'Have you seen what they're going to do? Knock down that lovely piece of 'thirties architecture and replace it with some ghastly modern construction.' She pushed a pamphlet into Effie's reluctant hand.

''Oh, but I think the new scheme is great' asserted Effie with more conviction than she felt. 'I mean the existing building is hardly an architectural gem, is it?'

'Some of us think it is'.

'But we have to move on, let another generation make its mark.'

'Mark!' the lady spat out the word. 'I'd call it more of an excrescence.'

'Oh, come on!'

'An act of barbarism.'

'We can't live in the past.'

'We are to a large extent our past.'

'Some of us want to progress.'

'Ladies, ladies...' Oliver interjected 'shall we have another drink and agree to differ.'

'So, what do you think, Oliver? Surely you don't want to destroy our precious heritage?'

'I certainly do not, but I don't want to destroy the good atmosphere of the party either. Don't you think Sal's garden is too gorgeous? She really has green fingers.'

This seemed to be Sally's cue to appear carrying yet another plate of mouth-watering goodies which did a great deal to calm the atmosphere. But Effie's engagement with the black-haired woman had triggered a surge of blood to her face which she knew would take a while to disperse. She suspected she had not behaved entirely well in this interchange and wanted to go home. Oliver seemed to have been cornered again by that woman and Effie was not sure whether he registered her hasty 'goodbye'. She was retrieving her jacket from the hall stand when Sally appeared.

'Effie, not going so soon? Are you all right? I notice you and Lucinda having rather an intense discussion. She gets a bit passionate about things. But hang on, I know Oliver wants to say goodbye. Ah, here he is. I'll leave you to it, but do hope we'll see you again soon, Effie.'

Oliver sounded quite breathless and dramatically wiped his brow, 'phew! There's nothing like a woman with a cause. But I didn't want you just to disappear again, Effie. I mean...' he hesitated, 'I don't suppose you'd like to pay a visit to the condemned cinema before it succumbs to the builders. There's a good French movie coming up.'

'That sounds like a very good idea.'

Back home, Effie made a quick note in her diary before going to bed. She skimmed down to the heading 'Oliver' which had been left empty. She could now write something with a degree of conviction.

'Give him an A+ for improvement in appearance, not that he'd ever be really good-looking, but he has a nice personality, something of a peace-maker and we seem to share some interests. I <u>think</u> he has a sense of humour, thank god. I certainly like him a lot better than I did. I must do because my reaction to that irritating bitch - she scored out 'bitch' and substituted - 'black-haired flag waver' - was something I haven't felt in a long time; no bones about it, I was jealous.' And that was enough for one night.

Ch. 30

Much of this was re-played to Susie at their next meeting. 'I haven't felt as churned up about things since Jack left' Effie complained as the two of them perched on bar stools at Freddie's. 'I feel as though a layer of skin has been peeled off and I'm just so easily put in a wobble. I mean imagine getting upset by that awful woman Lucinda.'

'Oh it's not just her you're upset about, darling' said Susie wisely 'but it may be that you are beginning to like Oliver and don't want her spoiling your pitch.'

'That sounds awfully crude. But it's true I did have this horrible pang when I saw her grasping on to Oliver, like she owned him. I guess I must feel something for him.' She pensively prodded an olive with a cocktail stick. 'You know, maybe it's a relief to think that someone other than my son-in-law or my ex-husband can stir my feelings.' She shook her head, 'but it's all a bit much to cope with. I've seriously been thinking of going to Dr Gordon and asking him to give me a dose of tranquilisers.'

Susie tutted. 'Come on, Effie, that's not going to do anything other than delay you sorting things out.'

'So?'

'So, you don't want to end up a chemical junkie, do you?'

'Dependency has its attractions.'

'Sounds like your library researches didn't teach you much.'

'Well, I think I gathered that pretty well everything that happens to us when we're young can work away inside us, and once it's there it's damn hard to get rid of, a bit like being on auto-pilot. So the thing is to try and take control of it, like remembering things, kind of making them more obvious rather than letting them sneak up and take you by surprise. So I've been trying to think back and remember things that might account for my current emotional mess.'

'Like what?'

'Like the fact that my mother adored my brother and never seemed to think I came up to scratch. God, Susie, she was so critical of my weight that it's a surprise I didn't grow up with an eating disorder. Least, you don't think I've got an eating problem do you?... I mean I may be a bit on the large side and eat pretty well, but even Jack didn't complain too much about my size; though, come to think of it, Hilary was quite a skinny bitch. Perhaps all those years he was secretly hankering after a slim sylph for a wife.'

'I doubt it' said Susie adamantly, pushing the crisp bowl in Effie's direction, 'so why did you marry Jack? I don't think you've ever told me what the attraction was.'

Effie considered this as she noisily crunched on a mouthful of cheese and onion crisps. 'Did I never tell you that Jack was once upon a time a friend of Victor? Yes, he and Victor met at college and stayed friends after that, and I met him one holiday when he was home. They were good fun. Even my parents seemed to like Jack, and I can tell you my mother was quite fussy about Victor's friends. She was so possessive. Not that he took much notice.'

'From what you say, Victor paid most attention to number one.'

'Right, he was definitely selfish, and perhaps the most selfish thing he did from my mother's point of view, was to go off and live in America and marry an American who didn't like England. I guess that just about broke my mother's heart. Assuming she had one' Effie added with a brief laugh. 'But, hey, Susie, shall we have another one? Remembering all this stuff is thirsty work.'

'Same again please, Freddie.'

Her replenished glass in hand, Effie addressed her friend soberly: 'You know, I'm just beginning to realise how important Victor was in my life. You see, Jack had got used to coming round to our house quite a bit. He and Victor would pitch up on Sundays around lunch, hugely hungry, a bit hung over, noisy, kind of lively and my mother just loved it. So when Victor went off to the Sates my mother issued Jack with an open invitation to go on coming round for Sunday lunch and he often did. My mother would tell me he was coming as though she wanted us to get together. So we sort of did. I suppose Jack was the next best thing to Victor. He even looked a bit like him in those days when he had a head of hair and I think I did fall in love with him. Of course now, with the benefit of hindsight, not to mention my dipping into books on amateur psychology, I suspect I was really in love with Victor.'

'Makes a lot of sense. I mean isn't that what we're all meant to do? Marry our fathers, or why not our brothers? I only had a sister which has been complicated enough.'

Effie was warming to her task, enjoying the beginnings of a feeling of booze going to her head. 'Funny thing was, you know, although I can see my mother was definitely encouraging me to become an item with Jack, she didn't seem that pleased when we got married.'

'Perhaps you underestimate the competitive element.'

'How so?'

'I'd say it's one thing to wield that baton and conduct an affair between you and Jack, but once you're married, well, then it's less under her control and you're the one who's got Jack and she hasn't got her beloved son.'

Effie was impressed with her friend's analysis. 'Goodness, Susie, perhaps I should consult you more regularly. That makes a lot of sense though it's not something to be proud of, I mean, the idea of competing with your own mother.'

Susie shrugged and sipped her Chardonnay. 'Oh I think you were competing with her for Victor practically from birth, and poor old Jack got caught up in it.'

'God, don't be sorry for Jack, that bastard. He doesn't deserve any pity, the two-timing, f'...ing....'

'Ok, OK - I only meant he was part of the triangle.'

Effie burst out laughing 'when you mention 'triangles' I can't help thinking of our maths teacher at school and how she used to get us to sing a song about Pythagoras and a right-angled triangle, the square on the hypotenuse and all that. It was such a neat formulation. Oh that real life were so. I just can't find an OK place for what's happened right now, how to think about my own feelings.' She was sombre again.

'Look don't beat yourself up too much about it. You don't want to get sick or anything.'

'Well, I haven't exactly been sleeping my best. Which isn't surprising I suppose and I've been dreaming a lot. Odd dreams, that leave me feeling uncomfortable.'

'Such as?'

'Last night I dreamt I was sitting at a piano trying to play a piece of music and I couldn't do it, it was too hard, and I kept looking away from it, as though someone was watching me from behind.'

'Oh I think you just can't face the music' retorted Susie quick as a flash.

'God, Susie, do you really think so? I've been telling myself I'm doing everything to face up to things.'

'I'm sure you are, but it's not just going to happen like that. I spent a good six months sorting myself out on that couch and at the end she made damn sure that I didn't kid myself it was all neatly tied up. A life task, I think she said.'

'Oh dear.' Effie looked glum.

Back home she opened her diary before going to bed. Where had the discussion with Susie taken her? Straight to my mother, was the obvious answer, and she had not so far even given her a heading of her own, subsuming her comments so far under 'childhood'. She tapped in 'my mother', adding as a sub-heading 'things I liked about my mother' which gave her pause for thought. Nothing immediately stood out while when she went on to list 'things I did not like about my mother' her fingers flew over the keys: 'never told me I was pretty, told me I was too fat, compared me unfavourably to my brother, didn't share my joys. What a bitch of a mother.' Having vented this thought she went back to the 'what I liked' column and added 'she never criticised my mothering of the children which for her amounts to being given the thumbs up. She was OK as a grandmother.' Yes, she could see that her mother had been very different with her grandchildren. She pictured her mother getting down on the floor to play with the children when they were small, patient and un-phased by the mess, in a way she had never been with her and Victor. Was that a way of making up for earlier shortcomings or was it just that much easier with the next generation? She had only to look at herself and Cathy and the pleasure she got from the two little ones. She flicked back to 'Cathy', re-reading her comments about how difficult she had been as a small child. 'She <u>was</u> difficult and clingy but she was also the most loving of the three, always took things to heart and was probably the one most upset by Jack and me getting divorced. Perhaps I was so taken up with my own hurt about Jack I didn't give enough attention to how it was for her, and Jane and Leo. I think I relied on the fact that they were all grown up and had their own lives. Can see now that was a mistake.'

With this thought she closed the diary and settled herself for the night in the hope of drifting into untroubled rest. What she found was that she dreamt vividly: she saw a woman running away from some people who were chasing after her shouting that she was a murderer. She was trying to call out herself that she was innocent but they did not listen and she was terrified that they were going to catch up with her. She woke in quite a sweat to find the sun streaming in through the curtains. Five minutes later she was propped up in bed with a cup of tea, her lap-top on her knees, tapping in a new heading for 'dreams' which were obviously going to be an important part of the SOP. By the time she had finished typing out the details it seemed all too clear that the message of the dream was something about getting away with it or, more precisely, not getting away with murder. This troublesome thought came out as a dialogue as she wrote.

'But I haven't murdered anyone'

'But you've done something which you know is totally wrong.'

'I didn't mean to hurt anyone.'

'It was a hostile act towards your daughter.'

'Oh god! Do I have to think about it like that?'

'How else would you think about it?'

'I don't know.'

And with that she closed the diary again to set about the business of the day.

Ch. 31

Oliver's fifteen-year old Ford was spinning along at no mean pace. Effie was in the passenger seat, wearing black jeans that she had just managed to squeeze herself into, and wellington boots. Oliver was at the wheel clad in an old blue sweater which he assured her was cashmere - one of Alice's favourites - and casual trousers that fitted well on his slim hips. He was certainly not fat himself but was quite at ease with Effie's 'embombpoint' as he called the flesh that she frequently complained of, the roll of fat that lingered round her waist.

'It suits you' he protested' I really don't like skinny women'.

They were on their way to visit Moldsworth House, a stately home dating back to the seventeenth century, on the last weekend before it closed its doors for the winter. October colours were slowly brightening the landscape as rain clouds parted and the sun appeared. It was the fourth time they had been out together and Effie was beginning to feel some pleasure in his company. It wasn't exciting as it had been with Kenneth, just being with him, but she had enjoyed the outings which had ranged from a visit to the cinema to see the French film mentioned at the party, an art gallery, a jazz club and now a trip to the country to inspect how the aristocracy had lived in the seventeenth century. It had been a culturally rich few weeks which she had thoroughly enjoyed. She could view Kenneth now as not only flawed in his character but a lightweight compared to Oliver. What had she seen in him? Her diary writing and discussions with Susie were also focussing her attention in provoking and disturbing ways.

Today, however, her troubled psyche was not at the forefront of her mind and she was pleased to be feeling relaxed sitting next to Oliver, acting as map reader. No such thing as a sat-nav in this car. She occasionally looked over to Oliver, trying to gauge what sort of man he was. Not as hopeless as her initial impression had surmised, more interesting, but she was being cautious of her own judgements after an emotionally bruising few months. Externally Oliver looked much more attractive. He was hugely improved by the removal of the wisp of hair that had only emphasised his baldness. The shape of his head with its finely chiselled features was accentuated by the shaved look, giving him a faintly aristocratic air. This reminded her that she was looking forward to seeing the seventeenth century portrait collection that hung in Moldsworth House which they were rapidly approaching. Oliver had done his research, revealing a substantial familiarity with the period. 'You'll be stunned by the Gainsboroughs and Van Dycks' he assured her 'and marvellous plaster-work and carving by the master, that Gibbons man.' Effie, whose artistic tastes favoured the more contemporary, was quite ready to be impressed, enjoying his enthusiasm. There was something else she was beginning to enjoy though it was hard to put her finger on it, something about the way he managed to turn round a problem. And the problems certainly had a knack of dogging him. That morning as Effie left her house in response to his honking the horn she had been greeted by a car with a front tyre as flat as a pancake. A stray nail was evidently the culprit. Effie's reaction was one of immediate disappointment – the trip cancelled - whereas Oliver was instantly burrowing in the boot for the spare wheel and had the whole thing fixed within twenty minutes.

Effie was reflecting on this as the imposing contours of Moldsworth House came into view. She would have been quite happy to take a tour of the house but Oliver preferred to wander around with a book in one hand and his glasses gripped in the other, frequently tugging at Effie's arm like an excited child when something took his fancy. 'Just look at this carving. Grinling Gibbons at his best. Quite stunning.' Which Effie had to agree it was as she inspected the intricate garland of plump grapes and vine leaves that twined around a huge fireplace.

'And what about this!'. Oliver was peering at the woodwork round the door 'a pea!' He was almost hopping around.

'Oh dear, didn't you go before we came out?'

'No, no, Effie. Look it's a peapod and it's closed which means he didn't get paid. Or so the story goes. They say that was how Gibbons indicated whether or not his sponsor had paid up: if the pod is open and shows the peas he was happy. A rather nice myth, don't you think?'

They both laughed, moving on to admire the paintings, Gainsborough, Reynolds, Van Dyck. Effie knew them all but was happy to listen to Oliver who was voluble in their praises: 'a superb collection, Effie, just look at this Van Dyck, the third Duke. Cuts a fine figure doesn't he? Look at all that marvellous lace, and what an expression. Can't get much more imperious than that, and even the frame is pretty perfect' he added as he pushed his index finger a little too enthusiastically into a corner of the ornate gold-painted woodwork, dislodging a sizeable chunk which came away in his hand.

'Oops!'

'Oh god' Effie winced.

A tiny waif of a girl with Harry Potter glasses was suddenly prominent in front of the portrait staring hard at Oliver.

'Mummy, that man is making the picture broken' she proclaimed as she tugged at the hand of a worn out-looking woman who to Effie's huge relief was so busy wrestling with a wriggling baby in a pushchair that she was giving only cursory attention to her daughter's remark. She placed herself firmly in front of the damaged corner prepared to outstare the small child who was in the process of being swept up by a large man who carried her off protesting. By the time she turned round to Oliver she found him rummaging around in his pockets with a concentrated expression on his face.

'Ah, here we are!' he exclaimed as he held up a tube of 'Fixit Forever'.

'My god, Oliver, do you always just happen to have a tube of glue handy?'

'You see, you never know. Now just stand there, can you. Pretend to be looking at the little dog in the corner of the painting. Won't take a minute.'

So Effie did as she was told, bending down in front of Oliver to peer into the corner of the painting at the small creature which turned out to have wide open eyes that Effie could swear were looking at her, as was the duke himself when she glimpsed up. There he was gazing down at her with superior disdain. But true to his word within a few minutes Oliver was asking her for a handkerchief to wipe away any excess sticky bits which he did most efficiently so that she had to admit, when they stood back to inspect his handiwork, it was hard to tell that anything had happened.

The experience, however, was unnerving for Effie so that a coffee break was suggested and they made their way out to the stone courtyard which served as a cafe. It was teeming with children and their families, but the sun was out and Effie found a bench to sit on, having first ascertained that the waif child was not in the vicinity. Oliver went off to get coffees while Effie sat with eyes closed, her face turned towards the warm sun. She could laugh now about what had happened but an image came to mind of Victor again. There was something about Oliver which reminded her of her brother, his knack of fixing things as well as breaking them. She recalled Victor in his shed at the bottom of the garden. He had been given the shed to do chemistry experiments in at a time when he showed an interest in things scientific. She was not allowed in but she remembered once she had been with her mother in the kitchen when they had heard a loud explosion from the garden. They had rushed out to see Victor emerging from his shed with a blackened face and singed eyebrows, revealing his white teeth in a broad grin as he triumphantly proclaimed 'that's fixed it.'

She opened her eyes and could see that Oliver was still in the queue. He didn't look at all like Victor but there was definitely something about his cheerful insistence that things were fixable that reminded her of him, and her thoughts drifted off again back to that garden shed, but later on, when they were both teenagers, with Victor still proprietorial about his bolt hole. There was a Sunday afternoon in June when she had been there with a friend from school, the beautiful Clair, who had long blond hair and long legs. She had cycled round on her bike which turned out to have a puncture when she arrived. Victor, of course, had offered to mend it. She remembered how he had allowed them to glimpse in his shed as he set about fixing the bike, searching for a suitable tool and telling them that the vital item – was it a wrench? - was not there and sending Effie off to search in the basement of the house where their father kept his tools. She spent a good twenty minutes searching, dreading having to go back empty handed, she so much wanted to please Victor. But she couldn't find it and finally gave up, tramping back into the bright sunlight, hot and dusty to find the door of the shed closed and no sign of Clair or Victor. She remembered standing there for a few puzzled moments looking round, calling out Clair's name, and then the door of the shed opening and Clair stepping out with dishevelled hair, smoothing down her top. Victor, unabashed, came out grinning and clutching in his left hand a metal wrench: 'sorry, Effie, it was here all the time.... won't take a minute'. Whereupon he had set to work to fix the puncture which he did in ten minutes, presenting it triumphantly to the two girls - 'voila!'

As though everything was all right, was her current melancholy thought, which she must have spoken out loud because Oliver was speaking to her as he placed two steaming cups of coffee in front of her 'everything all right? Yes, I'm sorry about that little mishap. I really think it is all right though. I once did a course on picture framing, you know.'

'Goodness, Oliver, you constantly surprise me.' But she did feel cheered up and able to consider that Oliver's resemblance to Victor was only partial, and she didn't have to challenge her view that he was basically decent and it was Victor, sadly, who was the one wanting. It had taken many years for her to accept this painful fact of Victor's fickleness despite all the evidence. How hard to see that someone you loved had feet of clay. She considered this as she sipped her coffee with Oliver beside her, and was pleased that he was quiet and seemed happy just to be enjoying the sun and fresh air. They continued their exploration of Moldsworth House without further mishap, and by four o'clock Effie's visual cortex was creaking under such a weight of rich images of carved garlands, reredos, lush wall hangings and of lordly figures surveying the world with aristocratic hauteur that she was delighted when even Oliver's enthusiastic curiosity was sated and they made tracks for home.

On the way back Effie reflected that she had enjoyed the day although it had left her tired and still busy with her own preoccupations despite the stimulating things she'd seen. She needed something to get her mind off her brother, Jim and the seventeenth century.

'Are you any good at crosswords?' she ventured to ask as she dug in her bag for the paper.

'Sure. Love them. Have you got one?'

So this was something else that they could share. From Effie's perspective it was a useful way of distracting the mind from complex personal problems while encouraging it to tackle neutral complex problems in the form of cryptic clues. 'Well, let's see... one across...'

The crossword turned out to be another thing Oliver was good at, although Effie could hold her own. She could not help feeling, however, that her attempt to get her mind off troublesome personal matters was not entirely successful as the clues unfolded: 2 down - 'female cat with tangled preoccupations' - two words, 7 and 7' she read out.

'Oedipus complex' Oliver shot back. And then there was 6 across: 'number of apples told one can't eat' - two words, 9 and 5, which turned out to be 'forbidden fruit', and worst of all 10 down: 'I'm in mixed up perfume becoming taboo' which Effie worked out was an anagram of the letters of 'scent' together with 'i' giving the answer 'incest'.

'An interesting theme' chuckled Oliver 'which reminds me for some reason, there's something I want to show you. I hope you'll come back to mine for a bit so I can let you see.'

Effie hesitated. Her meetings so far with Oliver had taken place outside of his house and much as she felt he had smartened himself up and she had enjoyed their outings, she couldn't help but remember the semi trauma of his downstairs toilet, not to mention the left-over shepherds pie.

'Well, I promised Cathy I'd pop over to see the children before bed, haven't seen them in a while' she lied 'and I need to talk to Jane about something, you know, she's getting quite serious about this young Scottish man of hers, and then there's Leo...' her voice trailed off and she realised she must sound feeble and indecisive.

Oliver glimpsed in her direction. 'My dear Effie, I certainly didn't intend to make you anxious but I thought you might like to come and have a quick glass of something and inspect my new facilities. Well, actually I mean my shower room. All mod cons. It was Sally's suggestion. She was quite forceful after that time when you, you know, got a bit stuck.'

This gallant invitation could hardly be refused and so half an hour later Effie was being ushered into Oliver's house to be greeted, first, by the dog that leapt around in excitement, yelping and wagging its tail like windscreen wipers, and secondly by the sight of a much tidier house which no longer smelt of neglect.

'You've obviously been working hard' she could say sincerely.

'Yes, my dear, but wait till you see this' he said as he threw open a door to reveal no longer the broken down cistern and cracked basin but a startlingly modern all-white room with a glass shower cubicle, a huge shower head like a silver sunflower and an array of chrome taps and knobs that instantly reminded Effie of Kenneth's Japanese bathroom with its sprays and water massagers. She had a brief image of herself sitting astride the bidet with that warm water tingling sensation that made her clench her thighs together at the thought. Yes, she had to agree with Oliver, standing next to him in the close confines of the space, that it was a vast improvement. He danced around her excitedly as he demonstrated the various workings of the impressive chrome-ware, inevitably brushing up against her in the process which was not unpleasant for Effie and perhaps even a bit interesting.

She edged her way out of the shower room. Oliver was smiling but made no attempt to touch her. 'How about a drink?' It was after 6 and Effie had to decide whether she would stay for a drink or drop in to see the girls as promised before their bedtime. 'I told the girls I'd bring them something from Moldsworth House, so I won't stay, thank you.' She had two little dolls in an eighteenth century dress tucked in her bag.

He did not press her, but as she was about to drive off, he reached in through the open car window and put his hand on her arm: 'It was a marvellous day for me, Effie, and now you've seen I'm getting my house in order I thought you might risk coming for dinner. I mean to the house? Promise I'll get Sal to help me with the cooking.'

'I think that would be extremely nice' said Effie quietly 'but honestly, why don't you just get some M & S. I love their food.' She could not entirely eliminate her doubts about the wisdom of letting Oliver anywhere near a kitchen. He merely smiled and withdrew his hand. 'Let's make it Friday, shall we?'

She sped off in the direction of her daughter's house.

Ch. 32

'What ants are the biggest?' Daisy was telling jokes to her grandmother as the two girls splashed around in the bath.

'I don't know. Tell me.'

'Elephants!'

They all giggled.

'And why was six scared of seven?'

'So do tell us. Why was six scared of seven?'

'Because seven ate nine!'

Again they all laughed and Daisy was getting into her stride. Effie was trying to wash her neck.

'And what do you call two burglars?'

'I want to guess this one' yelled Rosie as the bar of soap slipped from her fingers.

'Well? Go on then. Guess.'

But Rosie only grimaced and Daisy triumphantly shouted out 'a pair of knickers!'

'Good one!' chortled Effie, 'now get on and wash that face of yours.'

'I don't think that was very funny' complained Rosie.

'That's just because you're stupid and..'

'I am <u>not</u>' an incensed Rosie shouted back, spurting water over her sister's head from the mouth of a plastic duck. 'Hey....' Daisy retaliated with a cupful of her own and a full scale water fight was soon underway with a large quantity of the contents of the bath ending up on the floor amidst much noise of shouting and yelling, which Effie was doing her best to control, while secretly enjoying it, when the bathroom door opened and Cathy came in, booming out 'what's going on? Now you two just stop that at once, just look at the place. Water everywhere. You're totally in my bad books' and turning to her mother 'and, Mum, what on earth happened? Can't we have a bit of order around here.'

'Actually, Cathy, I think they were just having some fun. I'll mop it up, don't worry. Come on girls, out you get.' Effie did her best not to sound defensive or apologetic but was inwardly annoyed for having put herself in a position yet again where she was on the defensive with Cathy.

The girls were prancing naked around the bathroom, dodging Cathy's attempts to get them to put their pyjamas on, apparently immune to her fury. Nor was Effie much help and the level of excitement was rising when Jim put his head round the door.

'Hey, girls! If you want to behave like wild animals you'd be better to get dressed and come and watch fifteen minutes of that wildlife programme I recorded. `That OK, Cath?'

'Anything to get them to return to civilisation.'

Ten minutes of noise and struggle passed before both girls were in their night wear, teeth and hair brushed, ready for the promised TV.

'Now, fifteen minutes, that's what I said' asserted Jim 'and I don't want any more nonsense or fights or silliness – otherwise...' he made a sudden scary face, 'you're dead.' Which only made the girls laugh but they did settle down in front of the television as the image opened up of the African plains and a herd of elephants lumbered into view. The two were immediately quiet, glued to the screen.

'I think we all need a drink' said Jim as he pulled the cork out of a bottle. `You're not rushing off, Effie? So what's got into those two tonight?'

'All I can say is..' said Cathy looking towards her mother and then hesitating as though she'd changed her mind. 'Anyway, let's leave that. What I really wanted to say, Mum, really to ask you, is if you'd be able to look after Daisy and Rosie at half term in a couple of weeks. Margie and her husband - you know the lady who lives near you - have asked us to stay a night at this posh hotel where they have great food and a pool and all, and Hannah's going to stay with her grandmother for the Saturday night. So, well, we wondered if you'd be all right with our two, just for one night.'

'We'd really appreciate it if you would and the kids would love it. They always do'. Jim was looking straight at Effie. She had not allowed herself to look at him in weeks. She felt Cathy's eyes were on her and she forced herself to look back. But the eyes she engaged with were not accusing. If anything they were pleading. Out of the corner of her eye she glimpsed something similar from Jim's blue eyes, though she couldn't meet them.

'Of course I'll have them. Absolute pleasure. So when exactly?'

'I think it's end of October. I'll just check in the diary.'

Cathy rose just as Rosie came hurtling through to the kitchen sobbing and threw herself at her mother 'he's eating it, Mummy, he's eating the baby!'

'Who is, darling?'

'The big lion. The daddy lion!' she sobbed.

'We'd better see what they're watching' said Jim as he strode off into the living room with the others trooping after him, Cathy clutching a distraught Rosie in her arms, to find Daisy staring at the TV as though transfixed. She was watching a huge bull elephant that was swaying around a smaller elephant, occasionally nudging its rear quarters with its trunk. The larger creature seemed to have a second trunk swaying from its body and for several minutes the whole family stood staring as the bull swung this enormous appendage and nuzzled into the female who seemed not the least bit interested but did not move away. They watched in a mixture of amazement and awful realisation as the enormous animal lifted up its great hulk of a body like some ancient wrinkly old man to mount the female and direct the wandering snake into her backside. She submitted amidst some huffing and puffing sounds at which point Rosie, who had stopped crying and was avidly watching, called out 'What's it doing, Daddy. What's that long thing?'

'They're mating' answered Daisy in a matter-of-fact tone.

'What's mating?'

'Everyone knows what mating is' pronounced a scathing Daisy 'anyway, that's what the man said.'

An earnest commentator's voice could be heard in the background: 'and so Samso the bull elephant finally finds his mate and deposits his seed to guarantee the next generation, a process which will take nearly two years before a new life sees the light of day on the Mazumbulu Plains.'

Jim suddenly roused himself: 'Hey, kids, it's time for bed, I said fifteen minutes and time's up.'

Cathy switched off the television muttering something about 'really suitable bedtime viewing!' to Jim as she ushered the girls out of the room, while Daisy, not to be silenced, announced that she knew what the long thing was, though she wasn't going to tell, and she also knew that mating was to do with planting seeds and making babies and the long thing was a pipe that blew them in, like blowing through a straw, or maybe that was what the trunk did, she added, momentarily confused. 'Well, I want one' Rosie was calling out as the two were ushered upstairs. It was Effie's cue to go. She waved goodbye to the retreating children, receiving an enthusiastic wave in response from Rosie who called after her 'gran'ma, can you get me one of those pipes for Christmas?'

She didn't wait to hear Cathy's response. It had been a long day and Effie felt relieved to get back to her own house. She hesitated between a cup of tea and a glass of Sauvignon from an open bottle of wine in the fridge, plumped for the wine and headed for her desk. She needed to take stock, and settling herself, she opened up her diary, turning to the page headed 'Oliver' in the green colour. There was a certain inevitable tendency for her comments to turn into a list of things she liked or disliked. In the 'like' column she put as positives

1) his enthusiasm and knowledge about historic houses,
2) looking smarter and more attractive,
3) has a new shower room – ie. He has one foot in the 21st century.

In the 'don't like' column she put:

1) rubs his hand over his bald patch: but he does look better
2) is a bit accident-prone: but has an extraordinary capacity to fix things
3) is a bit too gung ho: but might be worse if he were timid.

Then there was something else she wanted to put down which she wasn't sure where to place and decided she needed another column which was headed 'neutral' and here she wrote: 'not rushing to engage in physical closeness.' Was she fine with that or was she beginning to wonder what he was waiting for? She had definitely not minded being ensconced in the shower-room with him. On the other hand there had so far been nothing like the excitement of her initial encounter with Kenneth nor, dared she consider, the business with Jim which still lingered as that guilty, troubling nut. How warmly Jim had spoken to her about the children and half term. She wrote: 'I didn't realise how much I miss physical contact. I thought Jack had killed it off completely and now I'm not sure what I want. I need to think about Jack and then I need to think about Jim. I've got to get things in order. Ordering is my best bet.'

She could hear Susie telling her that people weren't to be judged like a shopping list. But ordering things was important, wasn't it? A sense of order and pattern in the universe mattered, which was why it certainly was puzzling to face the obvious disorder currently besetting her life. She could still hear Cathy's voice echoing around the kids' bathroom: 'can't we have some order around here!' But there had been something else from her daughter too: that pleading look in her eye. Had there been a slight change of gear? Her cynical self put it down to the fact that she wanted her mother to babysit at half term so they could go off on a jaunt. But so what, and what about Jim? He had certainly sounded sincere in his request, and that was a relief as was the idea that they were trying to get on better. So could she look forward to some relief of that awful guilt?

Ch. 33

'I'm really looking forward to having the girls at half term. It's ages since they've stayed the night.' Effie was talking on the phone to Susie. 'I've been beginning to wonder if Cathy was keeping them away or being particularly possessive about them. So it's quite a relief. Feels almost back to normal.'

'Well...' There was no doubting the reservation in Susie's tone.

'I wish you sounded a bit more enthusiastic.'

'Just trying to be realistic.'

'Me too. But I think this half-term trip is a good sign, don't you?'

'Sure. But the last time we spoke about things we were delving into the knotty area of mother/daughter rivalry. Can't have just evaporated.'

'But I wasn't thinking of Cathy. We were thinking of me and <u>my</u> mother.'

'That's the point, darling. Doing things repeatedly. Didn't your researches tell you that we are destined to repeat our own histories including our mistakes: you competing with your mother for Victor and now, well, something going on between you and Cathy that's probably got a competitive element.'

'But not for the children. That really is my best bit, least contaminated.'

'Lusting after their father is a complication.'

'Oh, Susie.'

'Sorry, Effie. Not meaning to be boringly moralising, but it's probably better to admit things than pretend. That's one thing I learnt from my time on the couch.'

'Look, I'm doing my best not to pretend. That's why I'm keeping this bloody diary and talking to you. And I really think any lust I may have experienced has been quite shocked out of me. Like it was a different me. And I'm really thinking about what you say about rivalry. That's tough.'

'Well, if it's any comfort, I know that I'm dead jealous of my two boys just because they're half my age.'

Effie sighed 'Perhaps I should be grateful I hadn't thought of that one. And then there's Oliver. I guess I've got to make my mind up about him.'

'Now there I can encourage you. I think he's good news.'

'He's threatening to cook me dinner next week.'

'You're a survivor, darling. Must go.'

Susie made it all sound so easy and normal, which was exactly what Effie needed before she could phone Oliver. He answered promptly and his voice brightened up when he heard it was Effie.

'I did enjoy the weekend, and I'm going to hold you to that dinner for Saturday night. Sal has promised to give me a hand with the cooking and I promise it'll be simple.'

And so Saturday night found Effie, bottle of Cabernet Sauvignon in hand – he had told her it would be meat – walking down the path to Oliver's house. The weather was cooling and she wore thick tights, a skirt and a sweater which she hoped looked smart without being too dressy. Oliver grinned when he opened the door. He was wearing a large chef's apron with Moet and Chandon emblazoned on the front. 'You made it! Brave woman' he greeted her, giving her a friendly hug. 'You know, I think I could get to like this cooking lark. Come and see.' He ushered her into the kitchen from which a delicious smell was emanating. Steam rose as he lifted the lid of an old cooking pot; 'It's a venison stew. Sal's recipe.'

'That's ambitious, Oliver, but certainly smells good.'

'And I'm glad to say, though I say it myself, it <u>is</u> good. I trust my sister-in-law on matters culinary absolutely and, I have to admit, she was in earlier just to check on things' he laughed. 'But, come, let's sample the wine, if I can find the damn opener'. He bent to search in cupboards by the sink, triggering for Effie a flashback to the occasion months ago when he had rummaged around in an empty drinks cupboard to produce a decanter containing a bare couple of centimetres of whisky.

Tonight, however, there was a rich aromatic claret served in two lovely old cut glasses, a plastic bowl of peanuts and a saucer of black olives which tasted good and Effie rapidly felt at ease. They took their drinks into the living room where to Effie's delight a log fire was burning in the grate. 'First fire of the season' said Oliver giving it a good poke with a brass poker. 'And move over, Milton, make room for our guest.'

Oliver was addressing this remark to the dog who was lying stretched out on the hearth rug. 'Milton?' queried Effie, patting its flank. 'Yes, we thought he liked poetry when he was a puppy. My wife used to read it out loud and was convinced he used to perk up when she got to 'Hence loathed Melancholy', and he'd wag his tail at 'Sport that wrinkled Care derides, And Laughter holding both his sides' – or so Alice liked to think.'

'A poetic dog? Why not. He must miss Beth. Or do you keep up the reciting?' asked Effie, patting the dog's head.

'Sadly not.' He looked suddenly dejected. 'I haven't got her appreciation of such things. I haven't felt like going there since she died. Didn't even much want to look after Milton for a while, but... 'and his face brightened again 'I don't want to spend the evening talking about Alice. It's just so good to have you here. I haven't used this room enough recently.'

'It's a nice room, particularly with the fire going.' Effie could say this with some sincerity as the wine warmed her, the fire glowed and the dog dozed. It was really quite cosy. Oliver had taken some photos on the trip to Moldsworth which they spent some time looking at, Effie trying not to examine each one with her normal critical eye. God, she must go to the gym more often, but ending up laughing as they recalled the incident with the picture. Dinner, too, was quite a jolly affair: Oliver's casserole was as delicious as it smelled, it was followed by fresh fruit salad with crème fraiche which Effie loved and an hour or so later they were back in the living room with Oliver piling more logs on to the fire, a cafetiere of coffee on the side table and two glass balloons filled with a rich amber liquid, a fifteen –year old brandy that Oliver had magicked up from somewhere. 'Oh, you didn't know I have a secret wine cellar'.

'No I didn't' said Effie, taking a sip which slipped down her throat in a warm wave 'particularly since last time I was here I didn't get the feeling you were into wines.'

Oliver looked serious, leaning forward and gazing into the fire. `you know, you are right. When you were here before I really wasn't terribly interested in anything that I usually am. I fear Alice's death kind of knocked it all out of me. We used to do things like that together. She'd cook and I'd do the wine. And it's just taken a while to get back to things. I mean, what does it really matter what you drink if you're on your own? The whole point is to enjoy it with someone you care about.'

Effie had to think about this, knowing perfectly well that she was far from averse to solitary drinking and not wishing to have to consider this a personality flaw. Would Oliver think that rather shocking if she told him? And what about having to admit to a dreaded sexually transmitted disease? Or even to hint at her illicit attraction to Jim? She shuddered at the thought, momentarily envisaging Oliver as some puritanical John Knox figure on his pulpit ranting on about this monstrous woman with her sinful behaviour. But the good food and wine, the brightly flickering logs, not to mention the still prostrate gently snoring Milton added up to an atmosphere that was far from puritanical. She could see that Oliver had really loved his wife, that he really had been shattered and bereft by her death and that this, in its way, was truly impressive for Effie who had had to fight off cynicism about relationships after Jack's abrupt departure.

Oliver sat back and was raising his brandy glass, smiling now.

'Sorry, Effie, I don't intend to be morbid. I think I really have 'moved on' as they say. And meeting you has been one of the best things that's happened to me in a long while. I mean it.'

A lovely glow crept over Effie mixing with her already warm brandy feeling so that the world really looked good, and she lay back closing her eyes, just letting the pleasure waft over her. She found herself reaching out her arm towards Oliver who took her hand and squeezed it. Neither spoke. She squeezed his hand back. Nothing more. He squeezed again, she squeezed back. She opened her eyes to find Oliver still motionless, with eyes closed and his brandy glass in his hand. She wasn't sure whether she wanted him to do something else, gather her up in his arms or if she liked it just as it was. As if he anticipated her thoughts he opened his eyes and looked into Effie's.

'Effie, I do like you a lot, and I like to think you like me at least a bit. But I can't go very fast, you know. To be frank...'

'Oh please, do be frank' she interjected.

'.. to be frank, I don't think I can quite face the sex thing yet...'

Effie waited, unsure what to say. He took his hand away and reached for the decanter. 'Here, let's enjoy the moment. This brandy's damn good, isn't it. I haven't felt so relaxed in a long time.' He swallowed the remaining brandy before topping up both their glasses and settling himself back on the sofa next to Effie. 'I did want to bring it up – sex, I mean. I mean we know each other quite well now and I've been thinking about it. I thought you might have too?'

In her mellow mood Effie stretched herself and answered in a rather languid voice, patting Oliver's thigh which was right next to hers. 'Of course I have, but do go on.'

'Well, we're neither of us spring chickens...' Effie laughed and involuntarily patted the varicose vein behind her left knee, but refrained from saying anything. He hesitated, sipped his brandy looking thoughtful, and continued. 'I don't know what it is, perhaps it is just getting older, and of course there's Alice. She really was a lovely woman – extremely good mother – quite sexy in her way... 'Another pause in which Effie's imagination got busy with shifting the quite ordinary image of the woman in the photo on the piano to a more vamp-like version of Alice. Oliver was finding his voice again.' Yes, really quite sexy, she had the most beautiful... quite unusual...' Effie had to restrain her bursting curiosity.. 'but I fear some of that has gone into retreat with her departure'. He turned to look at Effie. 'I'd really hate to start something and find, you know, that I couldn't perform. I've been thinking about it since meeting you and I realise right now I just feel a bit too nervous, and it's not that I wouldn't like to try, I assure you, but..'

'Oliver, say no more. I quite understand and it is not a problem. I think we both need some time, and I think it's most decent of you to let me know, and I feel quite touched by your openness' she added patting his thigh. The two were silent for a few minutes while Effie's imagination was far from quiet, juggling images of a mysteriously beautiful Alice and a half-naked Oliver. Some logs spat from the fire and she watched as Milton stretched himself out on the carpet, the epitome of a creature at ease. Surely now was the time for her to be frank as well?

'Oliver, there's something I ought to tell you, since we are trying to be open with each other.' She took a gulp of Courvoisier and shifted position 'Since we are talking about sex, I'm afraid I've got a problem.'

'My dear Effie?' Oliver sat up. 'What can you mean?'

'It's dreadful to admit, but I've got herpes.'

'Ah.'

'I know it's an awful thing, particularly for someone of my age and I only just got it. I had an attack not so long ago' she rushed on 'I'm fine now but it can happen again, I know, because I went to this clinic.. and they said there is no real cure and so you might get another attack though they said it wouldn't be as bad as the first, but it could happen again. Quite likely it will.'

'Oh I know' was Oliver's response 'a damn nuisance. You poor thing.'

'You mean you're not shocked and horrified?'

'Good lord, no. I'm just sorry. Very unpleasant for you, I'm sure.'

'Well, yes, it has been a huge worry. Not what I expected at my age.'

'But no worries on my account, I assure you. These things happen. If it ever crops up again when we're together and – you know – well, we'll just deal with it.'

Effie lay back feeling a couple of stone lighter and a wave of gratitude swept over her towards this man who had relieved her of a weight of guilt. At least she could shed one spade-full of the stuff. And they toasted each other in the firelight.

Ch. 34

Half term a few weeks later brought the girls' planned stay at their grandmother's. Effie made sure to give both parents a warm and encouraging farewell, determined to express only good feelings. She was pleased for them to be off on a jaunt and truly delighted to have the girls to herself for longer than usual. She shamelessly indulged them: a cinema visit with popcorn, hamburgers from Hank's Hickory Hamburgers and ice-creams from the Italian cafe. Back at the house it was to be a bubble bath and extra long story time. When they arrived at Effie's house around 6.30 it was to witness Oliver's bent figure struggling to extract something from the boot of his car.

'Who's that man?' was the immediate question.

Effie explained it was her friend Oliver, a kind man who had been fixing her lawn mower and was returning it. Oliver greeted them all cheerfully, deposited the mower, but did not stay, on the understanding that this was to be a weekend for Effie and her grandchildren.

The girls were excited and rushed upstairs to turn on the bath taps, chucking in half a bottle-full of Little Miss Happy bubble mixture and throwing off their clothes with gay abandon. A cloud of shimmering bubbles gradually rose over the edge of the bath and was soon covering the two girls who were whipping it up with their small arms flailing and much merriment until Effie decided she had to calm things down a bit to prevent the whole bathroom disappearing under a layer of foam.

'Right, time for some washing' she asserted as she took a towel to Daisy's tousled blond hair. 'Rosie, you too'.

'Look at me' shouted Rosie who had given herself a white moustache and white frothy eyebrows. 'Let me see, grandma, let me see!'. The shouting turned to laughter as she spied herself in the bathroom mirror. 'I look like your friend. He's got white hair.'

'No he doesn't' retorted Daisy 'he doesn't have <u>any</u> hair.'

'Oh, he does have <u>some</u>.' Effie felt the need to defend Oliver from juvenile disdain.

'Is he your boyfriend?' asked Daisy, with a coy look.

'Well, he is – sort of, I suppose' said Effie grabbing the sponge and wafting her arms through the foam in an attempt to find the soap.

'But you're <u>old</u>, grandma!' exclaimed Rosie, wiping the bubbles off her face and furrowing her small brow.

'Yeh, and if he's your boyfriend, that means you do <u>sex</u>' pronounced Daisy grinning.

'What's sex? queried Rosie.

'Sex is what you do when you have a boyfriend, that's what Annie told me, and she knows 'cos she's got a big brother who told her and he says...'

'That's enough of that, Daisy. I have no wish to know what her brother says, and...' Effie grasped Rosie by her blond topknot and began to scrub her back vigorously 'I may be old to you but these days sixty isn't so old, you know.'

'Sixty!' Rosie was stunned.

'She can't even count to sixty' Daisy blithely dismissed her sister.

'Oh yes I can' responded Rosie heatedly, and the two began counting up as fast as they could, with Daisy inevitably charging ahead leaving Rosie floundering in the 30s. Upset and angry, she began hitting the water in Daisy's direction which was Effie's cue to pull the plug and defuse the situation before it got out of hand and the bathroom was totally flooded.

'Right, that's it. Anyone who isn't out and dry in one minute does not get a story,' a threat which, to Effie's amazement, worked.

The girls were deposited back with their parents on Sunday evening by an exhausted Effie who stayed just long enough to absorb the fact that Cathy and Jim looked relaxed and seemed to have had a good time but also long enough to notice that almost the first words from her daughter had a critical edge: 'they look as though they didn't get much sleep', to which Effie could not resist replying that none of them had got much sleep and that she was pretty tired herself.

'I'm not tired' insisted Rosie, yawning.

Not to be outdone, Daisy boasted 'We went to bed at nearly ten o'clock', which caused Cathy to frown and tut 'honestly, Mum, that really is a bit late, even for specials...'

'Well, it <u>was</u> special. We were enjoying ourselves, and the girls are hard to resist when they really set their minds on something.'

'Boundaries never were your strong point, Mum.'

...

Later that evening Effie was busy filling in her diary. Under 'events of the day' she was describing her time with the girls together with her assessment of how she had handled things which came out again in the form of a dialogue. 'Those kids had a great time, I know they did. I'd give myself 9 out of 10, but two minutes with Cathy and I barely get a pass mark.

So what are you doing wrong?

What am <u>I</u> doing wrong?

Yes, you.

I feel she is always sniping at me, disapproves, makes me feel I can't get it right and isn't at all grateful.

That's quite a list.

I know, and I've also put on two kilo, though I suppose I can't blame her for that.

No you can't, she said to herself out loud, sitting back in her chair and letting her inner eye take her off, remembering the food she had readily consumed with the grandchildren over the weekend. Those two liked their food, unlike their mother who had been a picky eater as a child, rejecting dishes she had prepared and then complaining she was hungry, and fussy too about her clothes, never happy with what Effie chose but refusing to take any interest when they went shopping together. Damn difficult child. Much more so than the other two. She remembered one summer when Cathy had insisted on wearing the same pair of torn jeans for the whole time, refusing to be parted from them. As she pictured it Effie's hand moved to the waistband on her own trousers, aware that she could barely squeeze in her fingers. Action was called for and her final entry that night was a clearly spelt out resolution that she would:

1) take off 2 kilos next week... which she calculated was just over one quarter of a kilo per day which sounded manageable
2) try harder with Cathy... which she did not spell out but which triggered a vivid dream that night of herself at the gym on the treadmill watching a distant figure who she knew was Cathy but who she could not reach however fast she walked.

Ch. 35

'R U up 4 glass of V 2 nite?'

'Yup'

'C U @ usual at 8.'

A few hours later the two women were sipping prosecco in Freddie's Bar. 'It feels quite hopeless' Effie complained 'I've been killing myself at the gym to lose a kilo or two and managed a grand total of 650 grams, and on the Cathy front, she hasn't called me all week since I had the kids and I barely got a thank you.'

'No?'

'I'm afraid I just hear that tone of recrimination, that I'd let them stay up too late, tired them out, and it was pretty exhausting for <u>me</u>, you know,'

'But you enjoyed the weekend. I mean, you can't expect children to constantly express gratitude. Trying to think when my two last said anything remotely grateful, but they do give me lovely flowers on my birthday.'

Effie pondered this as she gazed around the heaving bar and leaned in towards her friend. The place was noisy with Friday-night revellers. 'We had a great time. I loved it. It's just that I'm desperately wanting to be able to stop feeling so guilty about Cathy and somehow when she's so critical I think she must know something, and won't forgive me.'

'Effie, I really don't think you should persecute yourself with such thoughts. There is no reason to think Cathy has any idea you've been lusting after her husband.'

'Susie!'

'Sorry, but I actually want you to stop over-dramatising things.'

'You think I am?'

'A bit'

'But there seem to be all sorts of dramas going on in my head, like remembering things about my mother and Victor, and Jack popping up again and the awful events of that holiday, not to mention the riot of dreams I'm having.'

'Hang on, one thing at a time'. Susie put her glass down firmly. 'So what's the awful holiday you mean?'

'I must have told you about the holiday we went with dear Hilary and her husband-as- was. Jack and I went on several holidays with them, they were a couple we liked, we got on, as they say.' She stabbed a black olive. ` This particular holiday – must be six or seven years ago now, it was before the babies - we rented a villa in the south of France, the weather was great, house lovely, gorgeous pool, and I guess Hilary was looking specially good. I remember Jack commenting on how well she looked, if ever there's a more ambiguous phrase, and a few weeks after we got back to England he announced that he didn't think we were getting on and he wanted a separation, that he and Hilary were going to make a life together, and off he went.'

'You poor darling. I didn't know it was quite as grim as that.'

'You bet it was grim. Hilary was my best friend. Our kids had always been friends. What a bastard and I keep thinking I've got over it and then he raises his ugly head again. Seems to be back in my mind and I just want to forget him, Susie. I've been doing a reasonable job at it, and to be fair to Cathy, she rarely mentions him. All the kids know it's still a sore point. But you know the other day I got quite a jolt. Rosie suddenly said something about 'grandpa' and I had to think for a minute, who on earth is she talking about?'

'I can see that, but the fact is he is their grandfather. So where else has he been raising his ugly head?'

'He's been sneaking into my dreams of all places.' Effie sounded affronted at the notion. 'If you can hear me over the din I'll tell you.' She proceeded to recount her last night's dream in which she saw Cathy as a little girl playing with a friend. She was calling her but Cathy ignored her, more interested in continuing the play with her friend. The two girls got further and further away until it seemed there were three of them in the distance, one of them now a boy who looked like Jack. She had woken feeling upset and angry that the three were taking no notice of her.

'I can see what you mean about him sneaking in' said Susie sympathetically 'but I suppose there's no harm in seeing him playing with Cathy, I mean he is her father.'

'Sure, and I used to think he wasn't such a bad Dad. He even did things like try and play cricket with Leo though he wasn't actually the least bit sporty. But after what he did it's hard to think of him as other than totally toxic. When I think how he used to preach to the children about honesty and loyalty. He'd really make them suffer if he found out they'd done anything wrong, even tiny white lies.' Susie tutted. Effie finished her glass of prosecco and pushed her empty glass towards her friend. 'I feel I'm getting to the nub here, Susie, I haven't ever really told anyone just how awful it was with Jack and - god, I hope you can stand me telling you all this?'

'For god's sake, don't get all pathetic. Keep going and let's have another. Two more proseccos,please, Freddie.'

'You know, the more I think about it, the more I think Jack's to blame. He's behind my problems with Cathy. I wouldn't put it past him not to be filling her in with all sorts of bad stories about me, bastard that he is.' She gulped her wine and closed her eyes, shutting them tightly as though to squeeze the image of him out of her sight, half chanting to herself 'get off my back Jack, put you on the rack Jack.'

'Let's not go too far with that' said Susie putting a restraining arm on her friend's.' I can see why you're angry but I honestly don't think he'll be feeding the kids horror stories about you. I mean, I don't think he's got the imagination for one thing.'

'Well, I sometimes wish I didn't have such an imagination because a certain awful scenario has been worming its way into my head recently, since the business with Jim. I mean what if the kids found out, Daisy and Rosie. I've let myself imagine the horror on their faces if they saw their grandmother clinched in an embrace with...'

'Come on, Effie, this won't do.' Susie spoke firmly. 'Let's just throw that one out. That's your worst thought, you've had it and now just get rid of it.' She took a handful of peanuts out of the nearby bowl and munched them pointedly. `Some things, once thought, and chewed over are best swallowed.'

'But some bits are pretty indigestible.'

'You can't keep chewing over the same thing.'

'So am I becoming boringly repetitive?' Effie looked downcast. She hated any evidence from her friend that she was too much. 'So much for self-analysis.'

'It's not a criticism. It's just trying to keep things on track' said Susie in her efficient business voice, and then, relenting 'but, come on darling, you're doing fine. So where are we?' They both sipped their drinks and gazed around the bar which had filled up with plenty of pleasure-seeking youngsters. Effie had a brief flashback to her first date when she had met the amusing Brendan. That seemed so long ago.

Susie was speaking: 'So what about that dream then, the one with Cathy and her friend and Jack. So who was the other girl?'

'Oh that was Amy, Cathy's best friend from years ago. In fact Amy is Hilary's daughter. I suppose I met Hilary through Amy and Cathy. The girls met at school and were close as thieves for a while and I got to like her mother, Hilary. We started doing things socially and Jack hit it off with Hilary's husband too and the kids got on, so we went on a few holidays with them all and then without the children as they grew up and didn't want to come with parents, and..' Effie hesitated, 'and then we got to that fateful holiday that I just told you about. The end of a lovely friendship.'

'I see.' Susie furrowed her brow. 'So the girl in the dream who's Cathy's friend is the daughter of the woman who went off with Jack, and he's there too, and they're all ignoring you.'

'I hadn't thought of it quite like that.'

'You might say you've got good reason to be angry with your daughter. I mean, it's her friend's mother who's the culprit in the affair, apart from Jack of course.'

'You know, I never made that connection to Amy.'

'You needed Dr Susie Freud to point it out to you.'

Effie spoke slowly: `I think, my darling, you are right. Damn right. And I've been blaming Cathy for her friend's mother all this time. It adds up to me blaming Cathy for Jack's departure. Makes absolute sense in a horrible sort of way.'

'It's not horrible if it helps you understand things better.'

'So where do I go from here?'

'I don't know that' said Susie getting up 'but I do know I'm going home to make Fred some dinner. All this psychologising is making me hungry and he'll be wondering what's happened to me.'

They gave each other a friendly hug at the door of the bar. 'I think I actually feel a bit different' Effie reflected aloud 'as though something has lifted a bit. But it needs some thinking about. Can't thank you enough, really.'

Susie called back as she exited, scarf flying, 'my services available any time, and I never got to hear how things are going with Oliver. Next time?'

Ch. 36

'I need time to digest things' Effie wrote in her diary the next day. This assertion was translated into action as a period of several weeks in which she retreated from some of her normal activities, went onto a kind of auto-pilot at work, excused herself from seeing Oliver on grounds of not feeling too well and made strenuous efforts in the gym to drop some unwanted kilos, braving the treadmill despite, or perhaps because of, its associations to the dream about Cathy. She turned down an invitation from Bea to go to another private view on the grounds that she did not need any further stimulation. She looked after the girls a couple of times at Cathy's request but made it a point not to stay and chat when the parents returned. She found herself regarding her grandchildren with more than usual attention. Were they all right? did they display any signs of disturbance? What did they convey about their parents? She could not resist asking Daisy how her mother was, and then regretted it because Daisy seemed to feel it was not the usual sort of question.

'Mummy? Well, she was cross with me for forgetting my homework book but then she said she was too tired to be cross which doesn't make sense, does it, 'cos she already was.' Effie couldn't fault the impeccable logic. She refrained from asking how Daddy was. Rosie chipped in, however, to tell her that her daddy was cross too when she and Daisy had been fighting over a comic which got torn, 'and he said we have to share 'cos we don't know how lucky we are. Are we lucky, gran'ma?' Effie felt obliged to reply that, yes, they were very lucky, but added that her mum and dad were also very lucky to have them, and she was a lucky grandma...

She was partially re-assured by Daisy telling her an appropriately innocent joke: 'gran'ma, what's the kindest vegetable?' 'I don't know, darling, tell me.' 'A sweet potato!' she giggled. This was followed by a less savoury offering which Daisy excitedly informed her was 'dirty'. 'Gran'ma, what did the willie say to the condom?'

'Good gracious, Daisy, I'd no idea you knew what a condom was.'

'Oh everybody knows that.'

'They do? So what's the answer?'

'Cover me, I'm going in!' Daisy tittered and Effie tutted. Did the child really know about such things? She hoped she was just showing off.

'Nothing obvious to worry about' she wrote in the diary 'and I notice Cathy did not make a big point about me bringing the children back late. Is there a mellowing, or am I just looking for reassurance?' Many of her diary entries were in the form of questions like this while what she wanted was the comfort of answers. 'You've made the connections, so get on with it.' This was partially Susie's voice. She knew her friend was expecting her to get on with things now that she had helped her make the crucial link to Cathy and Hilary. Quite how that played into events with her daughter's husband was scarily fuzzy and it was easier to pursue her thoughts about her brother. She could see how Jack and her brother were almost joined at the hip in her mind. It was so obvious that she was amazed she hadn't noticed before. Not that there was anything wrong in marrying someone who reminded her of her brother. What was less clear was how that linked in to what had happened with Jim.

She had left Jim till the last in her diary. What to write? How to understand? She knew she had been a bit surprised, though pleased, that Cathy and Jim had got together. 'Not an obvious match' she wrote. 'Always felt he was a lovely man, kind and intelligent. I think I had a soft spot for him from the start. Those lovely blue eyes. Of course, that's Victor.' And she saw the scene again on the beach as they stared naked at each other. She had seen not only his penis but the expression on his face, his gaze.

'So Jim reminds me of Victor and they are both forbidden' she wrote. 'In fact Jim is a much kinder version of Victor. When I think about it, Victor wasn't such a nice brother. He tricked and manipulated me a lot of the time. My mother never defended me against him. So, back to my mother, I see, and I'm trying to think about Jim. I think Jim really does like me and appreciates me which my mother never did and my father took his cue from her.' She re-read what she had written and frowned. Did it sound too much like an exercise in excusing herself? She could imagine Susie pointing this out. What's the idea of the diary? Not much point if you're not going to be honest. All too easy to pass the buck.

This thought seemed to trigger a dream that night in which Effie saw her family, including her parents. They were playing a game of ball on a beach and were throwing it around from person to person getting faster and faster and more and more angry. The ball gradually changed into a grenade which no one wanted to hold nor dared to drop. 'None of us want to take responsibility for what's happened. Just passing things round from generation to generation. So what if the buck stops here with me?'

'You know that it damn well has and there nearly was a terrible explosion.' She saw that moment in the car with Jim and the flash of the headlights. Had she been saved from disaster only by that chance beam   . of light? What if the neighbours hadn't pitched up at that moment?

I don't know.

Would you have stopped if they hadn't?

I'm sure I couldn't really have gone through with it.

You'll never know for sure.

Oh god.

She closed the diary with a flourish, got up from her desk and burrowed in her bag to fish out her phone. She texted a message to Oliver, telling him she was feeling better and expressing the hope that they could meet up again soon, and another one to Susie, apologising for being anti-social. The final text was to her daughter. She felt an overwhelming agony of remorse at how close she had got to catastrophe. What could she say? What she wanted to say was something like:

'sorry for being such a stupid, thoughtless, unprincipled, un-boundaried, reckless, dangerous mother...'

But since she had every hope that Cathy would not have a clue what she was talking about, she eventually settled for:

'Sorry if I've been a bit off recently. Would love to have the girls for the day on Sat.'

As she pressed the 'sent' button the phone rang and it was a chirpy-sounding Susie. 'Effie, where have you been? I've been wondering what you've been up to and hoping you are not just ruminating like a morbid cow.'

'I have needed to think.'

'Well, darling, I was hoping I could doff my Dr Freud hat and get back to more superficial things.'

'Can't think of anything I'd like better, actually.'

'So, look, there's my new collection going to be on display at the end of the week. You must come and look. Fantastic new stuff.' Her voice was excited and fast. 'But where have you got to, then, with all this thinking? If you can tell me in three minutes, love to hear. Got'a photographer coming.'

'Yes, to the collection, and 'no' I can't tell you in three minutes.'

As she rang off Effie knew she was disappointed that Susie was not more available, that she was busy again with her own life. She sighed as she rose to busy herself with her own domestic affairs, gathering up washing and tidying her desk which usually gave her a degree of satisfaction that she could replace disorder with order. As she shuffled papers, the phrase 'tell me in three minutes' stuck in her head. Of course you couldn't describe or explain a process of trying to resolve a deep emotional problem in a matter of minutes. And yet, when she thought about it, a lot can happen in three minutes. She spoke out loud to no one in particular: 'it took Jack precisely three minutes to tell me he was leaving me to go and live with Hilary. The bastard. The bitch.'

Ch. 37

Oliver, in his furry lined jacket which made him look like a teddy bear, gave Effie a warm hug which she returned with enthusiasm. It was Christmas week. The two had gone separate ways for the day itself, Oliver to his daughter's and Effie to Jane's. Cathy and Jim had taken the children up to stay with his parents for a few days.

'It's their turn to have them'. Effie felt she had to explain to Jane who tended to disparage conventional family customs.

'God, Mum, if Alastair and I ever tie the knot I hope you won't expect us to shuffle between our respective parents every Christmas.'

'No, Darling, I won't expect other than your usual considerate behaviour.'

'Right.'

They both laughed. Always easier to laugh with Jane than with Cathy. Maybe that wouldn't change however good a job she did on digesting the recent emotional upheavals. 'Give yourself time' Susie had advised with her counsellor hat on. 'You know it's not Cathy's fault her best friend had a mother with a roving eye and no moral principles.' Effie knew that perfectly well, but it still did not quite stifle those bubbles of indignation. She could follow the process quite visually, imagining a set of scales with a great lump on one side marked 'guilt' with an equally huge mass on the other marked 'resentment'. Her birth sign, after all, was Libra.

But it was Christmas and having got through the day itself she was determined to enjoy herself. She and Oliver had been getting on well, if still tentative on the issue of sex. It was something they joked about rather than practiced beyond some hugs and kisses, which Effie felt no need to complain about because she had her own problems to struggle with and felt there was plenty of other evidence that he liked her.

She disentangled herself from the bear hug and hoisted her bag into the boot of the car. This was Oliver's Christmas present to her – a couple of days at a country hotel: 'set amongst the delightful rolling hills of the Cotswolds, this luxury hotel with every facility, makes every effort to sooth away the stresses and strains of city life. The de luxe spa with its magnificent swimming pool will pamper your body and soothe flagging spirits while the five star restaurant will cater for every taste. Try starting your evening in the glamorous Gloucestershire bar where you can sip champagne while you listen to the sounds of our resident impresario who will serenade you with romantic songs that promise a world of dreams.'

'Can't be all nonsense' had been Oliver's optimistic justification for apparently succumbing to the sales blurb. 'We can always leave if it's too awful.'

'Oh, I'm really looking forward to it' said Effie as she settled down in the passenger seat. 'I don't want to think about anything serious. It's been a difficult few months.'

Oliver said nothing but squeezed her hand before starting the car and speeding off in the direction of Chipping Notwood and the Golden Beagle Hotel. 'Shouldn't it be 'eagle'?' Effie chuckled. 'Maybe they couldn't decide whether they liked birds or dogs.' Which comment was clearly Milton's cue to bark enthusiastically from the back seat. 'Can't be bad if they let us bring Milton' said Oliver. More yaps from said hound who was clearly delighted to be included in the party, sensing wide open spaces.

Oliver had booked for two nights. The journey, which started off well, deteriorated once they left the motorway. Effie found it difficult to read the map from Oliver's well-thumbed edition of 'the A to Z of England and Wales' and after several wrong turns which left them back where they had started, she made the fatal mistake of muttering that it was a pity he didn't have a sat nav. Oliver's usual calm, benign self was instantly replaced by an outraged wildman.

'Effie! I have never needed the assistance of technology in order to be able to find my way around this country... in all my forty years of driving I have always got to my destination unaided and usually on time... all I require is an intelligent woman who can read a map properly. Please don't mention that word again - ever!'

Even Milton looked startled. Effie was so shocked at this revelation of Oliver's touchiness and temper that she was silent, leaving it to Milton to begin agitating, breathing hard and then howling, a mournful, penetrating howl.

'Now see what you've done. Upset the poor dog!' Effie sniffed, blew her nose and then relented a little. Their first row. And they hadn't even made love properly yet. 'I think we'd better stop; get our bearings and let the dog have a pee.'

The rest of the journey took place in darkness and silence. This was only relieved when Oliver turned on radio 3, which Effie hated, and they proceeded to the sounds of bellowing organ music. Oliver muttered to himself as he peered at signposts, swore under his breath a few times as he reversed into a main road and finally let out a triumphant 'aha!' as a large notice loomed into sight proclaiming 'The Golden Beagle'. He mumbled a hasty 'sorry' as he drew up outside a rambling country mansion. They headed straight for the bar after dumping their bags in the bedroom giving Effie just enough time to register that there was a large four-poster double bed and an en suite bathroom with a plastic shower curtain and a bath with an emerald green stain surrounding the plughole. 'We both need a drink' she stated.

The rest of the evening passed through several stages like a game of hide and seek, moving from cool to warm to very warm and finally, hilarity, no doubt fuelled by a generous amount of alcohol and good food so that by the time dinner was over they were both utterly exhausted and could only stagger up to their bedroom and fall unceremoniously into the four poster bed, to drop instantly to sleep.

They slept late and well, finally woken by Milton tugging at Oliver's bedcovers. Once they got going they occupied themselves very happily walking the dog, though as Effie pointed out, with Milton there was no question of 'walking' anywhere: the creature was in paradise, racing around like a mad thing. They swam in the large pool and explored nearby villages in the car, indulging in day dreams of the country cottage they would buy 'one day'. Back at the hotel Effie subjected herself to the manipulations of a nubile young man who pummelled and kneaded her unwilling flesh for half an hour which was about as much as she could stand.

'So much for 'soothed and pampered'. It was more like 'bruised and battered' she complained half-seriously to Oliver. 'Still, some of that Xmas excess must have budged.' Oliver, who seemed to have the constitution of a one hundred percent ectomorph, only chuckled.

'All very well for you.'

'But you know I like your embonpoint. It really suits you, and I fully expect you to have the whole three courses tonight.'

Effie did not need much persuading, so that the two of them ate and drank their way through a number of delicious dishes including a dessert comprised entirely of cream, chocolate and brandy which the two attacked with gusto. Oliver was telling Effie a story about an incident when a glamorous woman had mistaken him for a chauffeur when he had drawn up outside a department store to pick up his wife: 'This dolly woman dripping furs just plonked herself down on the back seat and waved me on to some smart address – just like this.' He gesticulated wildly with his cream-laden spoon and a large dollop flew across the gap between the tables to land with a neat splat on the hand of the woman next to them. Oliver leapt up profusely apologising, and clasped the offending hand in his. Effie had a distinct sense of déjà vu - wasn't it Kenneth all over again? - and for an awful moment she thought he was going to lick it off.

'My dear lady, I'm so sorry. Entirely my fault. Here, let me wipe it off.'

The object of this apology was a young rather brassy blond woman who was wearing bright pink lipstick and a fitted dress to match. Far from making a fuss she began to laugh, reassure Oliver and introduce her partner, Stan, who looked like an overgrown teddy boy from the sixties. The result of all this was that the four of them ended up back in the Golden Gloucestershire bar carousing for an hour or so and becoming the best of friends with the inevitable result yet again that by the time they eventually got to their room they dropped, like two heavy logs, into the mock Tudor bed and slept like babies.

Effie's sleep was interrupted by the sound of a dog barking and shuffling noises but she dozed off to dream of a golden Labrador nuzzling into her and pulling her along towards an ocean she could just make out in the far distance. The dog was barking again and pushing its nose into her so that she opened an eye to see Milton standing there at the bedside, panting expectantly. With the other eye she saw Oliver, already dressed and grinning, dog lead in hand.

'It's a marvellous crisp morning. Milton and I saw the sunrise while you were in the land of nod. And now, my dear, it's time for tea' said Oliver as he plugged in the kettle which nestled on a tray laden with cups and assorted tea bags. Let's see - English breakfast I think.'

Effie closed her eyes again, half-awake, and listened to the comforting sound of water coming to the boil, of Oliver humming as he clinked cups and tore open packets. She felt warm and comfortable. Pleasantly calm. She shut her eyes again and was aware of Oliver sitting on the edge of the bed beside her. 'Your tea, madam.' She raised herself, took a sip of the hot beverage and sank back on the pillows. 'Considering last night, I feel amazingly good' she smiled. 'Me too. Haven't felt so energised in ages.' He tore open a small packet of McVittie's digestive biscuits and offered one to Effie who took hold of it, but he did not let go. 'Let me give it to you'.

Effie took her hand away and allowed Oliver to break the biscuit which he fed her in small pieces. 'You really look good, you know. I think you look your best first thing in the morning. Fresh, unadorned.'

'You must be joking.'

'I never joke about such things' he laughed, cuddling in closer. 'Would you like some more tea... or something else, perhaps?'

'Well....' Effie put her tea cup down.

Oliver was not waiting for an answer but was already tugging off his trousers in a sudden burst of ardent enthusiasm. He threw his shirt to the ground and within seconds was snuggled up next to Effie in the bed, grasping her in his arms, stroking her hair and covering her in kisses. 'My god. Oliver, I didn't know tea could have such a dramatic...' she did not finish her sentence as Oliver covered her mouth with his own and for a few moments they held each other like young lovers, seeking each other's tongues, mouths, and feeling the still unexplored parts. Effie put up no resistance, had no desire to and sensed her own body for once reacting the way she wanted it to, gradually warming up, becoming aroused, excited by the sense of Oliver becoming aroused too, of something hard pressing against her. 'My darling, my darling' he breathed in her ear as he raised himself and Effie willingly opened her legs. She wanted him and tried to guide him in but somehow it wouldn't go.

'I'm too dry' she whispered in his ear 'it won't go.'

Immediately Oliver was up and riffling somewhere in a bag and back again with a 'this'll do the trick. Cheekie Charlie, my Durex friend.' And within seconds Effie gasped as Oliver entered her to the sound of a triumphant 'yes....! followed by plenty of panting and rolling around until Effie found a comfortable position where something really did happen and a minute later something happened for Oliver too. He breathed out her name as he came and she burst out laughing as he sank back, exhausted but smiling.

'Well, you really are the man who fixes things' she said as she nestled into the protective space offered by his arms.

'I hope you mean that as a compliment.'

'Oh yes' Effie could say sincerely.

'And was it OK?' There was a mild note of anxiety in the question.

'More than OK.'

'Sure?'

'Oliver, it's not like you to display unnecessary worries.'

'Sorry, but it's been so long, and I've wanted it so much for quite a long time and I've worried a lot that my body would let me down, as you know. I mean, one thing to want and another to do.'

Effie's response to this was to give Oliver a big hug and kiss him on the ear nearest to her. 'My dear man, please don't worry on my account. It's great if we can but honestly doesn't matter if it doesn't work, you know.'

'But I want it to work.'

Another kiss was deposited this time on Oliver's bald head which made him laugh and seemed to be Milton's cue to remind the pair that there was a third party present. He barked excitedly. 'Breakfast and some more exploring I think' said Oliver raising himself. `I'd forgotten about the dog. And all this activity is making me hungry.'

'Me too' cried Effie as she exited the bed with the nearest thing to a leap she had got to in years. She felt happy. At last she dared to think that things were going in the right direction. She reflected on this in the bathroom as she peered at herself in the mirror. Something felt relieved. It wasn't just that they had made love at last. The relief was that she had desired Oliver and there had been no lovely blue eyes sneaking into her fantasy as she reached towards climax.

Ch. 38

'Here we are'. Effie swung her legs out of the taxi, balancing on the one hand a creamy chocolate cake on a fancy gold platter, and on the other, her weight on the high heels that she was already regretting wearing. So much for vanity. Oliver gallantly gave her his arm as they walked towards Cathy's front door on which hung a Christmassy wreath, which was always a bit funereal for Effie, but this one was livened up by some red balloons and streamers beside which was pinned a sign covered in drawings of ballet dancers strewn around a bold -'WELCUM '-.

The door was opened by a grinning young man in jeans who introduced himself as 'Justin - and you're just in time for the party' he laughed gaily.

'Hi – Effie – sorry. Must deposit this cake and platter.' She made a bee line for the table, pushing through a group of revellers who already seemed to be well-oiled, leaving Oliver apparently sharing a joke with Justin – 'sounds like a pub' she heard him chortle, 'come and sample our cider at the Cake and Platter!'

Effie, relieved of her chocolaty burden, scanned the room, looking for Cathy.

'Effie! How nice to see you!'.

'Oh hello, Sheila. Where's Cathy?'

'No idea. So what's this I hear: a boyfriend, eh?'

'Well, I suppose so. Yes, come and say hello.'

Oliver, however, had already melded into the party and Effie was waylaid by the girls who had clearly been allowed to stay up late for New Year. Daisy was wearing a pink tutu and her hair was up in a bun tied around with glittery ribbons. Rosie was dressed in a tiger outfit and was enjoying jumping around and roaring. The girls gathered around their grandmother excitedly.

'Grandma, I got this tutu from granny Faye, and look at my nails!' She flashed her hands out displaying a set of tiny fingernails sparkling with silver glitter.

'My goodness, darling, did granny Faye <u>really</u> give you that?'

'Yes, yes..' trilled Daisy as she pirouetted round, unabashed, 'and I've got stuff for my eyes and shiny lipstick too, and perfume so I smell like a flower and mummy said you were bringing your boyfriend tonight. Is he the man we saw at your house that time?'

'Yes, I think you did see him that time a while ago. So come and say hello properly.'

But Oliver was still not in view, the noise level was rising and the girls were quickly distracted so that Effie did the obvious thing which was to head for the kitchen where the breakfast bar was piled with bottles and a pretty girl was busy filling glasses.

'White or red, Mrs McIver?' she grinned.

'Oh, Jasmine? I didn't recognise you in that black outfit. Very fetching. Are you acting barmaid tonight?'

'Barmaid/cum/baby sitter I think. Keeping an eye on those two for Cathy' she said as she filled a large glass of white for Effie.

'Well, it's very noble of you on New Year's Eve'.

'Oh I'm saving up, want to get myself a...' but Effie never did hear what it was she wanted as someone tapped her on the shoulder and greeted her with a loud 'hello, you must be Cathy's mum' and Effie turned to face a thin young woman with droopy hair who pressed in on her so that she was forced to retreat. 'She's told me so much about you.'

'She has?' Effie took a large gulp of her Chardonnay.

'I quite envy her having such a nice mum so near by. I mean nothing like your own mum, is there? My mum's miles away up north, not that she wouldn't help us a lot if she was closer, but that's how it is, and I often tell Cathy how lucky she is.'

'I suppose she is' was all Effie could think of saying, wishing that this young woman would move off and find some other mother figure to attach herself to. Did Cathy really say nice things about her to her friends? So why did she still feel guilty? Damn it, this was supposed to be a party. Where on earth was Oliver? And where were the children? Half the point was to introduce them to him.

Cheryl – such was her name - was still wittering on about herself and Cathy as though they were best buddies which Effie thought was unlikely, only having a vague recollection of ever having heard her name mentioned, when a welcome 'hi,Mum' finally interrupted the flow.

'Leo! How lovely you're here. How are you? Happy new year.'

They hugged affectionately and then Leo ushered forward an attractive young woman who had smooth dark skin, long glossy black hair and a slim figure.

'This is Anita.'

She smiled and Effie instinctively leant forward to kiss her on the cheek. She really was pleased to meet her after what seemed to have been a long period of what her son described as 'treading water' as far as girl friends were concerned, and Effie in depressed mood called 'what's wrong with him?' or in more up-beat mood 'what is he waiting for?'. The answer, she realised now, was Anita, who came across as charming and intelligent and showed every sign of having the huge plus of being very taken with her boy.

So far so good. Effie ticked off her son on her mental list of anxieties she wanted to sort out in the new year, Leo coming number three after Cathy and Jane. She just needed to see what Jane was up to with her Alastair and, of course, she was desperately hoping that they would all take to Oliver.

'There you are.' And there he was, brandishing a bottle, topping up glasses around him, which was Effie's chance to introduce him to Leo and Anita when Daisy came pushing in with her auntie Jane in tow.

'Auntie Jane wants to meet your boyfriend, gran'ma' she pronounced. Rosie, following suit, came leaping in to the huddle of grown ups, still in tiger mode, knocking Effie's glass so that chardonnay spilled all down her front. The sodden silky top clung to her body as though she were a girl in a wet T-shirt competition, which caused Oliver to whip out a red handkerchief and start blotting her chest. There was a shuffling backwards and some mopping up as Cathy appeared, audibly tutting at her mother: 'honestly, Mum, you do like to make an entrance.'

'I think in this case the culprit was Tigger here' said Jane bending to give her niece a hug.

'But I just want to meet gran'ma's boyfriend like Daisy' Rosie squeaked in response, still bouncing like a rubber ball.

'Well, Rosie, if you stay still for a minute – here - I'm fine now thank you, Oliver.' Effie brushed aside the red handkerchief with which Oliver persisted in dabbing her blouse which still clung damply to her chest and now displayed a reddish mark where the colour had run from the handkerchief, much to Oliver's chagrin. 'Oh dear, I am sorry Effie. If you let me have it I'm sure I can get the stain out.'

By now all three of Effie's children, partners, grandchildren and a few others were standing round her and Oliver expectantly.

'Goodness me, all of you at the same time and, thanks, no Oliver,I won't take my top off right now, it'll have to wait, because' - she took a deep breath - 'Leo, Jane, Cathy - this is Oliver.'

Leo nodded and said 'hi, I hear you support Arsenal'.

'Oh yes. Since I was a boy' which Effie realised, of course, was a bond.

Jane, forthright as ever, said 'so you're the man who's leading my mother astray?' to which Oliver replied 'Oh I hope so' and the two laughed, which Effie reckoned meant things were OK there.

And that left Cathy, who said with a sort of a smile 'I think you're a hit with my children. They want to know if you're their new grandpa' to which Oliver graciously replied that he would be honoured to be considered for the role, which caused Effie to forgive him immediately for any irritation she had been suffering on account of his handling of the spilt wine. At that moment a blast of music burst from somewhere temporarily drowning out conversation, causing Cathy to shoot off in the direction of the blast followed by the girls who clearly wanted to be at the centre of whatever was going on. A moment later they were back making a bee line for Oliver, urging him to come and look at their acrobatics. He willingly allowed himself to be pulled along to watch as the girls showed off their gymnastic talents, bending down to be at their level, clapping enthusiastically and soon playing quite the clown.

'He's certainly a hit their, Mum' said Jane 'obviously a nice guy.'

'Yup' came from Leo.' Go for it, Mum.'

The stamp of approval, and she felt a warm sense of relief. She had been quite nervous about the party: the scrutiny, her sensitivity, the dregs of guilt and her knowledge that she didn't have a rhino hide of a skin to protect herself. She watched Oliver as he clowned around and was touched that he should make all this effort for her grandchildren. She liked a man who didn't mind making a bit of an idiot of himself. He was clever enough to be able to do it without really making himself one, and a flash image came to mind of Jack looking bored on holiday playing cricket with Leo on a beach but so busy telling the boy what not to do that neither of them were enjoying it.

Squeals of laughter were coming from the girls who were unashamedly exploiting Oliver's good nature to the point where Effie felt it was enough and in danger of becoming too much both for him and also for Cathy who Effie suspected would intervene at any moment, telling him not to over-excite the children. In fact, Cathy was chatting quite cheerfully to her sister, only occasionally glimpsing at the noisy clowning. And Leo was coming to his rescue, giving the girls plates of crisps and helping Oliver up from the floor where he seemed to have got himself stuck in an awkward position. Effie could hear him say something about not being as young as he used to be and then lost sight of him as he followed Leo in the direction of the food table, which gave Effie a chance to have a brief conversation with Alastair, who was busy filling empty glasses.

'Did Jane tell you we're thinking of getting a flat together?'

'Together?' It was barely a couple of months ago that Jane had protested the absolute necessity of keeping separate dwellings in a relationship. 'I'm delighted' said Effie, which she was.' Just hope you find something', which she did. She really was pleased at the prospect of her most forthrightly independent child softening a little. Could she cross off number two? Alastair was swallowed up again by the crowd and the noise. The words of a song echoed round the room –

'I love you, yes I do. yeh, yeh'

The room was getting hot and Effie moved towards the window which was open and occupied by a gaggle of smokers who were leaning out, blowing puffs of smoke into the dark frosty air. The Justin, who had opened the door earlier, pulled his torso back into the room and cheerfully offered Effie a cigarette which she accepted without hesitation. 'Great party.'

Effie nodded and inhaled deeply before she breathed out a stream of smoke which blew in the direction of her two daughters who were still talking together. 'Yes, it's a good party but you know,' she leant in Justin's direction in a sudden burst of intimacy 'I dread Cathy seeing me smoke. She's bound to disapprove.'

'What, Cathy?' Justin closed his eyes as he too exhaled a stream of smoke. 'na a - never seen her tick any one off an' she knows my sister's kids. They like her.'

'Well, that's nice of you to say that, Justin, but I shouldn't be doing this, I know, in fact...' Effie promptly stubbed out her cigarette and dropped the end out of the window 'I ought not to indulge my weakness and, you know what, I think it's time for some food, to absorb all that alcohol. Don't you want something?'

'Yea. Later. See ya.'

She really did feel hugely hungry and began to manoeuvre her way towards the buffet table, at the same time searching the room for Oliver and noticing again her two daughters, Jane, as always, looking tall, sleek and confident, Cathy, shorter and a bit more ruffled, definitely not as slim as her sister. In fact, Effie could not help noticing that she had put on a bit of weight and knew she would have to guard the urge to say something about it. Could she suggest a gym subscription as a new year present? The immediate issue was to address her own hunger without over doing it. The table was laden with delicious-looking food. An Indian theme, and it was so easy to ladle on the spoonfuls of prawn curry, lamb korma, crispy chapattis. Even easier to pile on the pounds complained a voice in her head. She was thankfully distracted by a young woman next to her who was busy shovelling savoury rice onto her plate with gay abandon.

'Lovely spread, isn't it? Do you think Cathy did this all herself?'

'I think she did the prawns and rice, got a bit of help from the local tandoori place and some of us brought puddings.'

'Well, it looks gorgeous' she continued as she bit into a chapatti, revealing very white teeth. 'Makes a change. God! Delicious.'

Effie took in her eating companion more carefully. There was something about her that was familiar, which wasn't really surprising at her daughter's party she supposed. But what was it?

'.. and the wine's great. Going to my head a bit, that's why I gotta eat, but it's so festive. She's very good at it, isn't she? All looks so good. I mean, when I think what I have to stare at at work, all those poor people, all those private parts' she giggled. 'Shouldn't really say it but, honestly, it's not always a pretty sight.. Such a pleasure to see something like this which is just lovely to look at.'

And then Effie knew exactly where she'd seen this woman as an image flashed across her mind of herself splayed out on a table with her 'private parts' being swabbed. The kindly nurse.

Her own moment of recognition must have coincided with her dinner companion who had stopped suddenly, her mouth poised open to bite into a chapatti..

Effie had two responses: one was a pang of anxiety about being recognised, and the other was to feel a defensive desire to assert that her privates were perfectly pretty. Her companion was clearly embarrassed too. Gossiping about patients? 'I think' continued Effie taking the initiative 'we both know exactly where we met before and all I can say is that it's New Years Eve and it calls for a drink.' The two women clinked their glasses. 'Good health'.

'Let's hope so.'

The music blared out at this point and Effie extracted herself, scanning the room again to track down Oliver, finally locating him on the far corner of the room talking to a woman who she also recognised, Cathy's friend Margie. Was the room full of people who made her feel nervous? Another flash back to herself and Jim in his car that fateful evening and hearing Margie's voice outside. No good. She'd have to find out what they were talking about. She picked up the nearest bottle and headed in their direction. Oliver greeted her with a warm smile. 'Effie, there you are. I've been talking to Margie who obviously knows you and lives near you I gather. Old friend of Cathy?'

'Oh yes, I've known Cathy since we had babies at about the same time. The girls still get on pretty well, with a few ups and downs. Our Hannah's an only child and isn't used to some of the rough and tumble stuff. But Cathy understands that, I think, tries not to let them all get too excited' which was Effie's cue for another flashback to the occasion when the introduction of her cake at Cathy's house had triggered a rivalrous disturbance amongst the three children.

She really could not like this young woman but detected no veiled references to couples canoodling in cars on the street or unhealthy sexual goings on. The main issue for Margie was clearly some residual blaming of Effie for having upset her precious daughter, which was annoying for Effie, but mainly a relief. Oliver and Margie had obviously bonded over the subject of dogs, for which she had a soft spot. 'I've loved dogs ever since my father showed me there was no need to be scared of them. Used to have me sit next to our Labrador at tea time. I hated washing so dad got the dog to lick my hands clean. Quite clever really.'

'I suppose so' said Effie doubtfully.

'That reminds me, have you heard the joke about the dog...'

'Oliver, let's go and see if we can dig out Cathy. You've barely had a chance to speak to her.'

'Oh – right 'o.'

Oliver followed Effie, jogging his head from side to side with the music, as she headed for her daughter. She had never seen him so relaxed and cheerful, possibly fuelled by plenty of Chardonnay, but the rather floppy, distracted man she had first met was a thing of the past. He was soon getting on like a house on fire with Cathy on the subject of Daisy and Rosie who he assured her had talent and would benefit from in introduction to his daughter who ran a theatre group for children. 'Great idea' Cathy beamed. Then Leo appeared briefly making farewells as he and Anita were off to another party but he gave his mother a thumbs up as he left. Effie was then dragged away by the girls who were protesting noisily that they were not tired and did not intend to go to bed. Jim was attempting to grab them forcibly. It was Effie's first real encounter of the evening with him.

'Time for these two to make their exit' he asserted as he wafted them off, still protesting that it wasn't fair. 'Give us a hand, Jasmine' he called as he disappeared upstairs. 'I'm letting Jim do that bit tonight' said Cathy firmly, 'my night off' and she bent to rub her ankles. 'Quite honestly I couldn't face going up those stairs right now', a comment which somehow triggered Effie to open her mouth and say the very thing she had told herself not to do which was to mention her weight: 'well, darling, I was just wondering if you'd like me to take out a gym subscription for you. You know, nothing like a bit of exercise to get those extra pounds off'.

She saw Oliver open his eyes reprovingly, but Cathy, instead of reacting with a suitably caustic reply, turned to her mother with a half smile and said 'Mum, I'm glad for once you noticed there's been a bit of a weight gain. You may be interested to know, I'm pregnant.'

'Pregnant?'

'Yup'.

'A baby?'

'Yup.'

Effie could only exclaim and was near to tears.

'Fantastic' from Oliver.

'And it's a boy. We know that already.'

'A boy. How marvellous.'

The music thumped out and they were soon all dancing including Effie and Oliver.. Let yourself go, follow the flow, Effie was singing to herself as they jogged around together, until someone said it was nearly midnight and the television was put on and the music off and there was a picture of Trafalgar Square full to bursting with happy revellers. The picture switched to Big Ben and the first sonorous chime rang out to a great cheer in the Square and a general shout in the room with everyone turning to kiss the person next to them. Which in Effie's case was Jim. He kissed her on the cheek. 'Happy new year, Effie' he whispered 'no bad feelings I hope. Think we're OK. Cathy and me. This new one is good news. We're both really happy about it.'

Before she could reply someone was grabbing her and pulling her into line for Auld lang syne which was soon competing with the sound of fireworks and the circle rapidly broke up with a rush to open the door or gather round the windows. Effie extracted herself to slip outside, welcoming the frosty night air and a moment to herself. Jim clearly wasn't going to feel guilty himself or blame her, which was a relief, wasn't it? She wanted to know how he had resolved things in his mind but knew she probably never would. And she would have to live with the fact that she knew something about her daughter's marriage that Cathy did not.

A swathe of brilliant sparkling stars cascaded from the sky to bring Effie back from her reverie. She moved back towards the house, noting again the ballet dancers as she passed through the front door and smiled to herself as she pictured the same scene in a few years time with pictures of footballers to compete with the dancers. In the house, she scanned the room and laughed out loud as she spotted Oliver's bald head shining in the Christmas lights like polished mahogany and made her way towards him.

About the Author

Caroline Jolly was brought up in Scotland, studied in London and East Africa, and works as a psychotherapist in private practice in London where she now lives.

Printed in the United States
By Bookmasters